Kit Parker has loved writing almost as long as she's loved reading, though that took a little encouragement, and a lot of Roald Dahl, in the beginning. Since attempting her own sequel to Matilda, aged eight, she has continued to write stories with a large dollop of the fantastical.

Also being a fan of stories on screen found Kit working at a cinema during her student years and taking a writing degree in Southampton with a media twist.

She currently lives in Sussex and can often be found listening to a rather bonkers selection of music.

Also by Kit Parker:

Feels Like Home

Coming soon:
Fate Bound

BLOOD BOUND

KIT PARKER

Book one of the Pool Valley trilogy

First published as Blue Fire in 2014 by Hellcat Publishing
under the pen name Kit Small
Copyright © 2023 Kirsty Sian Small
Writing as Kit Parker

Kit Parker has asserted her right to be identified as the author
of this work in accordance with the Copyright, Designs and
Patents Act 1988

A CIP catalogue for this book is available from
the British Library

ISBN: 978-1-915462-02-2

Cover design by Hellcat Publishing
Cover image courtesy of Depositphotos.com

For the dragon in the sky, written with permission.

And to all the muses, may they continue to comfort the dreamers – no matter how long we take to bring them to life.

The city: Pool Valley
The population: 4,623,022
Of which are human: 79
Location: Classified

ONE

When a witch had a job to do, you stood back and let her get on with it. Even if you were a werewolf.

Especially if you were a werewolf.

Stepping aside to lean against the wall, Aiden folded his arms and locked his eyes on the street. Lorna shot him a look he knew well enough not to acknowledge as she strode past him into the bar.

The atmosphere shifted the moment she entered the throng of punters. They knew to keep their heads down when a guardian of the city strolled in. Few got up to leave, most knew they wouldn't need to.

Ignoring the bartender as he edged further and further towards the front of house, Lorna, eyes focused, headed for the pool tables in back.

Four vampires lounged around a table in the corner, taking it in turns to salute their night's work between swigs of alcoholic bottled blood and the clack of pool balls.

She already knew they were military vamps and to proceed swiftly. They were built to kill. But then, so was she.

'Hey boys, look who it is.' The vampire with the cue stood straight, distracted from his shot by her arrival. 'To what do we owe this honour?'

'You know why I'm here.' Lorna lifted one outstretched palm and the cue transferred itself from his hand to hers.

'I'm sure we don't . . . do we boys?' He held his empty hands up in mock innocence.

There was a round of laughter and the clank of glass as the three in the corner clinked their bottles in toast.

'So, you four didn't just butcher a pair of college students and leave them and their car in a ditch?'

'Of course not, sweetheart.' The grin he was wearing grew wider.

'But we were told . . . I mean, how could she possibly . . .' One at the back stammered.

'Know about it?' Lorna scowled. 'You morons know how this works right?'

'Oh sh—'

Before the vampire stood closest to her could finish his revelation, Lorna had snapped the pool cue in half and fired the splintered end into his heart.

'Oh shit, indeed.' She grinned at the remaining three through the resulting cloud of ash as it dissipated.

They all lunged forward in unison. Two grabbing for Lorna across the pool table while the third made a run for the door.

With a glance over her shoulder, she launched the remaining half of the pool cue. The vampire was two strides from the door when his ashy remains showered a couple who had been enjoying a quiet drink by the window.

Catching the movement out of the corner of his eye, Aiden leant around the door frame to peer inside. Taking in the scene with a smirk, he resumed his position.

Turning back to the advancing pair, Lorna planted the sole of her foot against the solar plexus of the first to reach her and, focusing her energy, kicked him into the dartboard. He landed on his ass with a crash, the disturbed dartboard bouncing off his head when it too took a dive for the floor.

Deflecting the remaining vampire with an energy blast from a flick of her wrist, Lorna recalled a piece of cue, ready to stake him before he could recover his balance.

As the third cloud of ash settled, she turned her attention to the heap on the floor as he began scrambling to his feet.

She let him stand, let him work out where she was and that his colleagues were dead, and when he came at her again, half blind with rage and fear, she caught him by the throat. Using her own anger to fuel her energy, Lorna lifted him off his feet and slammed him down on the pool table, pinning him with ease.

Smiling down into his panicked eyes, Lorna ran her fingers through his hair. He wriggled, but she had a good grip on his throat, combined with a strong telekinetic hold on his torso.

'Now, why would you think a guardian wouldn't come knocking after what you did? Who had you placed your trust in?' Lorna grabbed a fistful of hair and yanked his head back.

'Just kill me.'

'I'll get to that . . .' She let wisps of blue fire roll from her fingertips, singeing his hair and face. 'Now, I can let you become a werewolf chew toy for a couple of hours before I execute you, or you can take your punishment immediately with the utterance of a name.'

The vampire remained silent, weighing up his options. Lorna gave his insides a telekinetic squeeze. He roared through clenched teeth.

'Who?' she cooed.

'Go to hell.'

Looking up, as if to summon Aiden, Lorna smirked when the vampire followed her gaze with a flash of panic.

'Casey Baxter,' he muttered so quickly and so quietly that Lorna barely heard him. He even glanced around to see if anyone else had been near enough to hear. Aside from the ash-covered couple, who had since left, no one had moved.

'He's dead,' Lorna growled even as her stomach knotted.

The doomed vampire chuckled. 'Darlin', we're all dead.'

'Not dead enough,' she bit back as she hauled him to his feet.

Maintaining the bind even as he swayed on the spot, Lorna reached for a knife from her back pocket. The blade glowed red hot as it sliced through the air, his head bouncing twice on sticky floorboards before spinning to a stop, cauterised neck end upwards, against the leg of the pool table.

Looking up as the bartender came over to inspect the mess, Lorna shrugged.

'I kept it clean . . . ish.'

He looked at the body and then to the splintered back wall.

Lorna flicked her knife into the heart of the torso, disintegrating it.

'There. Now you only need to sweep him out the back door.' She smirked.

'Great,' he drawled as he walked away again.

Taking a deep breath as she glanced down at the ash heap for a moment before retrieving the knife, Lorna pushed the name rattling around her head to the back of her mind before leaving the bar.

'What's wrong?' Aiden asked as he removed himself from the doorway and fell in step with her as she headed up the Underground street.

'It's been a long night, that's all.' Lorna refused to meet his eye as she ran her fingers through her chocolate brown hair, trying to shake off the feeling of dread that had been oozing over her skin all night. 'What time is it?'

Tearing his eyes from her face to check his watch, Aiden's lips twisted into an unconvinced smirk. In the six months he'd been posted to work with her he'd seen her demons and met her ghosts. As a pack wolf, he knew the stuck record well.

'It's gone four.'

'Jesus.' Lorna stopped suddenly, making Aiden do a double take.

'Not another vision?'

'No, I'm just a bit wired. Fancy breakfast?'

'Only if it's Jenny's and you're paying.' Aiden grinned as they moved towards his car.

'You have yourself a deal.' Lorna pulled the hood up on her black sweater as they climbed into the classic Mustang and she sank down into the soft leather of the passenger seat for the journey. As Aiden turned the engine over, she stuffed her hands in her pockets and turned her head towards him. 'How come I'm paying?'

'Because it was your idea and I paid last time.' Aiden's

eyebrows inched towards his hairline, his eyes sliding sideways to meet hers.

'Oh yeah.' Lorna nodded and closed her eyes, hoping to get a nap in the twenty minutes it would take to drive to the all-night diner.

Sunrise had barely brushed the horizon when they entered Jenny's Diner and claimed seats in a booth by the window. The waitress was with them in moments, pouring a coffee for Aiden who, as always, had grabbed a mug from the counter on his way in.

'Hard night?' Ethel looked pointedly to the second mug he'd grabbed for Lorna.

'Something like that.' Aiden smiled at the look of surprise on Lorna's face. She hadn't realised she looked quite so ropey. 'Thanks, Ethel.'

'Thank you,' Lorna muttered to Aiden as she slid a hand across the table to claim one of the mugs before raiding the cream and sugar caddy.

Ethel reached over to the counter and placed a couple of menus down for them before disappearing behind the counter.

Stirring the coffee with one hand, Lorna lifted the menu with the other.

'I don't know why you bother with the menu, you always have the same thing.' Aiden's eyes peered over his own coffee as he lifted it to his lips.

'There's a difference between being the sad regular and at least pretending like you might try something new,' Lorna stated, arching one authoritative eyebrow. 'I'll have . . .'

'The bacon and egg baguette with a sickly-sweet hot

chocolate,' came a sarcastic chirp from over the back of Aiden's seat.

'Actually, Asha . . .' Lorna started, looking up with a smile, 'No, you're right.'

'In that case I'll have the same and find out what all the fuss is about,' Asha cooed as she slid into the booth beside Aiden, because Lorna, sat right in the middle, had declared her side of the booth hers alone.

Watching Asha closely, Aiden had temporarily forgotten his breakfast, waiting for the information she was there to deliver.

Asha, being a dragon, was a fabulous source of information. Good or bad, if something was going down, the dragons usually knew about it. As a waitress at Broomstyx, Asha had become Lorna's own personal informant. If she'd tracked them down at five in the morning, chances were it was important.

'Trouble?' Aiden asked simply.

'Not unless that's your new nickname for me?' Asha answered brightly as she tucked her leather trench coat into the booth.

'Morning, Asha,' Lorna yawned around her coffee. 'Where's Joomba this morning?'

'Sleeping in my pocket.' She grinned as Aiden shifted up the bench a little and Ethel reappeared with a notepad.

The snake-like serpent dragon Asha kept as a pet wigged him out. Especially as he wasn't really a pet at all, he was one of her own species stuck in form since puberty. Given dragons were immortal, no one knew how permanent it was.

'Full English please, Ethel.' Aiden shot the waitress a

boyish grin and pushed his empty mug forward for a refill.

'Sure, anything else?' Ethel looked to Lorna and Asha, who made their duplicate orders.

'So, what brings you out here?' Lorna frowned. 'To what do we owe the pleasure?'

'I'll let you eat first, but you're needed down at Broomstyx.'

'Couldn't Mia have called me?' Lorna groaned. 'Rather than sending you out at the end of your shift?'

'You've been off-grid for the last few hours.'

'She could have left a message,' Lorna bit out.

'It's been busy,' Aiden said bluntly.

'Yeah, no shit.' Asha looked between them. 'A guardian's been killed.'

Lorna squeezed her eyes closed for a moment. It wasn't unheard of for a guardian to die on the job, in fact it was a little too frequent for her liking, but there was something in the way Asha was looking at her.

'Trust me, it's not what you think.' Asha's eyes widened as she played with her tongue piercing, rolling it between her teeth, and shook her head.

Aiden also met the dragon's eyes questioningly, knowing they didn't need to voice their thoughts for her to know them.

'Just get down there when you can,' she encouraged.

'Thanks, Asha.' Lorna nodded. 'At least you can go home to bed, unlike some of us.'

'You kidding? I might just come back with you.'

'Are you really that odd, or just a glutton for punishment?' Aiden growled as their food arrived.

'Punishment? I'm here for the entertainment,' Asha yipped brightly. 'Kieran's back.'

Lorna froze, suddenly losing her appetite.

'Fuck.'

TWO

'I take it you've heard about your brother?' Mia's eyes fell softly on Lorna's expression after greeting them at the door to Broomstyx.

Owned and run by Mia and her husband Ben, Broomstyx was an Aboveground members-only bar for witches and onsite staff. Decorated to replicate a traditional British pub, the bar was one of Lorna's favourite places to catch up with Asha and other regulars, a plush red velvet wingback in the corner practically had her name on it. Especially in winter when the fires were lit. It was also a front for the training and resource centre for the witch population designated as guardians hidden beneath it.

'Where is the little shit?' Lorna hissed as they manoeuvred through the throng of punters to the biometric coded door at the back. 'Actually . . . never mind, I'll deal with him later. Where's the body?'

'We haven't taken her to the morgue yet, she's in theatre three.' Mia met Lorna's eyes as she raised an eyebrow, though Mia's were amused at the merry hell her adoptive grandchildren were going to cause when they finally came face to face. 'I'll take you down there, we've sealed it.'

'OK, now you're scaring me.'

'Between this and Kieran waltzing in just after the body . . . you're not the only one.' Mia wrung her hands at her waist as they made their way down several corridors and staircases.

They'd lost Asha somewhere in the bar, she'd paused to talk to another of the bartenders. Aiden was a step behind looking far more alert than either of them felt.

'Have you had any further disturbances around the house?' Mia asked as they approached the operating theatre.

'Not that I've seen.' Lorna kept her focus on the doors ahead as Mia glanced back at Aiden, who nodded.

Lorna suspected that he'd taken to dealing with the blood splatters they'd been finding daubed across the outer walls of her parents' old house without telling her, but in truth she didn't really want to know. If someone or something was trying to scare her, she'd wait until it showed itself to deal with it.

There had been enough murder within the walls of the house for her to give less of a shit about a little blood being flung at the windows.

At the end of the corridor Mia unlocked the theatre doors and they all filed in. As Lorna approached the covered body on the operating table, Aiden hung back and Mia relocked the door.

'Oh, Tanya,' Lorna whispered sadly as she drew back the sheet that had been covering her. 'What the hell happened? She was too good to end up on the slab like this.'

'It seems it was a targeted attack. She was on a kill vision .

. .' Mia trailed off as Lorna's head snapped up.

'How long had she been getting those?'

'More and more of the girls are reporting them. Even the less experienced among you,' Mia said quietly.

A shapeshifter herself, Mia wasn't directly related to Lorna, whose parents had both been guardians. Lorna's mother, Skyler, had been entrusted to Mia and Ben during the witch hunts at the turn of the millennium in which her own parents had been killed. The trio had reached Pool Valley safely, only to realise when she came of age that Skyler was part of a powerful guardian bloodline.

'Whatever happened to a good old-fashioned haul-in and lock-up, or a little violence-based warning?' Lorna huffed. It had been a long time since she'd had a night without a kill order.

Running her fingers through her hair to keep it away from her face, Lorna leant over the body to look for cause of death. When she found two puncture marks on Tanya's throat she jumped back, startling even Aiden.

'Was she drained?' Lorna's eyes were wide when she tore them from the body.

'Yes,' Mia said evenly.

'What?' Aiden stepped forward for a closer look. 'But vampires can't feed on other supernatural creatures. It's illegal.'

'That doesn't stop them all,' Kieran announced as he burst into the room, Ben sliding in behind him.

'It's illegal because it's fatal to all involved, right? There has to be evidence of a dead vamp somewhere near the body?' Lorna ignored her twin to question Mia directly.

'The clean-up team couldn't find one. The disturbance was called in by a civilian,' Ben admitted.

Before the world had gone nuts over proof supernatural creatures existed, Mia and Ben had been with Scotland Yard. The couple had been the perfect pair to get the guardian training facility up and running with their connections and Skyler's advice.

'I suppose it's too much to ask the vampire community whether one of their junkies has gone missing after biting the wrong species?' Lorna placed her hands on her hips.

'A skilled guardian wouldn't let such an accident happen in the first place,' Kieran pointed out.

'Is that why you're here? Have you decided to grace us with your presence because you think you know something we don't?' Lorna turned on her brother.

The look Mia and Ben gave each other didn't fail to catch Aiden's attention. He narrowed his eyes as he leant back against a filing cabinet.

When Kieran didn't answer, Mia stepped in.

'You two aren't doing that guardian thing and talking in your heads, are you?'

'No.' Kieran glanced at her, his crystal blue eyes alight. 'Lorna knows better than to let me get inside her head.'

'Damn right,' Lorna shot back, fighting against the smirk that tugged at her lips. Being a twin was one thing, being telepathic twins thanks to your species, that was a whole other ballgame.

'Why now?' Lorna asked again, walking towards her brother, her steps echoing in the sterile room.

He met her eyes but didn't speak. Lorna rose an eyebrow,

suspecting he was trying to telepathically communicate with her. When the silence grew awkward, she poked him hard in the chest.

With a mildly offended chuckle, Kieran rubbed at the spot as if it hurt and, taking a step forward, reached down to kiss her on the forehead. 'I missed you too.'

'I've had to get tougher with who I let in my brain these days, you'll have to just come out with it.' Lorna folded her arms. 'And I never said I missed you. Didn't even think it.'

With a scowl, Kieran took a step back, his eyes meeting Aiden's as he did so. They regarded each other for a moment with equal levels of disdain. Lorna could feel Aiden's accusing look even though he was out of her field of vision.

When Kieran looked down at his twin for an explanation, Lorna shot him a black look. She had a feeling she knew exactly what he was thinking.

He wasn't the only one with some explaining to do.

'My training was cut short. Lucious didn't explain why, though it might have something to do with this.' Kieran dragged his eyes back to the body over Lorna's shoulder, before they snapped back to Aiden. 'Who's that?'

'Kieran, this is Aiden Barnes, he's our resident werewolf. He's been working with Lorna for the last six months.' Ben stepped forward as if to make a formal introduction. Kieran and Aiden both took a step forward, that was as far as they went.

'Aiden Barnes as in Barnes Pack Alpha?' Kieran's brows headed for his hair line, though his voice dripped disdain.

'I'm on sabbatical,' Aiden replied casually.

'Can you be on a break from being alpha?' Kieran cocked

his head to the side. 'And why would you choose this place to do it in?'

'Knock it off, Kieran. You have no idea what's happened here in the two years you've been gone,' Lorna hissed. 'You left . . .'

'I left to become a better guardian.' Kieran aimed a glare at his sister. 'Not all of us can be as naturally talented as you are. Though perhaps you're slipping if you need a werewolf to back you up.'

Lorna inwardly cringed. Aiden remained stoic.

'Funny, I never expected you to run off to be . . . how did you put it when you got the invitation? *Taught to suck eggs.*' Lorna folded her arms.

'The oldest living supernatural in the city offers to teach you to hone your skills to the best they can be, you don't turn that shit down.' Kieran's glare remained fixed.

'Good. Some sense at least. Shame you didn't think we needed to know where you went when you made the midnight flit. Hopefully now there can at least be some useful action to go with that smart mouth of yours.'

'He doesn't live with you, does he? I can't see Daniel putting up with that.' Kieran shrugged off her barbed words with a smirk.

'Yes, he lives with me,' Lorna snapped. 'Daniel's dead, Kieran.'

THREE

Mia poured five slugs of whiskey into a set of tumblers and handed them out. Deciding to save Tanya's corpse a retelling of the March events, Ben had suggested they move to their office where there were a couple of sofas. It often doubled as a debrief room.

'We were attacked by a gang of vampires in broad daylight, six months ago. I didn't see it coming. Vampire kills were already on the rise, but not in daylight,' Lorna said quickly with an aggressive sigh once they were all seated. It took a lot for a vampire to want someone dead enough to attack during the day. Such excursions were high risk even if short bursts of daylight wouldn't kill them. 'They left me bruised but mostly unharmed. With the way they came at us, there was nothing I could do to stop them. It was over too fast.'

'Given the circumstances, we placed Aiden with your sister a week later, when he walked in the door looking to lend a hand around the place,' Ben explained.

'I'm sorry,' Kieran said quietly, gazing into the amber liquid in his glass, the air temporarily knocked out of him. 'What

16

happened to the vampires?'

'They have been dealt with,' Lorna huffed before draining the contents of her glass with one hand, the other toying with the tiger's eye she wore on a leather cord at her throat. Given to the head guardian by Lucious, the stone was enchanted. It allowed him direct access to her visions if he saw fit. Not that she ever expected to meet him in person.

'It took a couple of weeks, but Lorna got them all,' Mia pointed out. 'Fate always catches up.'

Lorna had been with Daniel almost five years having first met in college. Reaching out, she gave her brother's hand a squeeze, making him flinch before he offered her a sad smile. They had been friends.

'What else has been happening that I don't know about?' Kieran asked Mia and Ben. 'I have a feeling there's more.'

While Mia filled Kieran in on the heightened kill levels and the way the house was being targeted, Lorna turned to Aiden to make sure he hadn't yet fallen asleep.

'I'm fine.' His lips quirked in a light smile as she turned towards him. 'I'll get on to Nick later, see if he knows anything.'

'The Angeling?' Kieran's attention was suddenly on them.

'Yes, if he's ever come across attempts by a vampire at draining other creatures, he might have consulted Lucious.' Aiden shrugged.

'I forgot he was a member of the Barnes pack,' Kieran harrumphed to himself.

'He's my brother.' Aiden grinned when Kieran did a double take.

'Surely you can go back to the pack now that you've had

the chance to play bodyguard for a bit? We'll handle this as a family.'

Before Mia or Ben could interject, Lorna had turned on her brother.

'He's signed on for a year. That isn't your call to make,' Lorna said. 'Until we know more about what we're dealing with, the team stays the same. You're the rookie, for now.'

Kieran looked to Ben, who looked to Mia.

'What she said,' Mia agreed.

'*She* also needs some damned sleep,' Lorna yawned. 'We've chased vision after vision tonight.'

'Have you been living at Mum and Dad's place?' Kieran looked up as Lorna and Aiden stood in unison.

'Yeah. Don't worry, Aiden hasn't stolen your room,' Lorna teased. 'You need a ride?'

'No, I've got the motorbike, I'll catch up.' Kieran waved them off. 'I need a full debrief.'

Lorna and Aiden looked to Mia and Ben for clearance, but they instantly busied themselves with statistics.

'You never struck me as a family ties kind of setup,' Aiden said as they headed back towards street level.

'Says the Barnes alpha.' Lorna smirked, seeking out his curious mocha-coloured eyes, hidden beneath shaggy blond curls.

'Kieran isn't just closing rank. It's not my job he's got a problem with, is it?'

'He's just being overprotective. He doesn't know you,' Lorna reassured, though her gaze shifted to the floor.

'That doesn't answer the question.' Aiden shot her a look. 'It's what I am, isn't it?'

'He had a run in with a werewolf on a vision some years ago,' Lorna admitted. 'It wasn't pleasant.'

'On a vision? But we deal with our own kind.'

'Like I said, it wasn't pleasant.'

'Hey Lorna, not hitting the ropes this morning?' Ricky asked as they rounded the corner and headed past the training arena.

'Fuck off, Rick, I've been out all night.' Lorna flipped him the bird.

'See how the head guardian talks to us underlings?' Ricky laughed as he turned to a teenage girl who was tailing him. 'Head on in, I'll be with you in a second.'

'New recruit?' Lorna asked.

'Yeah, she's just started getting visions, but she needs a lot of work, no co-ordination whatsoever.' Ricky glanced over his shoulder to make sure she'd gone. 'Got a face full of crash mat on the first test. Missed the ropes entirely.'

'Ouch.' Lorna winced. 'Hopefully if these night visions ease off, I'll be able to run some more training sessions myself next week, let me know how she gets on.'

'Sure thing.' Ricky nodded as he backed through the doors into the arena.

'Speaking of being out all night, we should get home before you get another order,' Aiden said, fighting a yawn.

'A good twelve hours sounds perfect,' Lorna replied whimsically.

Aiden began walking again but Lorna didn't follow. When he turned back, she was rubbing her temples.

'Not again?' He frowned, his eyes concerned.

''Fraid so,' Lorna sighed. 'Tanya's killer.'

FOUR

Watching Lorna closely from his vantage point, Aiden sank lower into the shadows. She was standing against a dank wall, practically inviting the trouble they both knew was coming while he perched in a recess opposite.

Ten levels below ground, the access alley that would be the scene of Lorna's next kill serviced some of the shadier businesses the Underground had to offer.

Lorna had informed Aiden that she was on the lookout for a vampire with shoulder-length white hair. In stark contrast to the last set of goons, this one would be elegant, poised, not the usual type to end up on her hit list if she was honest.

The bloodsuckers certainly weren't her favourite creatures to hunt down, having a distaste for the way they killed when they did. She had yet to execute a vampire who hadn't made a beyond-reason mess of their victim.

Until Tanya.

Given that Tanya's body had seemed free of defensive wounds, Lorna expected she and Aiden would need to take him down together.

She'd been relieved to discover the description she'd received of the killer hadn't matched Casey Baxter's last known mugshot. That was a complication she wasn't willing to think on. The vamp in the bar had been fucking with her, she was sure of it.

Skyler herself had promised her daughter she'd killed Casey before Lorna even came of age at sixteen. The bogeyman of the vampire community, he was one of a small number of creatures guardians dreaded seeing in their visions.

Feeling Aiden grow rapidly restless, Lorna did a mental perimeter check for signs of life. Living with something as volatile as a werewolf, she had quickly learned to let his emotional output roll off her shoulders. She'd also worked out how to use it to her advantage just as fast.

As Aiden shifted his weight from one leg to the other, Lorna's eyes were drawn to his. In her mind's eye she saw his ears prick up. He lifted his eyes to look at her, but they were both distracted when a tall dark figure passed between them.

Feeling him relax when she didn't react, she settled back against the wall again. She didn't recognise the newcomer, chances being they were headed for the rear entrance to one of the buildings.

With a loud crash, a bin further inside the alley toppled over. The ringing of the lid as it rolled towards them was preceded by a fox making a bolt for the street.

Stifling a hiss of breath, Lorna glared after the furry blur.

Some shapeshifters were too coy for their own good.

Meeting Aiden's eyes in the dark, she breathed out in agitation. His head tipped to the side, listening for something, his gaze lifting to the point at which level 10 met level 9 three storeys and several feet of solid rock above them.

Before she could narrow her eyes at him for a clue as to what he was listening for, a figure stepped between them. Without looking at either of them the target paused to take a pocket watch from his waistcoat, the suit he wore perfectly tailored to his elongated form.

Scowling, Lorna looked him up and down. Definitely the vamp from her vision, but he seemed no worse for wear for having guzzled down several pints of guardian blood.

'Lorna, my darling, you're early,' the vampire said, remaining statuesque, his rich English accent mocking in its pomposity.

Snapping the watch shut and turning to Aiden, the vampire waited until Aiden made eye contact.

Aiden's eyes darkened in a threatening manner, werewolf telling vampire to back the hell off. Aiden's nose and impeccable hearing meant vampires and werewolves usually managed to steer clear of each other, the two species were lethal to each other, a crossed bite between them almost always fatal.

'But not in time,' the vampire added before his mouth spread into a macabre grin beneath cold, glowing green eyes as his fangs elongated.

'In time to see you choke on the poison you've been drinking, I hope,' Lorna snarled.

'Do I look like your garden-variety throat-biter? Lorna, darling, you insult me.' He sniggered, 'I'm just a lowly businessman.' His eyes flashed with a hunger that wasn't for the pulse charging adrenaline through her veins.

Aiden's ears would have slid back in realisation had he been in form, instead he shifted his weight and gave a low growl in warning. Lorna couldn't see Aiden or the vampire's face, but she felt the shift. As she prepared to break cover, movement from the back of the alley caught her eye.

While the vampire between them kept Aiden cornered, another figure appeared from the shadows.

It was carrying something large which it dropped unceremoniously at his feet, causing nausea to flood Lorna's senses, she'd long learned to recognise the sound of a body hitting the ground.

Shifting from her position enough that Aiden could see her, she gave him the all-clear to deal with the original target however he chose.

Throwing a handful of fire onto a nearby pile of rubbish, Lorna lit up the alley to get a better look at the victim. The newcomer chuckled when she realised it was a guardian, one she had trained with, drank with, laughed about pricks like him with.

There was a growl behind her as Aiden made his move and the fight between werewolf and vampire began in earnest.

'Wanna make something of it?' The vampire in front of her leered.

Resisting the urge to grimace in disgust, Lorna wondered how quickly she could reach for and fire the gun in her back pocket, thankful she'd grabbed it out of the car. He didn't look like he'd be hard to take down, he looked as though he'd been living in that alley for years, greasy hair clinging to his forehead and brown stains on his dirty trench coat smelling of dried alcoholic blood.

Not that it mattered where she shot him, the gun was

preloaded with bullets containing werewolf DNA, having been laced with Aiden's willingly given saliva. It had been his idea, though she suspected Nick had asked him to try it out of morbid curiosity.

Bench tests had proven very effective.

Legally, as he wasn't her mark, she couldn't kill him unless he made to attack. For the murder, he would pay, but the kill order had not yet been received. She began to suspect that he was just a bum, dragged into the fray on some promise of reward.

A quick glance at the girl at her feet confirmed that her death seemed to have been quick. The unnatural angle of her head suggesting a broken neck.

'Boo.' The drunk inched forward, opening his mouth to laugh at his own joke before he exploded.

Lowering the gun, having reacted on impulse, Lorna swiped away the ash cloud, glad she'd made a direct heart hit. Werewolf DNA had a nasty side effect, it wasn't an ash cloud when you hit a vampire anywhere else with what was essentially a werewolf bite, it was a cascade of blood and bone.

'Shit.' Lorna exhaled a heavy sigh as she knelt beside the body to confirm identity. 'What the fuck were you even doing here?' she asked on a whisper.

Turning the girl's head gently to confirm cause of death, Lorna's blood ran cold when she found two more puncture marks to accompany the broken neck.

'How the hell . . . ?'

'I can offer you a demonstration if you like?' A self-satisfied voice came from behind her.

Spinning out of her crouch, Lorna fired at the sound of the voice but her shot rebounded off the wall.

'Tsk tsk, so predictable,' a new male voice laughed from the shadows. 'And a little jumpy, I have to say. Bet I'm not your mark, either.'

'No. You're mine,' a delicate voice said out of nowhere.

Pivoting, Lorna found another vampire facing down a girl in a long, fitted coat, the large hood up to hide her face.

He started to laugh, the sound mocking, calling her a liar. She shrugged and a crate in the corner shattered, a perfect splinter embedding itself in the vampire's heart.

Throwing up an energy shield against the debris and ash, Lorna calmly returned her gun to her back pocket.

'Did your mark drain this girl?'

'Yes.' The guardian dropped to the body and began preparing her for burning. 'Though he wasn't my mark. I lied.'

There was a pause in which Lorna knew she should pull rank, berate the action visionless. But the continuing ooze of dread silenced her. Where were they all coming from?

'A threat's a threat, right?' the guardian continued.

Lorna nodded. 'I should take her back to the centre . . . inform . . .'

As the body ignited, the guardian stood.

'She was an Underground guardian before she joined your ranks. She has no family to inform.'

'I'll give you a moment.' Lorna nodded in acknowledgement.

Underground guardians were often loners who didn't want or need the help of Mia's facility. They didn't exclusively patrol the Underground streets, it was a term they had been gifted for being elusive.

Scrubbing her hands over her face in exhaustion, Lorna headed for the mouth of the alley to find Aiden sat calmly on the curb watching the comings and goings on the street beyond.

'Aiden one, vampires nil?' Lorna asked as brightly as she could manage.

As she approached, he looked up with a wry smile.

'Try three-nil. But I got your mark.'

'Three?' Lorna's brow creased as she took in the vampire remains behind him.

'When do these things ever go as smoothly as we anticipated?'

'It's getting rarer,' Lorna drawled and patted him on the shoulder as there was a clang from the fire escape above the alley.

Heading back inside to see whether the noise was simply the other guardian making a swift exit, Lorna scanned the metal platforms and ladders for signs of movement. As her eyes adjusted to the gloom, she spotted a figure far too large to be the hooded guardian watching her from the topmost platform.

The dirt at her feet shifted as something landed behind her.

Before she could turn, she was lifted off her feet and slammed into a wall as talons sank into her flesh and pinned her against the brick. Dazed, she barely had time to consider a counterattack before fangs pierced her throat.

Instantly paralysed, Lorna couldn't even scream.

FIVE

Blood, dust, pain.

The glow of a fire somewhere nearby.

Lorna struggled to make out shapes as the alley slowly came back into focus. Her world was numb and soundless, but she knew she was on the ground.

No, not numb, all-consuming pain made everything else dull.

The frantic silhouette of Aiden, who had shifted involuntarily into a wolf on seeing what was happening to Lorna, was in the process of mauling the vampire who had attacked her. Tearing him to pieces, he separated the head from the body before his bite marks could cause a vampire-sized splat.

Her first attempt to sit up caused a scream to burst from her throat when a flood of pain unlike anything she had ever experienced ripped through her and sent her body into spasm.

Closing her eyes, Lorna fell onto her back to breathe deeply while every muscle in her body slowly, agonisingly, ceased cramping.

When she felt ready to move again, it was to drag her right arm up to her neck. Cold, damp air on blood and saliva led her to believe she'd find a chunk of flesh missing, but she only found two tiny, deadly puncture marks.

Sucking in another deep breath in preparation to attempt to sit up again, Lorna found herself winded as her eyes settled on a figure watching her from one of the upper platforms of the fire escape. Knowing there was another guardian in the alley and that Aiden was distracted, her first instinct was to scream a warning, but her lungs wouldn't fill enough to let her.

Grinning, Casey Baxter lifted a finger to his lips before disappearing into the shadows.

Blood rushing in her ears, Lorna rolled back onto her side, a wave of nausea rising in her stomach. Before the bile could reach her throat, hands gripped her by the arms and dragged her into a sitting position up against the wall.

Expecting to see another vampire ready to finish her off, Lorna flinched when a face drew close to hers in the gloom.

'It's only me,' Kieran hushed as he brushed her hair to one side to confirm what had happened for himself. 'Shit.'

'What are you doing here?' Lorna asked, finding her voice, though it didn't sound like hers. 'Did you see him?'

'You were my fucking vision, of course.' Kieran glared at her. 'See who? What the hell happened?'

'I thought I . . .' Lorna looked around for the other guardian. 'Never mind. What will a bite do to me?'

'Other than kill you?' Kieran bit out as he stared a little

too hard at the puncture wounds. 'I don't know.'

'I think we both agree I'm as good as dead. I mean how long do I have?'

'For obvious reasons, this never happens, so I don't know.' Kieran's eyes dropped to the ground.

Movement down the alley told them Aiden had finally calmed down, having turned the vampire in question into blood and bone soup, and returned to his human form. Before he could join them, the hooded guardian reappeared and tugged him out of earshot.

'Are you OK?' She tipped her head back enough for Aiden to see the concern in her violet eyes.

'I'm fine,' he growled, tearing his gaze away from Lorna. 'I can't say the same for Lorna.'

'You need to be with her.' She tiptoed up and kissed him on the one spot on his cheek that wasn't bloodied. 'It's going to get rough. We'll do all we can. Call if you need us.'

Glancing into the alley at the twins she raised a hand in acknowledgement before reaching for Aiden's arm as he tried to move towards them.

'Do you want us to stay?'

'I didn't think you were ready to expose yourself?' Aiden bit out with a scowl. 'Does he even know you're here?'

'Of course. He's here,' she said gently. 'He took out another two that were gunning for you. And given what happened anyway, just as well, don't you think?' Raising her eyebrows, she punched him lightly on the arm and walked away.

Swallowing hard, hands on his hips, Aiden shook off a shiver as he watched her go. With a deep breath and a once over of the surrounding buildings, he finally locked eyes on Lorna.

'Who the hell was that?' Kieran barked as Aiden dropped to his knees next to his sister.

Ignoring him, Aiden took hold of Lorna's hand, gripping it tight. 'I'm so sorry.'

'You're all bloody.' Lorna stuck her tongue out in mock disgust. 'And it's OK. There was nothing we could do.'

Offering him a weak smile, Lorna returned the grip on his hand before glancing around the alley.

'So, you know that guardian?' she asked finally when neither Kieran nor Aiden spoke.

'Yeah,' Aiden muttered, though he continued to stare at Lorna as though she might leave them at any moment.

'I've not met anyone else you know,' Lorna said as brightly as possible, her brow glistening with sweat.

Having often wondered about the pack dynamic, Lorna assumed she'd been kept separate for political reasons. He'd never mentioned whether there were many women in his life or the pack. Though he had admitted to having a string of ex-girlfriends.

'What are you insinuating?' Aiden all but growled, distracted.

'That if you . . . you told me you had girlfriends . . .' Lorna trailed off.

'She's my brother's partner,' he replied with a slow smile.

'That was the angeling's . . . Sorry, Nick's, other half?' Lorna said around a grin before whistling to herself, impressed. 'Was Nick here too?'

Nodding stiffly, Aiden's eyes found the bite marks on her

throat.

'That's a shame, I'd have liked to have met him.' Lorna sighed whimsically.

Nick Barnes, legend had it, was something of a wonder. Aiden wouldn't blow smoke up his own little brother's ass, but the current angeling was rumoured to be the strongest asset the Barnes pack had. A half angel-half demon concoction, he was the only one of his kind. An angeling only appeared on a birth certificate at the registry once in every 300 years.

'Are you two just waiting for me to snuff it? Or are you in more shock than I am?' Lorna huffed, failing to cover the strain in her voice as she lay her head back against the wall.

'We need to get her out of here.' Kieran, finding his voice at last, watched Aiden draw Lorna onto his lap and squeeze her tight when she screamed through another all-body spasm.

Rocking her gently as she relaxed, he tucked her head onto his shoulder, making her feel cocooned and safe within the heat and strength he provided. Closing her eyes and wishing for sleep, Lorna breathed through the agony as best she could.

'I said, we need to get her out of here,' Kieran repeated and reached out as if to transfer Lorna into his grip.

Turning his manoeuvre into a lift, Aiden got to his feet, picking Lorna up as she finally slipped into unconsciousness.

'I heard you the first time,' he snarled.

SIX

Clearing a path for Aiden to carry his sister through the double doors of one of the rooms in the medical wing, Kieran was relieved to see it wasn't theatre. Regardless, Aiden cringed at the sight of an empty gurney in the corner as he looked for anywhere else to put Lorna down.

'Now what?' Aiden growled as Keiran looked just as lost.

'Sit her in the recliner in the corner,' Kieran instructed, spotting a lab tech's choice of plush-looking desk chair.

Doing as he was asked, Aiden gently sat Lorna in the seat as Kieran continued to do laps around the lab, opening and closing cupboards and drawers. When inspiration failed to strike, he snatched up a cloth from the sink and ran it under the tap.

Aiden was bracing himself on the arms of the chair, staring at the sweat running down Lorna's pale brow, when he was bustled out of the way by her brother brandishing the wet rag which he tore in two, handing half to Aiden.

'If Mia sees you covered in blood, she'll pitch a fit.' Kieran shoved the wet cloth into Aiden's unresponsive palm.

While Kieran cleaned the bite wound to get a better look, Aiden tore his gaze from Lorna's sickly appearance to tug his phone free from his pocket and dial his brother.

'Hey, are you home yet?' Aiden asked quietly, pacing across the room whilst wiping at his face. Kieran shot him a look over his shoulder before returning to his task. 'She's out cold. We've managed to get her back to the guardian compound . . . he's looking now? Can you hand me over please, thanks Kia.'

While the phone was handed over, Aiden discarded the bloodied rag and knotted his free hand in his hair, his eyes never leaving Lorna's face.

'Nick . . . tell me you've found something?'

Tossing the rest of the bloodied flannel in the nearest bin, Kieran straightened up and listened in.

'What can I do?'

Kieran looked up as Aiden paled several shades at whatever his brother was saying.

'We need to find something to strap her down with.' Aiden balanced the phone between his ear and shoulder as Nick continued while they both began searching the room afresh, this time for restraints. 'OK, thanks Nick, I'll call you back.'

After tossing lab coats, tourniquets and their own belts into a pile on the floor, Aiden hung up.

'What does he think we'll need all this for?' Kieran asked, placing his hands on his hips for a moment before they began sifting through the pile for the best options.

'She might be woken by pain so intense that she could injure herself or us with full-body convulsions,' Aiden admitted as he gently strapped her right arm to the chair with his own belt. 'But this isn't an exact science,' he muttered, 'she may not wake up.'

Guardian and werewolf regarded each other for a moment before reaching for Lorna's ankles. By the time she was secure, she had started to stir.

'Ugh, how long was I out . . .?' Lorna sighed as her head fell back against the chair, though her eyes snapped open when she realised she couldn't lift a hand to swipe the hair out of her face. 'Why am I tied down?' Her eyes blazed at her twin.

'It's a precaution, in case . . .'

Before Aiden could finish his explanation, Lorna convulsed with an ear-splitting scream they were certain the whole complex heard.

Gulping down deep breaths, the white heat that had seared through every nerve in her body subsiding, Lorna fought against the restraints as her vision returned. Relieved to see that she hadn't combusted and taken the rest of the room with her, she squeezed her eyes closed in an attempt to mentally shut out the pain.

'What the fuck was that?' she growled through gritted teeth, looking straight at Aiden when she spotted the phone in his hand.

When he didn't answer, she rattled the restraints in frustration, but he still didn't move. Frozen to the spot, Aiden's eyes were terrified as he stared right through her. Scowling, Lorna gave him a visual once over and found the fist gripping his phone to be shaking.

'We don't know, Nick just told us to expect . . . well, whatever that was,' Kieran explained. 'He didn't know whether you would . . .'

'Well, I wasn't going to turn into a freaking bat and trash the joint now, was I?' Lorna snapped at her brother. 'Untie me.'

As Kieran did as he was told, Aiden found his voice.

'Is there anything we can give you to ease the pain? Neutralisers, painkillers, morphine?' he mumbled.

'You can't save me. A neutraliser would be pointless. But some terrific painkillers wouldn't go amiss,' Lorna snarled, glancing down at Kieran as he untied her ankles and she rubbed at her wrists. 'What's the strongest thing we have?'

'I don't think I could give you anything strong *enough*,' Kieran said gently.

'If you overdose me, it's only going to shorten the sentence,' Lorna bit out. 'Go raid the medi-cabinet.'

'No.' Aiden flinched at her words. 'Nick is looking into it. You're not dead yet.'

'Yet,' Lorna agreed. 'Look, just dose me on whatever you are willing to try, and we'll carry on as normal for as long as I can.'

Sitting forward as Kieran raided the medical cabinet, Lorna felt the room spin and a new wave of nausea added itself to the pain. Focusing on the form of Aiden within her reach, she noticed he was still shaking, though it seemed to have progressed to a full body quake.

Reaching out, Lorna placed a hand on his forearm causing him to flinch again. He was hot to the touch, much warmer than usual. Shaking himself off, he attempted a reassuring smile and took her hand to help her to her feet.

When Kieran handed her a box of near-knockout strength

painkillers, she crossed the room on wobbly legs to fill a discarded coffee mug with water and knocked two of the pills back as though they were vitamin chews.

'This isn't bothering you?' Aiden's eyes were narrowed as he watched her.

Leaning back against the sink, Lorna finally engaged with reality and made eye contact with both men in turn. Aiden wanted answers, Kieran could barely mimic her calm.

'All the while I can control the symptoms and pretend I'm fine, I can't be worried about the end result. If they can be controlled. I don't want Mia or Ben panicking and I certainly don't want any of the other guardians to know yet. If it kills me, it kills me. My time.' Lorna shrugged, fighting back a wave of nausea.

'It can't be that simple,' Aiden growled.

'Yes, it can. It has to be,' Lorna returned. 'Witches who become guardians don't retire, they die on the job, we're used to it.'

'You might be,' Aiden ground out.

'Doesn't mean we have to like it,' Kieran said quietly as Lorna turned to leave.

'We've had reports of screaming, what's happened?' Mia asked as she and Ben burst through the door.

'Just a little bone reset.' Lorna smiled unconvincingly.

'Yet none of you seem to be cradling any broken limbs,' Ben stated as he folded his arms across his chest. 'Does someone want to explain what's going on?'

'Not really,' Lorna deadpanned as she watched Aiden zone out, he hadn't acknowledged they had company. 'Aiden?'

As they all looked to the werewolf he began to sink to the

ground. Rushing forward, Ben reached Aiden just in time, letting him fall against his shoulder as Kieran helped steady him into the chair and Mia hit a button on the wall, setting off an alarm for immediate assistance.

'Aiden, is any of that blood yours?' Lorna pointed to his stained jeans.

'Probably,' he muttered before passing out.

SEVEN

In the confusion that followed, Lorna managed to deliberately lose herself in the waiting area of the medical department. Ben had gone with Aiden, and Kieran had been dragged away for questioning by Mia.

Fat lot of good that had ever done her, Lorna thought as she lay her head back against the sofa and contemplated harassing the coffee machine in the corner.

Between the drugs kicking in and the waves of nausea, she'd welcomed the chance to lay down. She might even have passed out at one point but decided that was unlikely. Mia would be giving Kieran the grilling of his life for him not to have reappeared.

Extending her arm out in front of her, Lorna pinched her thumb and forefinger together. Her internal temperature was dropping, and with that was a creeping numbness of her nervous system.

Raising an eyebrow to herself, she sat up and eyeballed the coffee machine again.

With her body beginning to feel less like her own, Lorna

stood up with a deep breath to steady a rush of vertigo and slowly moved across the waiting room to the coffee machine.

Selecting a large black coffee, she shoved her hands in her pockets and stared at the machine as the drink poured.

It was a slow day for work-related injuries. Not only was there no one else waiting, but it was quiet enough in the medical department that the only thing she could hear over her own breathing was the machine in front of her and the wall clock ticking.

She watched the second hand make a full revolution before realising it was getting on for midday.

She still hadn't made it to bed.

Scrubbing her hands over her face to banish the thought that the next big sleep she'd see was reliant on a meeting with Death himself, Lorna held her breath for a moment. Releasing the tension and the unwarranted thoughts on a sigh, she reached for the espresso button on the machine and added an extra dose of caffeine to her drink.

Coffee in hand, she took a testing sip as she returned to the sofa and glanced again at the clock.

The planter next to the sofa she was perched on rattled enough for the leaves of the bush living within it to rustle.

Shooting the foliage some serious side-eye, Lorna bristled. Telekinetic disturbances had accompanied her mood swings since she was a teen. A light warning to rein it in.

'What the fuck am I doing?' she whispered into the coffee in her lap before raking a hand through her hair.

With a sigh, she leant her head back to stare at the ceiling. If she wasn't about to die imminently, she wanted to be useful. She should have been out hunting Casey down as a parting shot. Pissing the vampires off and leaving her fellow guardians in a safer position seemed like an excellent use of her last day.

She stood up and took another large mouthful of coffee, deciding that if neither Kieran nor Aiden had returned in the time it took her to finish it, she would head out. Screw the consequences.

With only one mouthful left, she began pacing the floor.

Lorna paced the floor until a wave of vertigo forced her to sit back down and question her own motives for letting the coffee go cold.

She couldn't leave the complex without knowing Aiden was OK.

Fear had been building in her gut, knotting itself up with the nausea.

She couldn't bear it if he'd been caught in the crossfire somehow.

'You know what, screw this.'

Deciding it was better not to know, she turned on her heel, decisively heading for the door, and walked straight into Aiden.

Taking a step back in surprise, she stumbled against the sofa, dropping the cup and the last of the coffee on her sneakers. Wordlessly, he reached out and caught her wrist, saving her balance.

Huffing out a sigh, she waited until he'd let go to fold her arms and raise her eyebrows expectantly, forgetting she hadn't asked him what had happened out loud.

Aiden's lips twitched in a slight smile, knowing she had to

be really rattled to talk to herself. The glare she met him with told him to wipe the look off his face.

Looking him up and down, about to argue her case, Lorna stopped short. After whatever he'd been through, his shirt was unbuttoned, the belt still missing from his jeans making them sit lower on his hips than usual and making her wonder whether he went commando. With a white gold wolf's tooth on a choker at his throat and the natural tan of his skin, Lorna found herself unable to ask the question anyway.

Reaching out to grasp her by the shoulders, Aiden gently sat her down, making her realise she'd been swaying. With a huff, Lorna expelled all her breath and tried to loosen up.

Letting her go, Aiden stepped back and placed his hands on his hips.

'Are you OK? What happened?' She gave herself a little shake and looked up at him.

'I picked up a splinter during the fight tonight. A shard of silver.' He relaxed his stance with a shrug.

Lorna felt her blood run cold. 'Do you think it was deliberate?'

'Hard to tell, to be honest.' He shrugged again. 'I knew I'd picked it up the moment I started to feel feverish. It wasn't my main concern at the time,' he said with a pointed look, sitting next to her.

'Will you be OK?'

'I'm fine,' he said with a smile. 'Once located, one of the doctors managed to extract it all. I thought a mild faint would get you out of difficult questions anyway.'

'Could it have killed you?'

'If left, possibly, eventually. If the fever took hold.' Aiden shrugged and began buttoning his shirt back up.

'Even the smallest shard?'

'It doesn't have to be very big if it gets under the skin.' He watched her puff out a breath through pursed lips as she stared at the floor for a moment.

Standing, he retrieved his belt from his back pocket and slid it on.

Lorna shuddered, she didn't want to think of the repercussions if anything happened to Aiden in the line of duty. She suspected that his father would sue the life out of Mia, and squashing Lorna would be high on Nick's list if Aiden came to harm because of something she'd done.

'Let's get out of here, shall we?' Aiden suggested as he finished replacing his belt. 'How are you feeling?'

'Woozy, and my body temperature keeps dropping.' Lorna stood carefully. 'I'm starting to feel the need to pop some more painkillers.'

Nodding, Aiden began leading them out of the medical department, though he kept close in case she needed support.

The exit door was in sight when Kieran appeared from one of the examination rooms brandishing a first aid box.

'I've stuffed it full of more painkillers,' he said, looking them both up and down. 'Now what?'

'Home and get some sleep?' Aiden looked to Lorna.

'I'd rather not,' Lorna said evenly.

'You've hardly slept all night.' Aiden's voice was strained.

'Yeah, you should rest at least,' Kieran agreed.

'And spend what could be my last few hours wrapped in a blanket waiting to expire? I don't think so.' Lorna rolled her eyes and ducked into the examination room Kieran had just left. 'I'm definitely going to take more of these, though.'

Waving the blister pack of painkillers from her pocket at them, she headed for the sink.

'It's been barely two hours since . . .'

'We should probably contact Asha in a bit, see if she knows of any vampire gossip,' Lorna said between gulps of water. 'There has to be a reason why vamps think they can drink from guardians all of a sudden.'

'Like what?' Aiden frowned.

'The vampires in the bar this morning didn't expect to get caught. They were genuinely surprised when I turned up.' Lorna shrugged, careful not to overshare the facts.

'If they think they've found a way past visions, no guardian will ever be safe,' Aiden stated.

'That's what I'm afraid of,' Lorna replied.

'Who is currently deemed strong enough to succeed you?' Kieran asked quietly, closing the door to the room in case anyone should walk down the corridor.

'Given your training you, I guess. It would depend on the frequency of visions.'

'I've never had a high enough frequency.' He shook his head in response. 'I don't think I'd be first choice.'

'It could be any number of the girls,' Lorna agreed, looking at Aiden, who leant against the wall with his arms folded. 'Undoubtedly Mia and Ben will have discussed it with the council. They don't have to discuss it with me and, most likely, wouldn't want to.'

'Would Asha know?' Aiden asked quickly, the look in his eyes making Lorna want to reach out and touch him in reassurance.

'She might,' Lorna admitted. 'They wouldn't have to tell her for her to know.'

'We could ask her to find out.' Aiden pushed himself away from the wall and reached for the door.

'Good plan. She should be at home by now and I need to know why the vampires have a sudden fascination with our blood, and not just in the interest of spilling it. The more clued in we can get before I go, the better, even if you two have to relay it.' Lorna strode across the room to join Aiden at the door. 'I also want to know why some of them are still walking around afterwards when I haven't seen any guardians healthily sporting new neck markings.'

He wouldn't make eye contact but, resigned to the plan, Kieran fell in line. Halfway down the corridor, Aiden's phone rang.

'Nick, any news?' Aiden answered quickly, though his eyes fell faster, and he hung back a few paces. Lorna glanced over her shoulder to see if they needed to stop, but he didn't look up, so she knew it wasn't a related call and kept heading for the exit to the parking garage.

'Now?' Aiden growled. 'OK, alright, yeah I get it.'

Lorna head him mutter an expletive before he was at her back, one hand gently gripping her elbow.

'I have to go meet with the pack,' he said quietly over her shoulder.

'Off to teach some rogue a lesson?' Lorna smiled as she turned to face him, noting the hint of affection in her own voice and that it was more for Kieran's benefit. She knew he had other duties. She also knew the real reason he was on sabbatical, his father temporarily holding the alpha reins.

'Something like that. Dad and Nick have been tracking this one for a while, if I don't go now, we could lose him. It's central, I'll be back as soon as possible.' His eyes roamed her face reluctantly, as if committing her to memory.

'It's fine. I'm fine for now. We'll call in on Asha and let you know where that leads us.' Lorna shrugged.

'What if something happens?' Aiden's voice was pained as he tried to avoid Kieran's gaze over Lorna's shoulder.

'You'll be with Nick, won't you? We'll call. Or at least, Kieran will if I can't,' Lorna reassured him before glancing at her brother. Kieran gave a single nod but his eyes were dark.

'Why do you have to go anyway? How often do you run off like this?'

'Whenever he has to,' Lorna stated on Aiden's behalf.

'I'll return to being alpha at some point, it's my duty to my pack and my family,' Aiden growled.

'Just go. I'm fine. I promise not to expire before you get back.' Lorna stood tall and met his eyes seriously.

Moving closer, he cupped her face in his hands and rested his forehead against hers. 'I'll get as much out of Nick as I can while I'm with him. You're not going anywhere on our watch, not if we can help it,' he whispered.

'Don't make promises you're powerless to keep,' Lorna said gently, reaching up to slide her hands into his and give them a squeeze as she stepped back.

With a resigned nod of his own, Aiden moved past the twins and set off for the parking garage at a run.

'Well, there goes our ride.' Lorna turned to face her brother after Aiden had gone from sight. 'What?'

'You're just going to let him go?' Kieran ground out through gritted teeth.

'Yes.' She scowled. 'Now what?'

'I guess I should be glad he's gone. You were bitten in his plain sight regardless, he either sucks at his job or . . .'

'Or incidents like that are exactly the reason he was brought on board in the first place and without him it could have been far worse?' Lorna said softly. 'Drink? I could do with one.'

'With all the drugs in your system . . .'

'I could do with the distraction,' Lorna teased. 'Unless you fancy a tumble in the training ring?'

'If you live to see tomorrow, I'll totally take you up on that.' Kieran nudged her with his shoulder. 'We really need to talk to Asha, and she might not be back on shift until late tonight. We can use my motorbike, where's your car?'

'It's back at the house.' Lorna bit her bottom lip, she'd never been a fan of riding pillion on Kieran's bike. 'Just don't forget you have a passenger this time.'

EIGHT

'Sorry to wake you.' Lorna beamed and shoved a box of donuts from a deli down the street at Asha as she opened the door to her apartment.

'It's OK, I struggle to sleep during the day . . . holy shit, get in here,' Asha squeaked. She had been rubbing her eyes out of a yawn, but on making eye contact with Lorna, reached out and dragged her into the apartment, leaving Kieran to close the door.

'I take it I don't need to tell you what's happened?' Lorna watched Asha cross the living space to the corner kitchen and put the kettle on.

The dragon scrubbed her hands over her face and turned again, leaning against the counter in her baggy pyjama bottoms and vest, her burgundy curls piled high on her head for bed.

'I was getting increasingly concerned something like this might happen,' she admitted sadly. 'You didn't kill your brother then? Hi, Kieran.'

'Hi,' Kieran replied uncertainly as he and the tiny red

47

serpent dragon on the sofa eyeballed each other. 'What's that?'

'That's Joomba,' Lorna informed her twin, glancing over her shoulder in amusement. 'He doesn't bite.'

'Much,' Asha teased. 'Coffee?'

'Black, no sugar, please,' Kieran muttered as he sat himself on the opposite end of the seat to the tiny dragon, peering at it in fascination.

'What have you been hearing?' Lorna leant across Asha's breakfast bar. 'Or seeing.'

Seeing the pain in her eyes, Asha slid Lorna a glass of water for her to take more medication if she needed to. With a look of understanding, she turned back to the coffees.

'Vampires have been hushed of late, as if waiting for some big news. Rumours have been circling, rumours about feeding, but they've been confusing at best as it seems most of them don't yet know what the announcement will be.' Asha shrugged, her head down as she fixed up three coffees. 'When it's about blood, no one is safe. Then when I heard about Tanya this morning . . . I probably should have warned you, but I didn't know what to really warn you about, I'm sorry.'

Turning to slide Lorna another cup, this time full of strong black coffee, Asha then carried Kieran's cup to him and retrieved Joomba from the arm of the sofa.

Depositing him on the counter she glanced at her watch as Joomba watched Lorna expectantly.

'He can have a few.'

With a grin, Lorna reached under the counter to retrieve the jar of chocolate drops Asha stashed for her sugar-addicted ward.

'Doesn't seem to do him any harm,' Lorna cooed as she placed six chocolate buttons down in a pattern in front of Joomba.

With an appreciative caw, he tucked in, the first swallowed whole.

'Slow down, that's it until after dinner,' Asha warned. 'So, Aiden thinks Nick will have the answers?' She hooked a stool and sat at the bar.

'If he doesn't, I'm dead.' Lorna sighed. 'Well, I'm dead anyway, really.'

'It hasn't killed you yet.' Asha shrugged, lifting her mug to her lips.

'Should I be reassured that you're not worried about me expiring on your carpet?' Lorna laughed.

'I don't think the rumours are about killing off the head guardian, they don't feel like it anyway. And the creep let you go before Aiden dismembered him.'

'That's right, he did. Tanya was completely drained.' Lorna pursed her lips thoughtfully. 'Do you think they want to know what will happen next just as much as we do?'

'I think someone has been experimenting beyond the city borders and the eyes of the guardian network.' Asha met Lorna's eyes again.

'Yesss . . .' Lorna shot her brother a look as he got up to join them. 'Rumour is that Casey Baxter has risen from the dead.'

Feeling Kieran freeze for a split second as he slid her the other available stool and stood beside her, Lorna took a mouthful of her own coffee before accepting the chance to sit.

'I'd heard that too,' Asha mumbled, avoiding Kieran's gaze when it turned on her. 'There are bigger fish out there than you, you know that, right? If they can use you in some way, it will be to get to the bigger fish.'

'You mean the angeling?' Kieran queried. 'There aren't any stronger guardians.'

'That you *know* of,' Asha pointed out.

'Do you know one?' Lorna asked, genuinely curious. Asha just blinked at her. 'Of course you do, but you can't tell me who she is, for her safety. Is she my successor?'

'No. He's your official successor.' Asha nudged her chin in Kieran's direction. 'As far as the council is concerned, at least.'

'If the vampires are waiting to see if you survive, we should probably try to find out why. What's the endgame?' Kieran raked his fingers through his hair in a manner Lorna found to be more agitated than frustrated.

'I don't think we go looking for it, I think it will come to me,' Lorna grumbled, stifling a yawn. 'What time do you need to be back at the bar tonight?'

'I'm back in at eight,' Asha replied as she reached out to tickle Joomba under the chin. He was still eating the chocolate buttons, with one and a half left to munch.

'Is there anywhere we could go to pick up some more of these rumours?' Kieran asked her. 'Lorna's attackers were all killed, but someone might know the attack was planned?'

Asha met Lorna's eyes, Lorna looked away.

'Can I have an hour to get some breakfast and a shower?' Asha grinned at Kieran.

'Sure.' Kieran shrugged, though he fidgeted with his mug. 'Or we can get a head start?' He glanced at Lorna.

'Can I have a nap while Asha gets ready, please?' Lorna yawned again, this time almost falling off the stool.

'We need to know what's happening,' Kieran said gently, though his voice was strained.

'And I'm exhausted. I was out all night. Why don't you head out and we'll catch you up?' Lorna suggested, heavy lidded.

'I'll keep an eye on her,' Asha offered.

'What if . . .' Kieran's cheek twitched as he bit down on the end of his sentence.

'If I die in my sleep then yay me . . . and yay you for trying to help to the very end.' Lorna smiled sleepily and slid off the stool to give her brother a hug.

'Don't use the sofa, go through to the bedroom,' Asha instructed, scooting around the breakfast bar to steer her away from the living area.

'Sofa's fine,' Lorna mumbled, even as she let Asha push her by the shoulders into the bedroom, where she fell face-first on to the duvet.

'She's already out,' Asha said to Kieran from the bedroom doorway. 'Go do what you have to do.'

Without meeting her eye, Kieran left the apartment.

NINE

Aiden was still in Pool Valley central when his mobile rang.

He was stood over the battered and bloody body of one of the larger werewolves from a rogue pack. The bastard had been responsible for the murder of their youngest female member during a calculated attack at the beginning of the year, and Aiden was in little mind to grant any form of leniency.

Kia had herded and chased the wolf back to his own apartment, Nick had cornered him, and Aiden had attempted to gather any information the doomed mutt had been willing to share before he met his doom.

'It's Asha,' Aiden glanced at his phone, barely taking his eyes off the rogue.

'Answer it, it might be an update on Lorna,' Kia said, her arms folded as she took over, making sure the wolf was pinned telekinetically, not that he was going anywhere on two dislocated knees.

'OK.' Aiden nodded to the mangled form at his feet and wiped his hands and the phone on his jeans before answering.

Kia looked up at Nick, who shot her a look. Scowling at him, she crouched down next to the already beaten werewolf to get a grip on his jaw. One sharp twist and the already laboured breathing ceased with a final grunt.

'She's with me, asleep, Kieran's gone back out,' Asha explained down the line. 'I'll message you the symptoms I could see that she might not have told you about, you can forward it to Nick.'

'That's great, thanks Asha. I'll be over shortly.'

'Say hi to the angeling for me.'

'Hi Asha,' Kia called out with a smirk. 'Nick also says hi.'

Nick offered a reluctant wave as he moved to the door to see if anyone was coming.

'I'd better get back.' Aiden sighed as he repocketed the phone and looked down at the body.

'Well done, or extra crispy?' Kia enquired, playing with a ball of fire in one raised palm.

'Leave him,' Aiden snorted. 'After what he did, they can see what we're willing to do.'

'We burned all the others,' Nick stated.

'The others hadn't torn apart a teenage girl,' Aiden growled. 'I'll forward you Asha's message. Are you two following Dad back to the house?'

'No, we'll stay close, I have some contacts I want to call about this morning,' Nick said, glancing at Kia as Aiden led them out into the hall. 'We'll be at my place.'

Aiden was at Asha's door twenty minutes later.

'She's still out for the count,' Asha said as she stepped aside to let him in.

'At least one of us has slept,' Aiden said with a sigh, fatigue causing him to let his guard down as he met Asha's eyes.

Asha gasped. Aiden inwardly swore.

'She knows about the rival pack.' Aiden shrugged her off.

'As do I. But does she know . . .'

'No.' Aiden cut her off.

Biting her lip and glancing at the bedroom door, Asha picked up the plate of toast crumbs from the coffee table as Aiden helped himself to a seat and, popping the last piece of crust in her mouth, took the dish to the sink.

'Can I get you anything?'

'A caffeine intravenous?' Aiden chuckled. 'How is she?'

'Getting colder and paler every time I check in on her,' Asha said as she handed Aiden the coffee she'd made herself to go with her breakfast but hadn't yet touched, before returning to the kitchen to make another.

Finding the drink at the perfect drinking temperature, Aiden drained the contents of the cup in time for Lorna to wake up with a scream.

As Joomba ran for cover underneath the cushion he'd been sleeping on, Aiden dove for the bedroom where he found Lorna sat on the bed with her head between her knees.

'I'm . . . well, I'm not OK,' she said with a grunt. 'Hallucinating, that's all.'

'Not a vision?' Aiden asked as he sat next to her.

'Thankfully, no.' Lorna patted the sweat on her brow and pulled a face. 'It was messy.'

'How are you feeling?' Asha was leant on the doorframe in a pair of wide-legged trousers and a different vest that would later have a Broomstyx t-shirt pulled on over the top. Joomba was perched on her shoulder.

Contemplating for a moment, Lorna finally answered, 'About the same physically. How long did I get?'

'Only an hour.' Asha shrugged.

'That's better than nothing,' Lorna huffed. 'Right, where do we start?'

'I guess to catch vampires about during the day, we'll have to go underground?' Aiden peered at Asha over his shoulder.

'Most vamp deals go down in the casinos.' Asha nodded. 'We could head to the gambling district? With me around we won't need to go into any of them, perhaps just grab a drink nearby.'

'Or some more food?' Lorna asked hopefully, knowing that if she couldn't sleep, she could at least fuel herself.

'There's a great Mexican restaurant down there. It's popular with the vamps 'cause they make chilli infused blood cocktails.'

'Mexican it is then.' Lorna smiled as her stomach rumbled.

TEN

'I could happily order half the menu.' Aiden shot the waitress a grin when she appeared mid-speech with a bemused look. 'This half, specifically' – he motioned to the street food – 'but I'll start with a steak burrito.'

'It's a feeding day, is it?' Lorna teased.

'Hey, I haven't even managed a nap, the wolf is hungry.' Aiden pulled a face.

Lorna aimed a kick at his shins beneath the table, he caught her foot between his ankles with a wink as the waitress turned her attention to the rest of the table.

'Can I get a chicken burrito to go?' Asha looked up from the menu hopefully.

'To go?' Lorna glanced over after ordering a quesadilla.

'I'll take it to work for my dinner.' Asha shrugged. 'While you two eat, I'm going to do a little window shopping in the area, see if anyone's thinking of opening a witch blood brewery.'

'Asha!' Lorna hushed, but not without a smirk. It was Aiden who shifted uncomfortably in his seat.

'Can you two keep it down? We're on dangerous ground here as it is.' Lifting his beer, Aiden took a casual look around the brightly decorated restaurant at the surrounding punters.

Half the tables were occupied with cocktail glasses rather than dinner plates.

Wriggling her foot free, Lorna glared at him. No one area of Pool Valley belonged to any specific species, but that didn't mean there weren't popular hotspots.

'Someone is after you, mostly likely watching you. If you're spotted by the wrong person in here . . .' he whispered.

'Announce it to the world why don't you?' Lorna whispered back, her eyes wide and mocking. Supernatural hearing often stretched further than a few busy dining tables, even during a late lunchtime rush. 'Anyway, someone is always after me. It comes with the job,' she continued at her normal volume.

Aiden covered a cringe by picking up his beer bottle again and draining half of it.

When the waitress returned with their food, Asha excused herself and headed down the Underground street.

'She took Joomba with her, right?' Aiden paused as he lifted his burrito towards his face.

'He was coiled up her forearm, yes.' Lorna smirked through her second mouthful. 'I wonder where Kieran got to.'

'You let him know where we'd be.' Aiden shrugged as he took a large bite out of his burrito.

'I did, but he hasn't replied. Anything from Nick?'

'Not yet.' Aiden met her eyes.

'Hmm,' Lorna hummed, her eyes meeting with a vampire

across the restaurant she'd noticed watching her.

Pretending she hadn't noticed but making a mental note to keep an eye out for the raven-haired woman, Lorna kept her in her peripheral while she finished eating. The vampire could have been expecting a guardian visit for all she knew. The last thing Lorna wanted was a skittish vamp causing a scene.

If she'd been there on a vision, she'd have done her job before getting chow.

By the time Asha returned, Aiden had ordered an extra basket of chicken wings and finished those too. Lorna was sitting watching him and willing her stomach to hold on to the food she'd given it.

'Are those meat sweats?' Asha asked Lorna pointedly from the end of the table. 'Powder room?'

'Good idea.' Lorna got to her feet carefully, not wanting to have a sudden, telling dizzy spell.

Hooking their arms together, Asha took off in the direction of the restrooms, leaving Aiden to look on suspiciously.

'Are you alright?' Asha hushed, shoving Lorna into the disabled cubicle and locking the door. There was no one else in the restrooms, but Lorna shook her head and sat down next to the toilet.

'I think I just need a moment,' she said, grateful for Asha's quick thinking. 'What did you see?'

'The same thing you have.' Asha crouched down in front of her. 'Why haven't you told anyone you *saw* Casey Baxter?'

'Because I couldn't be sure that is who I saw, the state I was in.'

'Bullshit, I can see him in your eyes.' Asha worried her

tongue piercing between her teeth. 'And in the eyes of some of the vampires down here. Most haven't seen him, but they're certainly thinking of him. You need to tell Aiden.'

'I can't.'

'Nick's gonna find out anyway. What good is lying to him going to do?'

'I don't want him going after Casey. No one should be going after Casey.'

'You idiot. If you die, they will anyway,' Asha soothed.

'Casey didn't bite me himself. We can't go after him.'

'We? Who said anything about chasing the boogeyman? Though that monster has to slip up someday.' Asha glanced at the floor with a sigh before holding her hands out to help Lorna up. 'Think you can stand?'

'Yeah. I'll be OK.'

Allowing herself to be pulled to her feet, Lorna gave Asha a hug before offering her a smile.

'You really should tell them what you saw.' Asha prodded Lorna just as Joomba appeared out of her pocket, climbing up her back to sit on her shoulder again.

'I can't risk it.' Lorna met Asha's eyes as she reached to unlock the cubicle.

'Holy shit,' Asha breathed. 'You're as bad as each other.'

'What?' Lorna scowled.

'Nothing,' Asha squeaked. 'Let's get back.'

'I got the bill,' Aiden said as they returned to the table. 'Are we good to go?'

'Yeah, all done.' Asha beamed, scooping up her dinner parcel.

Lorna swept the restaurant for signs of the vampire who

had been watching her, but the table she had occupied was empty, the cutlery replaced.

'What did you find?' Aiden asked Asha as they exited onto the street.

'Well, I don't think guardian blood is going to appear on any menus any time soon . . .' Asha shot a look at Lorna. 'But there is rumour that it can be consumed.'

'Who could possibly be spreading that rumour?' Aiden looked disgusted.

'I think I have an idea,' Lorna grouched as she plucked her ringing phone from her pocket to inspect the caller ID. With a shudder she answered the phone.

'Hello, Jacob. To what do I owe this honour?'

'Hello, witch.'

'Now, now, I was civil,' Lorna cooed. 'You never call me just to insult me.'

'I hear you're a dead witch walking.'

Lorna didn't need to see Jake Baxter's smug grin to hear it in his tone.

'I wonder who on earth could have told you that,' Lorna said, heavy on the sarcasm as she turned away from Aiden and Asha. 'Given you've been promising to kill me for years, have you called to gloat?'

'Not quite.'

Lorna scowled to herself as he paused, her mind trying to work out what it was he possibly could have wanted if he already deemed her doomed.

It wasn't likely to be council business, the representative for the vampire community refused to talk to her on a professional level. One of the many reasons Mia and Ben held the interests of the guardians on her behalf.

A very old and very bloodthirsty vampire, his extensive military background had landed Jake the seat on the council when he'd single-handedly formed the Pool Valley armed forces. Most of its members were bored or deranged ex-fighters. Most of its highest-ranking officials were vampires.

Aiden was glaring at Lorna's phone with contempt. Werewolves were not particularly welcome in the forces. Nor did it sit well with Jake that werewolves could deal with members of their own kind who stepped out of line themselves while everyone else fell under guardian supervision.

'So, what exactly do you want? You know you're supposed to contact Mia if you want an audience with me . . . or had you forgotten your own rules?'

'I'm calling you because I'd be very surprised if you've admitted to Mia what your lapdog let happen to you last night,' Jake said in a way that told Lorna his signature macabre grin was splitting his cheeks in two.

Lorna bit the inside of her own cheek so hard she tasted blood.

When she didn't answer him, Jake continued, 'I'd simply adore the chance to run some tests on you, should you be willing. Preferably while you're still with us, however, dead or alive, it's all the same to me.'

'Hard pass,' Lorna spat in shock.

'You don't even know what the tests would involve yet.' Jake laughed.

'I don't need to know. Though I'm sure they won't exactly be in my best interest.' Lorna's voice darkened. 'Or ethical, for that matter.'

'I'll only ask nicely once,' Jake warned.

'I would say over my dead body, but I'll make sure they burn it before you even know I'm dead.' She smiled sweetly. Aiden next to her flinched.

'Of course, the biggest test is on you already. It will be truly fascinating if you live, we'd have wasted so many corpses . . .' Jake admitted thoughtfully.

Lorna felt her core temperature starting to rise at the thought of the many people who had died at the hands of vampires since the beginning of the year.

'One of these days, Jake, I'm going to be sent for you. And I promise you, I won't make it quick,' Lorna growled.

'Not if you're dead.'

'There's still time. Next time I see you, one of us will die.'

'Promises, promises.'

'Bye Jacob.'

'I'm not finished with you yet,' Jake shouted in warning as she dropped the phone from her ear.

'For today, you are,' Lorna hissed as she disconnected the call. 'Bastard.'

'What did that relic want?' Aiden was stood with his arms folded, watching her intently, when she finally turned back to them.

'Doesn't matter, he's not getting it,' Lorna snapped.

'What now?' Asha asked to change the subject.

'I could do with finding Kieran.' Lorna looked up and down the street as though he might be near. 'See if he found anything. Are you heading off?'

'Yeah, if you don't need me I'll make my way across town

. . .' Asha trailed off as Lorna swayed on the spot. Aiden reached out and placed a hand on her shoulder to steady her.

'Can't catch a break today, it seems.' Lorna smirked. 'I have work to do.'

'You can't be serious?' Asha played with her tongue piercing nervously.

Lorna nodded.

'Fate's being a real bitch today,' Aiden bit out.

'Right. I'll leave you to it, but please be careful, you've stuck around this long.' Asha reached out to hug Lorna tight. 'Don't let him anywhere near you,' she whispered in her ear.

'Jake isn't going to lower himself to chasing me,' Lorna replied as they parted. 'It's that demon manservant of his, Li, we'll need to look out for, or his nutcase of a daughter Hillary,' Lorna said.

Nodding, Asha shot her a look before heading back down the street.

'Where to?' Aiden asked simply, hands on his hips.

Phone still in her hand, Lorna silently dialled her brother.

When he answered, he was the only one who spoke, and Lorna was soon returning the phone to her pocket.

'He had the same vision, he'll meet us there.'

'That can't be good, right?'

'Not usually,' Lorna agreed.

'So, what are we walking into.' Aiden fell in step with her as she took off in the opposite direction to the one Asha had headed.

Lorna stopped again abruptly, her gaze glazed as she stared up the Underground street.

'I can't take you with me,' she muttered.

'What's that supposed to mean?' Aiden tugged at her shoulder to make her face him.

'Without trying to sound like a total bitch, it's beyond your paygrade.' Lorna grimaced as she spoke.

'There's a Baxter involved,' Aiden stated, his face turning thunderous. 'Even more reason for you to have backup.'

Meeting his eyes, Lorna swallowed down the ball of dread choking her words.

'You can't get involved, you know that.'

'The fuck I can't.' Aiden reached for her shoulders but she brushed him off and started moving again. 'It's a trap, you know that, right?'

'You know the rules,' Lorna snapped, looking over her shoulder at him as he growled and lurched to catch up.

'Those rules are bullshit.' His voice deepened. 'I'll go with you to Kieran.'

Lorna nodded. 'OK.'

ELEVEN

Cutting across town, Lorna led Aiden to a high-rise office block with Underground connectivity. Aiden frowned when he realised Lorna was walking directly towards the marble lobby.

'What is this place?'

'Just some office block. We'll find our target in one of the floors undergoing renovation.' Lorna shrugged.

'Interesting place to stir up trouble,' Aiden drawled.

'Not an easy place to get in or out of, the seventieth floor.' Lorna slid her eyes towards him.

'Is Kieran already up there?' Aiden's eyes slid to the set of elevators behind reception, trying to see how many floors there were in total.

'I'm here.' Kieran's voice slipped between them from behind.

'Where did you come from?' Aiden growled.

'I've been here a while.' Kieran's eyes darkened. 'You shouldn't be here.'

'Kieran . . .' Lorna warned.

'I have a duty to protect your sister,' Aiden replied.

'Like you did last night when you were too busy being an animal to protect my sister? Maybe your aim is to get us all killed faster? Tell me, are you generally a monster, or do those meathead wolf instincts kick in with the smallest drop of adrenaline.'

'Kieran, that's enough,' Lorna barked as Aiden's hackles rose.

'Beyond blaming me for the acts of a few bloodsuckers, just what is your problem with me?' Aiden pushed, taking a step closer to Kieran.

With a sigh, Lorna sank to her butt on the curb to watch Aiden bring her brother's issues out into the open.

'I've seen what your kind is capable of.' Kieran's voice was low as he held his ground.

'This is Pool Valley, everyone is a monster, we're all capable of horrific acts,' Aiden ground out, looking Kieran up and down for good measure.

'Not all of them have unpredictable instincts.'

'I'm not doing this with you here and now.' Aiden took a step to the side, towards Lorna. 'I don't know what you saw, or why you had a vision to track down a werewolf, but I know that if that order was made, it was a wolf beyond our control.'

'They claimed he was diseased.'

'If you are referring to the rabies-like disease werewolves can contract, then I'm truly sorry you had to see that. Unfortunately, as it travels in the saliva, that is the only circumstance under which we cannot deal with our own.' Aiden held a hand up in acknowledgement.

'I arrived just in time to see the mutt tear a shifter to pieces.' Kieran's voice was strained. 'I saw what you did to that vampire earlier, I don't want you anywhere near my sister.'

'Regardless of how dangerous you consider me, I will *never* harm your sister. The sooner you get that into your head and let us get out of here, the more chance we'll all have of seeing this through.'

'You couldn't protect her earlier. I doubt she'll live through the night with you around.'

Lorna leant back against a lamppost and watched Aiden stumble two steps back, knocked off balance. Knowing Kieran had shoved him with an energy burst, she looked to Aiden's balled fists as Kieran closed the gap between them.

A blue wall of energy cracked and shimmered between the two, knocking them both on their asses.

'Eugh,' Lorna grumbled, her head falling into her hands. The effort it had taken to throw her shield that far took its toll and her stomach rolled in response to the spiking pain between her temples. 'Who's got the painkillers?'

Digging some out of his pocket, Aiden joined her as Kieran bleated on about something.

Knocking back a couple of pills, Lorna held her hand up to stop her brother. It sounded as though he was speaking backwards.

'I didn't get a word of that,' she said calmly when he paused. 'Where have you been?'

'Nothing, never mind. I needed to do a little research of my own. It's not important. Can you stand?' Kieran climbed to his feet.

'Yeah, yeah, yeah. I'm fine.' Lorna started to heave herself up, but Aiden reached out and grasped her hand to help her.

'Who was the focus of your vision?' Aiden queried as he also got to his feet.

'I told you, you can't come with me,' Lorna reiterated as she reached for the lamppost again.

'What's wrong?' Aiden's voice cracked as he tried to help stabilise her.

'Something's not right. I need a minute.'

Taking a deep breath against a building wave of pain, Lorna turned to Aiden and, burying her head in his shoulder, gripped a fist full of his shirt as she held her breath to prevent herself from screaming. His arms slid around and enveloped her to keep her steady. Focusing on the warmth of his embrace, Lorna drank in the comfort she found in having him so close, until the pain passed.

When Lorna felt ready, she let go of Aiden's shirt and splayed her hand across his chest, ready to steady herself. In case another wave hit her, Kieran moved in too, offering some privacy. The Underground street wasn't bustling enough to cover the incident, nor was it quiet enough to be ignored by all who passed by.

Letting her go, reluctantly, Aiden rested a hand on her shoulder. Once he was sure she was steady he used his free hand to check his phone again. Wordlessly, he lowered the phone and looked back to Lorna. Glancing up at him, Lorna forced a smile, beginning to wonder how long she had left.

'The painkillers aren't touching it anymore?' Kieran asked.

'I only just took them,' Lorna said with a wince. 'Though I'm starting to feel a bit disconnected.'

'In what way?' Aiden scowled.

'It's a little like being drunk, like it doesn't really hurt, but at the same time it really fucking does.' Lorna's shoulders shook as she chuckled to herself. 'I'll be alright, let's get this over with.'

Moving in again, Aiden tucked her close, allowing her to support herself fully against his frame. Slipping into the crook of his arm, but offering him a glare, her face relaxed when he began massaging circles into the middle of her back with his thumb. Her eyes narrowed, he always knew how and when to distract her when she most needed it. Focusing on the repetition, she closed her eyes and took a deep breath.

'I appreciate the distraction, but I meant it Aiden, you can't come up with us.'

'Lorna's right,' Kieran said quietly. 'You need to sit this one out.'

'I can't do that.' Aiden's eyes were fixed on Lorna, his face pinched.

'Go help Nick with his research, find me proof that a guardian somewhere survived a bite, I'm going to need all the help I can get after this.'

Kieran shot his sister a look she ignored.

'Where will I find you?' Aiden asked finally, resigned.

'There's a welcome party above us. There may be hostages,' Lorna answered, her voice softening when she saw the horror in his eyes. 'I've got Kieran. I'll be OK. But you shouldn't go looking for a fight with a Baxter.'

With a snort of derision, Aiden huffed out a breath and backed up a step. 'Alright.'

'Thank you,' Lorna said with a sigh of relief.

'Call us if you need backup.'

'We can't,' Lorna whispered.

'I'll send Nick.'

Nodding, Lorna reached out to pull Aiden into her arms.

When his arms gripped her a second time, she inhaled the increasingly familiar scent of him, committing him to memory.

Squeezing her tight for a moment, he released her just as quick and, with a nod to Kieran, took a side-exit and headed for the nearest subway.

'You ready?' Kieran asked tentatively.

'For any of this? Fuck no,' Lorna scoffed but smirked.

'There are a lot of military vamps up there, Lorna.'

'Quickest way to get an audience with the head guardian.' Lorna shrugged and headed for the lobby.

Security had seen them coming and let them straight through the turnstiles, ensuring they also had an elevator to themselves.

'We got the same vision, right?' Lorna said once the doors were closed, looking up at him with a questioning look in her eyes.

'I think so. I can't get in your head. Even if you're trying to let me in, all I'm hearing is static,' Kieran muttered.

'Hey, there's an upside to this after all.' Lorna grinned.

'Not funny.' Kieran reached for both her hands. 'We have twenty vamps and five hostages. But no target.'

'The target will be whichever Baxter ordered them to take prisoners.' Lorna's eyes widened.

'Then they're not really an official target.'

'How can they do this without being marked for execution?' Lorna scowled even as she turned away.

'What did Jake say to you?' Kieran asked as he followed her lead.

'He wants to run tests on me.' Lorna rolled her eyes. 'I said no, of course.'

'What else did you find out in the Underground?'

'Just that someone is spreading rumours that witch blood is a delicacy these days. If it's Jake himself, he's probably using the reputation of his son to encourage experimentation,' Lorna snorted.

'Mum dealt with Casey Baxter before she died,' Kieran deadpanned.

'His reputation lives on.' Lorna shrugged but glanced back at her brother, who was taking a little too much interest in the ceiling.

'What are you going to do if a member of the Baxter family is waiting for you? You can't kill a council member without a vision.'

'I can't kill anyone without a vision,' Lorna retorted. 'It's probably just Jake hoping to get his own way, or Hillary wanting a front row seat to watch me snuff it.'

'Jake has been baying for your blood since you broke one of his fangs.' Kieran chuckled to himself.

'It grew back,' Lorna huffed. 'Eventually. He took that way too personally.'

'You lashed out visionless and accused him of sending his staff to stalk us at college.' Kieran laughed but wouldn't meet her eye when she shot him a self-satisfied grin.

'He did! They were, and we never found out why!' Lorna pointed out. 'Creeped me the fuck out,' she said as she lowered her voice.

TWELVE

'Level seventy,' Lorna whispered, looking at Kieran as they backed away from each other, pressing themselves against the side walls of the elevator. 'Ready or not, here we come.'

With a swish, the doors pinged loudly, opening onto an empty and eerily silent office space.

Meeting Kieran's eyes as they heard the distinctive click of an automatic weapon, they set their shields and stepped out together. Palms outstretched ready to return fire, they both scowled to find the open-plan floor fully lit and smelling of fresh paint, though completely void of furniture where the decorators had recently vacated.

Keeping her focus on the space ahead as Kieran glanced from left to right, Lorna listened for the slightest movement.

She didn't expect to hear a vampire, they were too light-footed, however all one of the hostages needed to do was breathe too heavy and she'd hear it soon enough.

With another ping, the elevator doors slid closed again. As soon as they clanged together, the shooting started to their right.

Ducking behind a support pillar, the twins kept their shields steady and peered back to see if the shooters were advancing.

'Shooting the hostages?' Kieran frowned, his voice as quiet as possible.

'I can't sense any hostages on this floor.' Lorna shook her head as the gunfire paused. 'They've been moved. Or killed already.'

When the shooting started again, it was closer.

'I think they're trying to give us directions.' Lorna raised both eyebrows.

Kieran nodded in the direction over her shoulder then tossed his head in the direction of the office space as if to ask which way.

Rolling her eyes, Lorna stepped out in front of the gunfire.

Two bullets ricocheted off her shield before the shooting ceased.

Kieran released the breath he'd held as she'd stepped out. A guardian's shield wasn't completely impenetrable, especially if the guardian in control of it wasn't in the best of health.

When Lorna began walking in the direction of their assailants, Kieran fell in step with her, adding his own firepower to the wall of energy.

Five military vampires rose from their crouched positions and lowered their weapons as the twins advanced.

The smell hit them before the scene did.

Death was an unmistakeable smell when you'd been hunting those responsible for it for years.

The bodies of the hostages, a range of staff grabbed at random from around the building, were heaped next to a watercooler in the kitchen area.

Lorna sucked in a deep breath and the five guns pointed at them fell apart.

Kieran grinned and let Lorna make the first move.

With a wave of her hand, her shield expanded outwards, engulfing the confused soldiers in fire.

As panic set in, the twins made their move, swiftly dispatching the group.

'Five down,' Kieran muttered, hands on hips as he stared down at the ashy, charred carpet. 'Fifteen to . . .'

Looking at his sister, Kieran watched her tug her phone out of her pocket and fire off a message.

'Clean-up,' Lorna waved the phone before putting it away. 'We don't have time to catalogue the victims.'

With a pained glance at the bloodied pile of limbs, Lorna dipped her head in sorrow and respect then set off across the open-plan office space again.

'Where are you going?'

'They wanted us to go this way, right? So that's where we'll find the most trouble.' Lorna shrugged.

Stopping suddenly, she cocked her head to one side.

'On second thoughts, perhaps we should split up.'

'Is that wise?'

'The whole floor is empty aside from whoever lays in wait, but I'm getting life signs above us as well.'

Kieran tipped his chin upwards as he considered her

suggestion. 'There are more upstairs than there are down here. They might just be there to direct you.'

'That's why splitting up could be advantageous,' Lorna said brightly.

'Normally I'd agree with you . . .'

'Oh shush, we had to send Aiden away, come on, be my decoy,' Lorna goaded. 'For old time's sake?'

Kieran smirked, but his head fell when he followed it with a sigh.

'I love you, you know that,' he said as he looked up.

With a nod, Lorna reached out and touched his forehead, something she'd done since they were children when she wanted to connect with him, before they'd been old enough to fully master guardian telepathy.

'And if that werewolf and his prodigy of a brother can't come up with anything else, I'm going to fucking miss you.'

Slipping her arms around his neck, the twins pulled each other in tight.

'I'm sorry I have to leave you,' Lorna whispered.

'I'm sorry I couldn't stop this,' Kieran muttered before taking a step back, out of her arms. 'Right, where do you want me?'

'Follow your own damn nose.' Lorna lifted an eyebrow. 'That way.' She jerked a thumb over her shoulder.

With a nod, Kieran took off in the direction of offices in the south-west corner of the floor. Lorna set off towards a fire escape on the north face of the building.

Whilst navigating the stairwell as quietly as possible, she noted how her fingers were practically numb, though she could see her hand on the rail, she couldn't really feel it.

Unsure whether that would be a help or a hindrance, she shrugged to herself and continued to the top floor of the building.

Finding the level occupied by a different business, and laid out as a warren of enclosed rooms rather than open-plan office space, Lorna ventured from the stairwell with extreme caution. Red lights lit the corridors, suggesting someone had finally triggered an evacuation.

She estimated that Kieran would probably deal with a further five vampires, leaving her with the rest and whoever was commanding them.

It boiled her blood that members of the Baxter family managed to escape punishment for their behaviour. Though, she reminded herself as she eased down the first corridor, they rarely got their own hands dirty.

Their hearing was better than hers, so it came as little surprise when the sound of boots running towards her met her ears in stereo as they approached from both sides.

Ducking in through the nearest door, Lorna found herself in one of the boardrooms.

With a soft-footed jump, her feet connected with the ceiling.

As she listened, the two welcome parties collided in the corridor. No one spoke, but she soon heard them opening doors up and down the hall.

Despite being on the ceiling, she knew she was too exposed if they all charged the room at the same time.

When the door was opened, Lorna reached down and grabbed an unsuspecting vampire by the shoulders, throwing him at the glass table in the middle of the room with enough force to break it.

As the cavalry arrived, she set her shield against the spray of expected bullets and whipped up a telekinetic storm in the middle of the room.

Blood, then ash sprayed as shards of glass from the broken table tore through the room and the flesh of six more vampires.

Waiting until all the debris had settled, Lorna leapt down with a crunch of glass.

'That wasn't very sporting of you.' Hillary Baxter pouted as she pushed the door open before Lorna could reach for it.

The vampire surveyed the mess. Lorna raised an eyebrow and waited for Hillary's attention to return to her.

'Oh, I don't know.' Lorna looked Hillary's five bodyguards up and down where they stood at her back. 'If we're scoring, I'm winning sixteen-nil and I don't care if you are the council leader's daughter, I've got nothing to lose, I will make it twenty-two before I go.'

Narrowing her toxic-green eyes from beneath the fringe of her white-blonde bob, Hillary glared at Lorna. Significantly younger than her sire, Hillary was no more related to Jake than Lorna was to Aiden.

'I'm not here to fight.' Hillary rolled her eyes and smoothed the sleeves of her fitted military robe. 'I'm just here to make sure you snuff it.'

'And I'm only here to avenge those hostages.' Lorna shrugged and prepared to strike back.

The glass on the floor rattled.

Pain tore through Lorna's torso, but she refused to show weakness, attempting a second wave.

The glass didn't even rattle a second time and Lorna felt a bead of sweat roll down her temple.

'It seems you're finally running out of juice,' Hillary stated. 'About time, too.'

Lorna's legs wobbled as Hillary turned to the two vampire guards on her left.

'You two, finish her, and make sure her blood is well and truly spilled,' Hillary instructed. 'Sorry Lorna, this isn't personal, and I won't stay to watch. I can't be associated with your death.'

Reaching for a chair to prevent herself falling to her knees into the glass, Lorna's brow creased in confusion as the two executioners flanked her and Hillary turned to leave.

'Trust me, this is the best way,' Hillary said with a nod of respect before she left.

'On your knees,' one of the soldiers instructed.

Glancing down at the floor, Lorna looked for a spot to fall and realised, as she sank down, that it really didn't matter.

She barely made it into a sitting position when they began firing their semi-automatic weapons into her shield.

Hoping Kieran would hear the firing, or that a bullet would ricochet and kill either of the shooters before her shield failed, Lorna closed her eyes and waited for oblivion.

She felt the shield starting to crack moments before she fell into darkness.

THIRTEEN

'Lorna! Lorna, wake up. You have to wake up!'

The voice grew nearer as consciousness found her.

Her eyes fluttered but wouldn't open fully. She tried to sit up instead and only twitched. She tried to speak but what came out of her parted lips was barely a moan.

The sound of movement in the glass made her flinch. She was on the ground, though her torso was on his lap.

Managing to turn her head enough to look up at the face of her rescuer, Lorna found Aiden's panicked eyes.

A breath rushed from his lips to see her move.

'What . . .' Lorna started but choked on the word.

He sat her up and cradled her tight in his arms.

'What are you doing here?' she managed after a moment.

'I brought Nick,' he answered as if she'd given him a direct order to do so.

'Where . . .?' Lorna tried to look around.

'Doesn't matter,' Aiden soothed.

'He needs to get you away . . .' Lorna reached up slowly, her limbs screaming at the requirement, and stroked his

79

cheek. 'Away from . . .'

'I'm not going anywhere,' Aiden muttered, wrapping himself around her, his hand sliding into her hair to lift her head.

Her fingertips still on his face, Lorna met his gaze and felt tears sting her eyes.

Before she knew what was happening, Aiden's mouth was on hers. His lips took and savoured hers as the heat of his body surrounded her with such intensity she was certain she'd burn up.

Wanting so badly to cling to him in a way her body wouldn't allow, she choked back a sob, her body aching with loss.

Before she knew it, the tears were flowing.

Realising she had started to cry, Aiden pulled back, but she chased him with her lips, catching merely a taster before her head went slack and she fell back into unconsciousness.

When she woke again, she realised she was outside.

'We need to find Kieran,' Aiden said, his voice drifting away from her.

Lorna knew without looking that he was pacing.

Forcing her eyes open, she blinked stupidly a couple of times, finding herself stunned into silence.

Peering down at her, his nose barely inches from her face, was a glowing vision with blond hair which reached the nape of his neck, framing elegant cheekbones and mesmerising aquamarine eyes. Despite the look of intense concern on his face, there was a warmth emanating from him that she'd never experienced before. She felt incredibly safe.

'Aiden . . .' she mumbled. 'Should I be worried I can see an angel?'

'Well, she's half right,' the vision said with a chuckle before moving away and giving her some space.

'What can we do, Nick? I don't think she has long left.' Aiden appeared as Nick stepped back, his hands on his hips as he faced his brother.

Lorna's eyebrows made a run for her hairline, so THAT was Nick.

'There's no *documented* case of a vampire biting a guardian and either surviving. There's a lot of hearsay on the internet, whispers of attempts at feeding on witches or guardians, but it seems the council has worked damned hard to cover up all incidences of cross-species feeding.'

'Acting like it never happens won't stop creatures experimenting.'

'Exactly. I had to dig really deep and use previous experience to find anything at all.'

'Yeah, some might say you've got a little too much *experience.*'

Lorna heard the amusement and light teasing in Aiden's voice.

'There's no talk of a cure, but there were rumours of survivors. Generally, it seems most bites result in full drainage.' Nick paused.

'Any suggestions to go with those rumours?' Aiden growled.

'Like I said, it's been heavily covered up, but I do have a suggestion, though it's a long shot.'

'What is it?' Aiden's voice wavered slightly, making Lorna

wonder whether Nick would recognise or even question the hitch in his voice.

'What's the one species that vampires can't control? Can't often beat? Besides guardians, that is?'

'Me.' Aiden shrugged. 'Werewolves.'

'If we mix your DNA with theirs, it might help to cancel out the vampire venom.'

'You want me to bite her? Based on nothing more than your gut feeling?'

'It's that or shoot her with one of those bullets.' Nick turned away from the look of horror on Aiden's face and returned to Lorna's side. 'Lorna, would we have permission to attempt either of those options?'

'I'm dead anyway, what choice do we have?'

'You trust me to—' Aiden's jaw dropped as he span to face her.

'Of course,' Lorna cut Aiden off.

'If it works, there could be some nasty side effects,' Nick warned as he reached out to stroke her forehead. 'I suspect it will hurt like hell, whether it works or not . . .'

'Nick . . .' Aiden's voice was warning.

'It's fine.' Lorna met Aiden's eyes with a sad smile as it began to rain. 'Sorry,' she muttered, and attempted to throw up a shield to keep them all dry from her pain, but it barely shimmered against her skin.

'Save your strength,' Nick soothed with a smile.

'We need to find Kieran first.' Aiden ruffled his hand through his hair.

'He'll understand.' Nick looked up as Lorna's eyelids fluttered in exhaustion. 'We could lose her before you find him. The only other thing *I* could do for her now is give her a peaceful death.'

'Prevent me or the vampires from killing her by killing her yourself, you mean?' Aiden's voice cracked as he stared down at Lorna where she lay on the roof of the office block.

'What will I understand?' Lorna heard Kieran approach from behind her. 'Nick.'

Though she couldn't see him, Lorna heard the respect in her own brother's voice as he approached the angeling.

Getting up, Nick met Kieran and took him to the edge of the roof to explain his plan.

While they spoke, Aiden dropped into a sitting position next to Lorna and lifted her gently onto his lap.

'I'll try not to hurt you,' he whispered, placing a kiss on her temple while her brother's back was still turned.

'You didn't start this. At least we can say we tried,' Lorna mumbled, her eyelids drooping.

When Nick and Kieran finally turned to look back, Lorna felt a wave of nausea on seeing the haunted look in her brother's eyes.

He walked towards her, his eyes searching her features. She wasn't sure whether he was committing her to memory or looking for alternative answers none of them had.

Attempting a smile, Lorna hoped to reassure him. She'd agreed to take the chance.

Kieran's eyes fell on Aiden and the way he was holding his exhausted sister. His face twisted, he looked set to speak, but on meeting Lorna's eyes again his face fell.

When he reached her side, he crouched down and took her hand with a squeeze before reaching forward to kiss her on the cheek.

Meeting her eyes, he nodded.

Lorna nodded in return, her eyes filling with tears.

As he stood up again, Kieran gave a single nod to Aiden and walked away. Stopping at the edge of the roof, he kept his back to what was about to happen.

Nick lifted Lorna gently off Aiden's lap so that he could shift forms.

'I can sit up, it's OK,' Lorna whispered, using Nick's support to cross her legs and lean forward. 'Thank you.'

'Alright,' Nick answered softly and got up again.

Though he also turned his back, he stayed close.

Focusing on her breathing, Lorna watched Nick's ankle-length coat whip in the wind.

When Aiden's muzzle nudged her shoulder she smiled and inclined her head towards him as he rubbed his ear against hers with a soft whine.

Reaching up, she patted him on the nose before turning her head the other way to expose the existing wound. She felt him place his teeth either side of the vampire bite and give a testing squeeze to make sure he had enough of a grip.

With a quick pinch, his needle-sharp teeth pierced her skin. Barely feeling anything at first, Lorna took a deep breath as he released her shoulder and stepped back, but it was short-lived. Within seconds her body was on fire, all the muscles around the bite going into spasm.

'Fuck,' she ground out through the pain.

Nick and Kieran turned to find Aiden already back in his human form, sitting beside her trying to survey the damage while Lorna rocked back and forth, her arms clutched to her chest, eyes closed.

Kieran strode forwards but it was Nick who spoke first.

'All we can do now is wait.'

Aiden nodded and reached for Lorna's hand to snap her out of her trance.

'Wow, that packs one hell of a punch,' Lorna squeaked, finally managing to look up. 'How long do you think it will take?'

Kieran wouldn't meet her eye.

'I can't be sure.' Nick looked her up and down. 'Can I take you home?'

'I didn't think you collected your experiments too?' Lorna managed to smirk, sweat trickling down her face.

'I meant to your own home, I'm prescribing some bed rest while we await the results.' Nick shot her an amused look of his own.

'My penthouse is nearest,' Lorna said with a glance at Kieran and Aiden.

'It's on London Avenue,' Aiden informed his brother. 'We won't be far behind.'

'Hey, it's stopped raining.' Lorna smiled as Nick reached down and scooped her into his arms.

'It's over, for now, OK?' Aiden said gently, reaching out to brush her hair out of her face.

Over Aiden's shoulder, Kieran was glaring at him, but when he met his sister's eyes, he turned away.

As Nick took a step back, readying to leave, Hillary appeared at the door to the stairs, her three remaining bodyguards at her side.

'Go, take Lorna, we'll get past her easily enough,' Aiden

assured his brother, but Nick met Aiden's eyes blankly and shuffled Lorna into Aiden's arms as something in him shifted.

The transition made Lorna shudder and remember that she was safe, but at the hands of something with the potential to be truly destructive. When Nick let her go, his eyes misting with black as he turned on Hillary, she clung tight to Aiden.

As Nick approached the party two large black, leathery demon wings, sharp and angular, slid from his shoulder blades.

When Lorna started to quake, watching the angeling at work, Aiden began stroking her arm. Kieran stepped forward for a better view.

When he reached the first of Hillary's aides, Nick reached out and with one sharp twist, tore the vampire's head clean off her body, before throwing it to one side.

Lorna flinched.

Thrusting his other hand into the solar plexus of the second, he punched through the chest cavity and tore their heart out, squashing it in his palm before the vampire disintegrated.

By the time he reached the third, Lorna could feel a raw fear threading through her veins like ice. Yet, in Aiden's arms she wasn't afraid for her own safety. Nick's aura, his demon unleashed, rolled over the rooftop like freezing fog, heavy and oppressive.

The last vampire standing looked to his commanding officer for assistance as Nick approached. Hillary remained stoic, even as Nick's foot connected with the sternum of her last guard, sending the vampire flying towards a pipe protruding from the maintenance outbuilding.

As her last man standing disintegrated, Hillary lifted her chin and folded her arms, standing her ground, but she went limp with fright when Nick picked her up by the throat.

'This is over for tonight, and you might want to think more carefully about who you mess with,' Nick said, his voice having deepened and taken on a rougher edge, though Lorna still found it soothing.

'This is none of your business,' Hillary gurgled.

'I've just made it my business,' Nick growled.

Given his species, Nick had every right to get involved, even do as he pleased with the Baxter if he considered her a big enough threat to the equilibrium of the city itself. Unofficially Lucious' right-hand man, he had the power to judge and grant death, be it a violent one in demon form or a peaceful one with the touch of an angel.

Hillary's eyes slid up the length of Nick's wings before glancing across at Aiden and Lorna.

With a hiss of realisation, she lurched backwards and out of Nick's light grip.

Looking to Lorna again, frustration and intent still in her eyes, Hillary turned her back on them and leapt down the side of the building.

With a growl in the direction of the fleeing vampire, Nick turned and walked back to Lorna.

She continued to quake as she watched him, transfixed, though the nearer he got the more she felt the icy dread melt away as his eyes returned to their natural blue and the wings slid away. He, too, kept his gaze on hers until the warmth and smile she had previously seen in his eyes returned.

'Sorry about that. Now I'll take you home,' he said quietly, and took her back from Aiden before once again spreading his wings, this time two large white, feathered angel wings.

With a sigh of relief, Lorna slid into his embrace easily, Aiden giving her hand another squeeze as he let her go.

'We'll see you at the apartment.' Aiden nodded.

Kieran, tense and silent beside Aiden, didn't move.

As Nick launched himself into the air, Lorna let herself pass out again.

FOURTEEN

The first thing Lorna saw when she opened her eyes was Kieran staring at her from over the top of her medical kit. With a groan and a scowl, she waved him off.

'I'm fully aware of how awful I must look, you don't need to look at me as though I'm the monster from the deep.' She hauled herself up and looked around.

'Lorna . . .' Kieran reached for her as she moved.

'I'm awake, I clearly survived,' she huffed, but the look on his face made her look down. 'Oh.'

Blood from where Aiden had bitten her was seeping over her collarbone and shoulder but there were patches of her clothing that were shredded and bloody from her own glass cyclone.

'Yeah, oh.' Kieran raised an eyebrow.

'My skin is still a bit numb.' Lorna poked at some of the bloody stains with interest.

'I was going to try to clean you up a bit, but you might need to take your clothes off and do it yourself, if you can,' Kieran mumbled as he rummaged around inside the medi-kit. 'How are you feeling?'

'Like I'll live,' Lorna grouched as she started peeling her jeans off gingerly. 'Nothing seems to hurt as much as Nick said it might. How long was I out?'

'About an hour. I dosed you with painkillers while you slept.' Kieran glanced up at her lacerated legs as she tossed the jeans to one side.

'Please stop looking at me like that, it's like having a mirror thrust in front of you,' Lorna griped without thinking.

Looking up with a scowl of his own, Kieran opened his mouth to snark back, but his brow relaxed when a hint of relief passed through his eyes.

'I'll get you something clean,' he said, handing her a pack of antiseptic wipes and standing up.

'Can I then go back to sleep, and you slip me a dose of painkillers every few hours?' Lorna smirked but hissed an expletive when the first wipe met her skin.

'I think that could be arranged,' Kieran said softly and handed her a clean t-shirt and pair of pyjama bottoms.

Lorna took the clothes with a yelp. As their fingers had touched, Kieran had given her an electric shock.

'Hey! What was that for?!' she squeaked playfully, but when she looked up his jaw was set and he was staring over the top of her head. 'Talk to me?' Her voice dropped to a whisper.

'*It's not you, give me time,*' he transmitted as he backed away from her.

When Lorna nodded, he sighed in an attempt to calm himself.

'. . . Would you just listen to me? I think you should spend a few hours in wolf form for that wound to heal . . . Aiden!'

Nick followed his brother into the room as the door burst open and he strode in. 'There, she's awake, satisfied?' Nick was watching him with restrained anger even as he folded his arms and leant on the doorframe.

'I'll feel much better being on hand while we all catch up on some sleep. Kieran can take the spare room.'

'You can play watchman in form,' Nick argued.

Watching the brothers as she continued to dab at her wounds, Lorna realised the pair had probably been going around in circles about their security for some time.

'Won't Kia be waiting on an update?'

'She knows we're in the clear.' Nick didn't move.

With a snort of derision, Aiden put his hands on his hips. It was only then that Lorna spotted the blood stain smeared down the left side of his shirt.

'What happened?'

'It's nothing, a glancing blow with a shard of glass,' Aiden said dismissively.

'Go and change,' she commanded, making him glare at her. 'If you don't, I'll lie awake worrying that it's more serious than you'll admit.'

Behind him, Nick smirked as Aiden tipped his head and stormed out of the room.

'I'll make sure he does as he's told before I head off.' Nick's eyes sparkled in amusement. 'And I apologise for what happened on the roof. Being so close to death you'd have felt the raw menace of my demon.'

'I know not to get on your bad side.' Lorna nodded, her eyes wide but playful.

'How do you feel?' Nick searched her face with gently curious eyes.

'I think Kieran gave me the hard stuff, I'm just very tired, for now.'

'Interesting . . .' Nick nodded. 'If anything changes for the worst, don't hesitate to call. I suspect there may be some symptoms . . . and some of them could be permanent.'

'Gee, lucky me, but thank you.' Lorna nodded in return before he turned and left.

Once they were alone again, Kieran tidied the medi-kit away, stashing it back in the ensuite bathroom while Lorna slipped into the PJ bottoms and exchanged her vest for the t-shirt.

'I didn't realise you'd met Nick,' Lorna said, tucking her knees to her chest when Kieran reappeared.

'We crossed paths during training. He has permission to return to the Black Mountain Reserve whenever he chooses. Lucious has immense respect for him,' Kieran replied and looked down at the end of the bed as if contemplating sitting back down.

'Nick and Aiden are cut from the same cloth,' Lorna pointed out.

'Hardly,' Kieran scoffed.

'Well, it's looking like their quick thinking saved my life tonight.' Lorna shrugged.

'He's still a werewolf,' Kieran stated.

Lorna pursed her lips in a tight smile, her stomach churning as she remembered that both a werewolf and a vampire had infected her with their DNA in the space of twenty-four hours.

When Aiden appeared in form at the door, Kieran headed for it.

'She's all yours, get some sleep,' Kieran mumbled, making Lorna notice how tired he suddenly looked, before closing the door behind him.

Barking once at the closed door, Aiden huffed after him.

Falling back against the pillows in exhaustion, Lorna smiled and patted the bed next to her. Jumping up, left hind leg dragging slightly, Aiden crossed the bed to snuffle at her hair before flopping onto the sheets beside her.

Getting up just enough to slip under the sheets, Lorna realised how slow and heavy her body felt and gratefully sank back into the mattress, thankful that whatever changes were in store her body would get the chance to rest first.

As she began drifting into sleep, she began to get flashbacks of things she didn't remember. . . and things she most definitely did.

Peering across at Aiden, she found him watching her.

When he blinked, heavy lidded himself, she took the hint and let sleep take her.

FIFTEEN

It was still dark when Lorna found herself awake and staring at the ceiling.

Hissing through her teeth as even the slightest movement caused her skin to burn and joints to ache, she sat up carefully, looking for the clock in the gloom.

Remembering she wasn't in her usual bedroom, Lorna peered across the bed to where Aiden was flaked out, still fast asleep.

Slipping out of the bed as gently as her body would allow, she was thankful he didn't stir, even as she gingerly made her way out of the room. She didn't want to wake Kieran up either if she could help it, she just needed to find his stash of painkillers.

'Hey.'

Shoulders slumping in defeat as she shut the door behind her, Lorna found Kieran sat next to the bi-fold doors leading to the roof terrace, a steaming mug cradled in his palms.

'Hey,' Lorna returned as she crept over ready to sit next to him. 'Where are the drugs?'

'On the coffee table.' Kieran's eyes moved to the bag sitting on the table next to where she stood. 'You need another dose?'

'Yeah,' Lorna said as she snatched up the bag and realised how desperate her voice had sounded.

'How many doses?'

'Oh, it's not *that* bad.' She smirked as she sat next to him and handed him the bag.

Setting his cup down, Kieran fussed with the bag as Lorna waited patiently, watching the lights of the city twinkling beyond her balcony.

'I've just made tea, would you like one?' Kieran asked casually as he stuck the needle in her arm.

'I'm hoping this stuff will knock me out again.' Lorna tugged the sleeve of her t-shirt back down. 'Have you slept?'

'Not yet.'

'Is that really tea?'

Kieran's eyes drifted to her bedroom door and back to the floor.

'Please tell me you're not keeping watch,' Lorna warned quietly.

Keeping her eyes on her brother she waited for him to look at or answer her, prepared to out-silence him for once. Eventually, he rolled his eyes, a fond smirk tugging at his lips.

'You had two of us with you yesterday and it nearly wasn't enough. I can't sleep while the two of you do, someone should be alert until the sun comes up, I'll sleep then.'

'If I hadn't had the two of you there, I'd have been much worse off. Even I can admit that.' Lorna smiled. 'But you seem to have forgotten the protocol, we've been made all too aware of where our fate will most likely lead us. You can't drive yourself to distraction or exhaustion over something I'm fully prepared to face.'

'You may be prepared to die in the line of duty, but I'm going to do everything I can to prevent that happening,' Kieran said through gritted teeth. 'Especially if it means . . .'

'Means what? Dying the same way our parents did?' Lorna sighed. 'You and I both know we can't control that. I have to be prepared to snuff it in action . . . I wouldn't be very good at my job if I wasn't.'

'I can't . . . won't, stand by and watch your life get wiped out like generation upon generation before us, especially not the way Mum . . .'

'I realise you've seen some horrific things . . .' Lorna softened her voice. He hadn't let her see her parents' bodies.

'We both have.' He shrugged and retrieved his cup to take a mouthful of whatever was in it.

Lorna pursed her lips to prevent the names of the ghosts that hung between them from spilling forth. Kieran didn't need to be reminded of those faces in that moment. He'd also lost love because of who they were.

'Please go to bed.' Lorna reached out and squeezed his ankle. 'Even if you don't sleep right away.'

Meeting her eyes finally, Kieran gave a resigned nod and got to his feet. Placing the mug down on the table, from where Lorna could smell it was just tea, he reached for her hands and pulled her up.

'I'm not going anywhere tonight. And whatever this was has nothing to do with Mum and Dad.'

'Right,' Kieran breathed and pulled her in for a cuddle, to avoid meeting her eye.

Scowling as he let her go, Lorna moved to the open-plan kitchen for a glass of water, glancing over her shoulder to watch him disappear into the spare room.

Drinking the contents of her glass in one go, she headed back to her own bed. Running her fingers through her hair as she crossed the living area, she glanced out at the cityscape again, sunrise felt so far away.

Lorna opened the door as gently as possible but needn't have bothered. Aiden was sat up on the bed in human form, peering under his shirt.

'That's not a glass scratch, is it?' she asked, closing the door and leaning against it.

'It's practically a scratch now.'

'How many bullets did Nick pluck out of you while Kieran psyched himself up to clean my wounds?'

'Just the one,' he admitted, meeting the challenge in her eyes.

'For fuck's sake, Aiden,' she sighed. 'There was a reason we told you to stay clear.'

'You made it sound political.' He shot her a boyish grin. 'Besides, I wasn't the one they were shooting at. I just got in the way of a stray bullet.'

Lorna opened her mouth to retort but he raised both eyebrows pointedly.

'Right.'

'You're welcome,' he deadpanned.

'Do you need fresh dressings?'

'Probably,' he admitted with a shrug.

Nodding, Lorna moved to the ensuite and switched the light on so that she could raid the medi-kit.

Turning back to the bedroom, she found him stood in the doorway, a bundle of bloodied shirt and dressings in one hand.

Frozen to the spot, Lorna let her eyes find the wound for herself. It was little more than an angry mark on his very tanned . . . very firm torso.

He let her look for a moment too long before he threw the shirt in the hamper and the bandages in the trash.

Backing up until she was forced to take a seat on the edge of the bath, Lorna handed him an antiseptic wipe and tore the backing off a fresh dressing. He didn't take it at first, his eyes challenging her to apply it.

When she arched an eyebrow of her own, he took it from her and applied it himself.

'How's your neck?' Aiden asked, reaching out to brush her hair away from her own dressings.

'I'll take a look in the morning. I've taken more painkillers for now.'

Nodding, he took a step back so that she could get up. Sticking her tongue out at him, she gave him a shove out of the bathroom so that she could head back to bed. The drugs were kicking in.

'Lorna?'

'Yeah?' She turned to look at him as she shut the light out.

He took a step towards her in the dark, opening his mouth to speak, but before either of them could utter a word his hands found her waist and his mouth was on hers. Lorna had to cling to him to save herself from falling over, but he held her steady, backing her up until her shoulders met the wall. A flush of heat rushed through her body as he kissed her hungrily, his body pressing her into the plasterboard.

As soon as he broke the kiss for a moment, Lorna placed her hands on his bare chest, feeling the heat of him beneath her fingertips, hoping to keep him at arm's length, though she doubted it would stop him.

'That can't happen again,' she said, breathless.

'Why not?' Aiden growled.

'You should know why not.'

'I don't care what Kieran thinks of me.' Aiden nudged forwards, testing her boundaries, his eyes gleaming when her breath caught.

'I don't mean Kieran . . . it's more complicated than that. Daniel . . .'

'Daniel?' Aiden's tone darkened as he paused his advance. 'What has your dead ex got to do with the way you kissed me in that tower block?'

'The way *I* kissed *you*?' Lorna exclaimed.

'Did you think I was him in your half-dead state?'

With a guttural growl, Aiden leant over her, planting his hands on the wall at either side of her head to brace himself.

'It doesn't matter why I kissed you back . . .' Lorna started, ready to fight her corner.

'It doesn't matter to you, because you thought you would be dead now,' he ground out.

Lorna closed her eyes, unable to face the look in his. 'At least with me dead, you would have been safe. You could go back to the pack, the vampires would never find out how you felt about me.'

'How *I* felt about you?! So, when you . . . what was that? Giving me what you thought I wanted? Or a pretty cruel way to say goodbye?'

Swallowing hard and feeling tears prick at her lashes, Lorna opened her eyes to stare directly into his. 'It was supposed to be goodbye.'

'You would have preferred death to the card I dealt you,' Aiden stated and, running his hands down the wall, pushed himself away from her. He held eye contact as he reached for the bedroom door. 'I can't, and won't, apologise for saving you. You mean more to me than that.'

With that, he left the room. Unable to move, Lorna listened as he opened the terrace doors and headed out onto the rooftop garden. Only then did she release a ragged sigh and move to the end of the bed to sit down.

With a gasp, she spotted the claw marks he'd left down the wall, either side of where her head had been. Trembling slightly, she got back to her feet and touched the gouged plaster before quickly locking herself in the bathroom where she sat on the floor and tried to calm her breathing.

Feeling dizzy from the drugs and the deep breathing exercises, Lorna had just made it to her feet when she heard Aiden return to the bedroom. Feeling calmer, and knowing she couldn't hide from him all night, she unlocked the door and stepped out of the bathroom.

Only to find Aiden pulling clothes out of the wardrobe.

'What are you doing?' Lorna scowled.

'I think it's best I go back to the pack for a few days. We have a key annual meeting next weekend anyway and I need to clear my head.'

'Will you be back?' Lorna's face relaxed as she heard her own voice tremble.

'I've sworn to protect you. Of course I'll be back.' He didn't look at her as he threw one last shirt onto the bed and dragged a holdall out from beneath it.

'Great, so you're leaving me with my moody-ass twin? How long . . .?'

'Monday, maybe Tuesday.' He looked up as he lay a pair of jeans in the bag.

Lorna was impressed that he'd managed to stash so many clothes in the penthouse, there were more garments going into the bag than she was sure she had on hand herself.

'No, I meant how long have you hidden . . .' Lorna gestured to the scratch marks down the wall. 'That?'

'It's not important.' Aiden shrugged.

'Clearly it is.' Lorna folded her arms.

'It doesn't matter. You clearly believe that your dead boyfriend was the one for you and that you will soon follow him to the grave.'

'You made that assumption on your own,' Lorna bit out. 'You know me better than that.'

'Do I?' Aiden paused to glare at her. 'The last thing I expected was for you to drop his name into conversation like that.'

'If you'd let me finish, I was going to say that Daniel was killed for a reason, they'll target you at the faintest sniff of leverage.'

'I'm already a target. I'm in their way, especially after what I did yesterday. Why should anything *I* feel for *you* make any difference?' Aiden's tone was mocking as he continued shoving clothes into the bag. 'If it's easier, I'll file my notice with Mia first thing Monday. You can have until then to decide if that works for you.'

'*I* can have until then?! You're telling me what I can and can't do? Maybe it is best you go off and play alpha for the weekend, you clearly need the power trip.' Lorna raised her voice as she moved over to the bed and began helping him pack.

Completing the short task in silence, Aiden roughly zipped the bag closed and straightened, reaching for a t-shirt he'd set to one side.

Lorna squared up to him before he had a chance to put it on. Her eyes blazed into his as he faced her, his face thunderous.

'Are you going to let me leave?' Aiden motioned to the fact that she had the bedroom door blocked.

'No,' she snapped, and shoved his bag to the floor.

Glancing down at the bag, Aiden's eyes widened, but when he looked up, she was smirking at the childishness of her own actions.

'What do you want from me?' he breathed.

'Your safety,' Lorna admitted.

'Why?' Aiden inched closer, his voice low.

'I can't lose anyone else,' she whispered, but her eyes met his, even as her head bent low. 'I'd rather die first.'

'I'd noticed.' Aiden tipped his forehead against hers, making her close her eyes.

'Don't.'

'What?'

'I can't.'

Aiden sighed and lay his hands gently on her shoulders.

'Can't what?' he whispered in her ear, the warmth of his breath sending shivers down her spine.

'Do this.'

'What, this?' Aiden's mouth was less than an inch from her own, and before she could respond, his lips were on hers, hot and heavy.

After a moment she pushed him away a second time.

Aiden leant against her palms until she let his body sink closer, feeling the warmth of him rush over her.

Dipping his head, Aiden planted a tender kiss to her throat.

'If you really didn't want me, I couldn't do this . . .' Aiden whispered against her throat as one of his hands drifted between her thighs.

'You're playing with fire,' Lorna panted, even as her eyes glazed with desire.

'I can take the heat,' he murmured against her cheek as he lifted his head to kiss her again.

Lorna moaned into his kiss when the hand between her legs moved away so that he could reach under her t-shirt with both hands and stroke the curve of her waist with his thumbs.

Inching the t-shirt higher, he slowly tugged it over her head.

'Are you going to stop me again?' he asked quietly, reaching for the straps of her bra.

With a sigh of frustration, Lorna fell into his embrace, kissing him hungrily as they manoeuvred each other out of the last of their clothes.

As they fell onto the bed in a frenzy of heated kisses, Aiden paused only to admire her breasts, vowing to give far more attention to them next time, their bodies connecting seamlessly.

Lorna let out a cry somewhere between defeat and ecstasy as she wrapped her legs around his hips, unwilling to let him go once he was inside her.

Riding high on a combination of the way Aiden's muscular body felt against hers and the painkillers, Lorna quickly tumbled over the edge, biting down on a scream she was scared her brother might hear.

As they lay tangled in the sheets in the dark both Lorna and Aiden drank in the silence. Each for different reasons.

Aiden had wrapped Lorna in the bedding to keep her close as he dozed, one of her legs still draped over his thigh as they faced each other.

The painkillers were beginning to wear off and Lorna couldn't have moved if she'd wanted to for pain. Pain that wasn't purely physical.

Turning her head to stare at the ceiling, she wondered what the fuck she'd just done.

Not the sex itself, that had been long overdue between them, even she could admit that.

But she had vowed not to let anyone else get too close and she'd broken her own vow.

Her pulse suddenly racing and a sheen of sweat threatening her brow, Lorna sat up a little too quickly for her body, causing her to whimper in pain.

'Are you OK?' Aiden was instantly sat up beside her.

'The drugs are wearing off,' Lorna said quietly.

'I'll get them.' He leaned forward to kiss her shoulder, an endearing gesture that caused her heart to leap into her throat and she jumped up out of the bed.

'It's OK, I'll go.'

Reaching for a robe hanging on the back of her door, Lorna quickly drew the garment around her and strode into the living area.

Thankful Kieran hadn't reappeared from the spare room, she knelt next to the coffee table and started rifling through the medi-kit. Finding the tablets quickly, she headed for the kitchen for more water.

As she drank the glass slowly, she stared at her bedroom door where Aiden appeared, completely naked. He watched her finish the glass of water, but didn't leave the room. Instead he leant on the doorframe, scratching the stubble at his jaw thoughtfully.

Lorna met his eyes as calmly as she could, though her knees almost buckled at the sight after the way he'd made her feel between the sheets.

When he let his arm fall in resignation and headed back to bed, she shook herself off and followed him.

Finding him lounging on the bed, the sheet casually thrown across his hips, Lorna slid onto the bed in her robe.

'I can look out for myself, you know. I won't let them do that to you again,' Aiden muttered as he reached for her.

She was resistant at first, opening her mouth to speak, but thinking better of it.

With a fond sigh of humoured annoyance, he pulled her to his chest and relaxed lazily around her. Lorna felt heat encircle her body even where he wasn't touching her.

'How long have you been able to get into my head like that?'

'It started about a month after I moved in. And I'm not technically in your head. I just catch your vibe.' His voice continued to be soft as he buried his head in her hair and kissed the back of her neck. 'I'm not going anywhere.' His voice grew softer still as he yawned.

'What if we don't have a choice in that?' Lorna whispered.

When he didn't answer straight away, she wondered if he'd nodded off.

'You should get some more sleep,' he said after a moment.

'I agree.' Lorna struggled not to yawn as she reached for his hand at her waist. 'Leave that bag packed for the meet. I know you have to be there, what's happened shouldn't prevent that.'

'You could come with me,' Aiden said, suddenly sounding very awake.

'To the pack meet?' She turned her head to look at him in the dark. 'No, I'll be fine, I'll move in with Mia and Ben for the weekend if you're that worried about me,' Lorna soothed.

'It's the last place the vampires would dare to look for you. We can offer total pack protection while you recover,' Aiden offered, casually propping himself up on one elbow. She wriggled out of his grip to turn and face him.

His eyes penetrated hers as they met across the bed.

'And Kieran's reaction to this is likely to be?' Lorna shot him a look that suggested it wasn't best to tease a wounded lion.

'Despite his prejudices, Kieran would also be welcome to

attend and keep an eye on you. That is, if he could stand to be around that many of us at once.' Aiden smirked. 'Pack members include friends as well as family, you wouldn't be bored. Besides, Kieran would be a fool to refuse you the protection of Nick.'

Mulling it over for less than a millisecond, Lorna grinned. 'Sounds like a plan.'

She doubted he'd be so hands on with her around his family.

SIXTEEN

Blinking her eyes open, Lorna found Aiden fast asleep, his nose practically touching hers, one arm slung casually across her waist.

With a sigh, she glanced up and found a dull grey light creeping through the curtains. Weather to suit her mood.

Taking a deep breath, she raised one arm to sweep her hair out of her face. The aches and pains were creeping back in, so she decided she couldn't have slept very long. Her body felt bone tired as she rolled onto her back. Stretching out as slowly as possible, hoping Aiden didn't wake up, she considered trying to doze off again.

Until she heard Kieran rattling around in the kitchen.

Interesting, she'd never been able to hear the kitchen from the bedroom before.

Slipping out of bed slowly, Lorna retrieved fresh clothes from the wardrobe and headed for the shower.

When she emerged, dried and dressed, Aiden was no longer in the bedroom.

'He's in the bath.' Kieran looked up from an old newspaper

he was reading on the breakfast bar. 'Do you think you could eat anything?'

'I'm famished, what are you making?' Lorna asked, her stomach rumbling at the smell of coffee. 'Did you speak to Aiden?'

'I have nothing to say to him.' Kieran turned a page. 'There's barely anything in your cupboards, I had some bagels delivered.'

'I don't say I love you enough,' Lorna moaned as she spied a bacon-loaded bagel with her name on it.

'I don't know what the resident carnivore eats, so I got a selection,' Kieran huffed, making Lorna smirk. 'Least I could do is offer him a last meal.'

'What's that supposed to mean?' Her eyes narrowed as she lifted her bagel.

'Well, now we know high-level vampires are involved, we can't let one of the city packs poke their noses in. It won't go down well, it doesn't look good. Plus, I'm sure that Mia will fire him as soon as she finds out he bit you.'

'Essentially, that was in the line of duty,' Lorna said around her first mouthful of crispy bacon and melted cheese. 'I doubt Mia will see it the way you do. Anyway, Mia doesn't need to know. I lived.'

'She needs to know you were attacked by a Baxter, she'll need the details to report it to the council.' Kieran glanced up from the paper.

'Even if we told them, what would be done about it?' Lorna took another bite before a muffled, 'Honestly?'

Pursing his lips, Kieran grunted, knowing she had a point.

'It's probably best that we try to work out what it is that's going on, get more evidence. Who knows, maybe even a vision to deal with the problem,' she added.

'You can't go rushing back out into the field. We don't know what your body is going to do yet.'

'So far, nothing a few painkillers can't fix.' Lorna waved him off. 'Speaking of which . . .'

Diving over to the bag still on the coffee table, Lorna retrieved a blister pack and took two of the tablets with a mouthful of the orange juice Kieran slid her way as she returned to the kitchen.

'Anything else?'

'My hearing seems to have improved.' Lorna's eyes widened. 'Oh, and Aiden has invited us both to MaryVaille for the weekend.'

'Excuse me?' Kieran's voice dropped several octaves as he looked up at her.

'They have an annual pack meeting every Halloween. He was going anyway. But I think it's the perfect place to hide out and recover.'

Kieran gawped at his sister. 'You sound like you've already decided,' he managed through gritted teeth.

'It makes more sense than hiding here or with our grandparents. Vampires won't set foot out there and Nick will be there for the whole weekend too,' Lorna said calmly. 'It's ultimately my decision and I think it's the best one. You're welcome to join me and make sure no other werewolves take a nibble.'

Lorna regretted the joke as soon as she uttered it. His face was so full of fury, she was surprised he hadn't gone purple. His eyes, when she met them, had darkened in a way she'd never seen before.

'Kieran, I need you to work with me on this. When we work together, we're unstoppable,' she said, appealing to the brother in him.

'Then we don't need him and his pack. This is a guardian issue, it's not his fight,' Kieran said, his voice barely audible.

Lorna bit her lip and glanced at the bathroom door.

'But it is still his job.' Lorna sighed. 'Please just give me this weekend to recover.'

'What if more girls die?'

Squeezing her eyes closed Lorna felt the bagel threaten to make a return trip.

'Then you stay, but I'm not in a fit state to risk another attack while out on a vision. I'll be passing them over for a few days where possible, you'd be doing me a favour if you'd take them.'

'Not so that you can go out there,' Kieran huffed.

'I can pull rank just as easily,' Lorna sang. 'It's your choice, but I have rank.'

'Hey, are you two OK?' Aiden appeared, scrubbing his hair with a towel.

'A minor disagreement.' Lorna smiled. 'Kieran ordered breakfast in.'

'Amazing, thanks, I'm starving.' Aiden tossed the towel onto the stool beside Lorna and dug into one of the remaining bagels. 'Have you discussed plans for the weekend?' Aiden looked up brightly, making Lorna shoot him a look. She knew his hearing was better than hers.

'I'm coming to MaryVaille, Kieran knows the offer is there . . .' Lorna glanced over at her brother, who abandoned his paper and stormed out of the apartment.

'What was that all about?' Aiden feigned innocence after the door slammed behind him.

'I'm hoping it was a vision, but rightly so, Kieran has pointed out it might not be as simple as hiding out for a few days.' Lorna stared after him, a ball of dread settling in her stomach. 'Me hiding won't stop them killing other guardians.'

'If it's you they're really after, they'll be too busy looking for you,' Aiden said.

'I hope you're right.' Lorna ran her fingers through her hair with a heavy sigh.

SEVENTEEN

Packing the last of her toiletries into her own bag, Lorna listened for the front door for the millionth time.

Kieran hadn't returned.

He hadn't been at the house when they'd made a clothing grab, and Mia hadn't mentioned him when they'd called to check in and let HQ know where they'd be.

Lorna had glossed over her reasons for going to the pack meet and hoped Mia had taken it as a simple security decision.

Picking the bag up, she took it to the front door ready for departure and slipped a pair of boots on.

'Aiden?' Lorna glanced over as she sat on the sofa to repack the bag of painkillers.

'Hmm?' He looked up from a book he was reading on the adjacent sofa.

He always had a book on the go, he'd arrived at her parents' house in the spring with two equal sized bags, one for clothing, the other for books. The idea of chilling out at MaryVaille had appealed to her so quickly that she'd even considered taking a book to read herself.

'When do you want to head . . .'

Her question died on a frown when the intercom chimed.

'It's only Kia, I buzzed her up.' He put his book down and headed for the door as Lorna bounced up off the sofa.

'Ready to go?'

Lorna only caught a glimpse of Kia before she threw her arms around Aiden. When he stepped back to introduce them properly, Kia grinned and held her hand out.

'Hi, I'm Kia Henderson.'

Lorna had been reaching for her hand, but froze, the expression on her face had turned to bafflement as she recognised the long black curls and violet eyes by reputation.

'See?' Kia glanced at Aiden. 'It's Barnes, actually. Officially.' Kia turned back to Lorna and shook her startled hand, before hooking her thumbs into the back pockets of her flared black trousers.

'It seems we both have a habit of alternating surnames.' Lorna smiled.

Kia nodded. 'Though we're not yet married, I have been officially adopted by Acheron, so it is Barnes.' Kia grinned with a playful shrug. 'Sanderson by your mother's adoption only?'

'Exactly. The official title stays, well, official. I've heard the rumours, but mostly about your mother.' Lorna nodded. 'But as I've met Nick, it's great to meet the other half of that puzzle.'

'When Kia met Nick, she got out from under the Henderson shadow,' Aiden explained as Lorna recovered herself. 'Even helped us set up the Barnes Shelters.'

'Wow, of course, yes, I recommend the Barnes Shelters myself, have done for . . . well, since they opened. Thank you, for that . . . and for stepping in the other night.'

Kia gave a single nod. 'No problem. Now, let's get ourselves to MaryVaille before they start dinner without us.'

'You just want to get your hands on my brother,' Aiden teased as he picked up the bags and glanced at Lorna to make sure she was ready.

'Hey, who doesn't?!' Kia returned.

'Good point.' Aiden rolled his eyes as Lorna finished locking up and met them at the elevator.

'What does that mean?' Lorna asked as she shrugged her coat on.

'Before he met Kia all the girls at college held out hope that they were secretly the angeling's intended. He's also, you might have noticed, pretty good at what he was made for, so he'll always have enemies.'

'It's OK, I'm used to it.' Kia chuckled at the horror on Lorna's face.

Downstairs in the parking garage, Kia headed for an SUV parked next to Aiden's classic. When Aiden put their bags in his car, Lorna took that as her cue to get into the passenger seat. Kia wound her window down and leant out as Aiden got into the driver's seat.

'I'll follow you out,' she said as she started the engine.

Only then did Lorna realise that Kia was Aiden's backup.

'Her idea,' Aiden promised as his car rumbled into life.

Glancing again at Kia as she waited for Aiden to make his move, Lorna settled into the soft leather of the passenger seat. It wasn't quite dark and a vampire ambush was unlikely, but watching even two members of the pack looking out for each other made Lorna feel at ease.

The MaryVaille estate was a purpose-built mansion and grounds on the south-eastern outskirts of the city. The Barnes Pack had built and lived on the estate for over three hundred years.

Traffic was lighter than anticipated and they made it to the estate before most of the pack members had started to arrive. Kia didn't even make it inside the house, Acheron appeared and sent her back out to pick a group up from the nearest train station.

The presiding alpha then turned his attention on his eldest son and guest.

Lorna held her breath. She didn't even know whether Aiden had told his parents she'd be coming with him.

'Lorna, a pleasure to meet you at last,' Acheron said, his voice warm as he clasped one of her hands in both of his and escorted her inside his home. Aiden followed with the bags.

'Thank you for allowing me to accompany Aiden this weekend,' Lorna said as they entered the central hallway, complete with grand marble staircase hugging the rounded wall to the floors above.

'Nonsense, we finally get to spend time with the one person Aiden would ditch his family for.' Acheron shot his son a look as Aiden headed up the stairs with the bags.

Shoulders tensing, Lorna met Aiden's eyes but he only smirked and continued his mission.

'It's about time,' Acheron's deep voice muttered as he inclined his head towards her. 'Let's go and find Sookie.'

Looking up, Lorna found his eyes full of amusement. She

should have found it comforting, but his father's words only added to the unsettled feeling she'd had since Kieran had walked out.

Heading to the back of the house and through the dining room, they found Aiden's mother, Sookie, in the kitchen overseeing a busy team of caterers.

Where Nick, Aiden and his father were all varying shades of blond – Acheron's hair reaching his waist in one long braid down his back – Sookie's was a deep auburn. Glossy mahogany curls tumbled over her shoulders and around her face.

'Lorna! At last!' Sookie beamed, welcoming Lorna into her home with a hug and bright blue eyes. 'Get yourself a seat at the table before the horde arrive, we'll have all weekend to chat!'

The churning in her stomach increased as Lorna considered the welcome similar to that of a mother welcoming a new daughter. Offering her host a twisted smile and nod of thanks, Lorna let herself be led back to the dining room by Acheron, but not before Sookie had returned a knowing smile of her own.

'We'll definitely want to know more about you over the weekend, but for now I must speak with a couple of packmates before dinner, I'll leave you in Nick's capable hands.' Acheron excused himself as Nick appeared from the hallway.

'This place is amazing,' Lorna cooed, gazing up at the ornate ceilings in the dining room as she wandered towards Nick.

'Careful we don't lose you this weekend, it's cavernous in

places.' Nick grinned and pulled out a couple of chairs for them to take a seat at the end of the fifty-seat table that barely filled the room.

Her jaw had dropped in the car on the way up the drive, the twenty-bedroom mansion was nothing short of imposing with its colonial and Georgian features and wrap-around terrace servicing all bedrooms with a shared balcony.

'Oh, I doubt I'll stray far from those huge plush-looking sofas in the lounge I spotted on the way through.' Lorna smiled.

'How are you feeling?'

'Guilty that I'm planning to use this trip as a weekend off.' Lorna's lips twisted as she drummed her fingers on the tabletop. 'Kieran's off trying to find leads, I'm hoping the vision-break I seem to be having lets me continue to catch up on some sleep.'

'You haven't had visions since the attack?'

'It was two days ago. I'm just glad nothing has hurt as much as we expected it to,' Lorna replied.

'But you were having, what, several a day?'

'Aiden told you that?'

'We talk, he's also knackered.' Nick shot her a look. 'He's just less inclined to admit it.'

'I've noticed a couple of side effects.' Lorna met Nick's eyes.

'OK.'

'My hearing has improved, and so it seems, has my footing.' She smiled at the memory of how she'd discovered that one. 'I've accidentally snuck up on Aiden three times already.'

'Well, I'm not sure they're detrimental side effects,' Nick

laughed.

'What's funny?' Aiden asked as he joined them.

'That Lorna can creep up on you.' Nick grinned. 'I may have to use that to my advantage at some point,' he said with a wink.

'I've put your bags in my room.' Aiden ignored his brother's mirth and leant over the back of the chair next to Lorna.

'Don't I get my own room? You don't need to babysit me.' Lorna laughed to cover her shock and agitation.

'We'll sort the rooms out later,' Aiden said tightly. 'Nick, your head is practically glowing, if you know she's on the grounds why don't you go out and meet her?'

Looking from one brother to the other, Lorna felt the tension stringing between them. Nick met her eyes and then his brother's, they narrowed slightly, puzzled.

Leaning back dismissively when Aiden didn't move to take a seat, Nick's smile returned.

'There's very little point running to a car still in motion.'

'You even know where she is?' Lorna asked, curiosity getting the better of her.

With a nod, Nick started to get to his feet. The front door opened just as he reached his full height. Before he could reach the door Kia flew through it, black curls swinging about her waist as she leapt into his arms. Nick caught her with a smile brighter than the sun before she kissed him hello.

Mesmerised, Lorna watched the couple in awe. The air hummed as the room seemed to grow warmer in their presence.

Aiden slid into the seat next to Lorna as Nick put Kia down.

'Kia, are you at Wychwood?' Lorna asked, noting for a second time Kia's black trouser and fitted white shirt ensemble, the colours being the only uniform stipulation of the college she had attended. Wear what you want, but stick to black and white.

'Yeah, final year.' Kia gestured flamboyantly to her outfit. 'It's not like they let us hide it.'

'Ah, I miss those dorms.' Lorna smiled but felt Aiden tense up behind her.

'I miss these boys being there.' Kia reached behind her to tug at Nick's shirt. 'Nick graduated this summer. And we'd often hang with Aiden when he was doing his masters.'

'I was much closer with my brother during our college years.' Lorna nodded but her eyes sank to the floor.

When the doorbell rang, Nick lay his hand lightly on Kia's lower back and they left the room.

'They're amazing together.'

'You have to see it to believe it,' Aiden agreed.

'Why did Kia take on the Barnes name before marriage?' Lorna turned to look at Aiden, who was leaning forwards onto the table.

'There's never been any question about whether those two were meant to be. It's an angeling thing.' Aiden shook his hair out of his eyes and looked at Lorna's hand where it rested on the table, his own hands were clasped together. 'As with many of the supernatural races who know when they've met their "one". Only with Nick it's deeper and undeniable, they work as one.'

'That doesn't answer my question.' Lorna poked his arm.

'Knowing more about Kia will take time, and her trust. Now come and meet some of the furballs you'll be sharing the house with,' Aiden said, getting to his feet as laughter reverberated through the entrance hall.

Following him, Lorna soon found herself surrounded by the seventeen other werewolves who made up the pack. Aiden had explained to her during the drive out that their three female werewolves had been killed during the attack in March and so all current female pack members were non-wolf.

As it was, the unexpected attack had halved their full number.

Amongst the ruckus, Lorna soon found herself on the outside of the group as they all began talking at once.

'Right,' Acheron boomed suddenly. The hall fell silent, even though some wolves were stood on the upstairs gallery and others in the doorway to the lounge. 'I think that's all wolves accounted for, who's for a drink before dinner?'

'Wait for me!' came a loud squeak from behind the front door.

The werewolves had all begun filing into a room near the foot of the staircase, which Lorna soon discovered was Acheron's study, but Aiden, at the back of the group, grabbed the door as the hall emptied.

'Asha?' Lorna couldn't help the smile that crept across her face at the sight of the dragon on the doorstep. 'Is everything OK?'

'I'm here for the meeting,' she announced brightly.

'Do you come every year?' Lorna tried not to look as

confused as she felt.

'This is my first year, but as I know the pack quite well . . .'

'Asha!' Kia suddenly bundled into the dragon as she leapt off the bottom stair.

'You know Kia?'

'You're surprised by that?' Aiden frowned. 'I didn't know Asha myself until I started working with you, but it turns out that she's known Kia for some time. It seems she made a point of getting to know the current angeling,' Aiden said pointedly. Asha bit her lip in a guilty fashion.

'You've met Nick by now surely . . .' she said in her own defence. 'I mean, you would, wouldn't you?' Asha grinned.

'You're staying, right?' Kia asked, and when Asha revealed a rucksack Kia took it off her and disappeared upstairs with it.

'So, you know Kia?' Lorna said with a sly grin as she poked the dragon.

'Don't emphasise the *know*. What I know about Kia is only what she verbally tells me, and she's picky with that, given who she is.'

'Damn.' Lorna folded her arms and watched the study filling up. 'Does she avoid looking at you too?'

'No, she blocks me.'

Lorna's attention was dragged straight back to Asha's deadpan expression. 'That can be done?'

'I wish more people could do it.' Asha arched an eyebrow. 'But she's the only person I've come across who can blot out dragons completely. Even Nick doesn't block us out deliberately, the signals he gives out are unintelligible, it's a species defence mechanism, he doesn't have to control it.'

Lorna looked up in time to see Kia and Nick reappear from the room at the top of the staircase, Kia reaching back with a knowing smile as he took her hand.

'It's not malicious, that supernatural knows everything there is to know about her and he loves her implicitly, she's just very private. The only other people I know who know half as much are Nick's family,' Asha said with a look at Aiden.

When Nick and Kia reached the door to the study, Aiden ushered them inside.

'You're both welcome to attend,' he gestured to the door. 'We won't be going over anything important just yet.'

'In which case, I'll go up to my room and settle Joomba in. That odd colour change thing has been happening more and more, he's literally off colour,' Asha said, hugging Lorna tight before she skipped off up the stairs.

'I'll take a moment to get my bearings,' Lorna said, waving Aiden off with a smile. 'Nick said it's easy to get lost. If I'm not in the dining room when you come out, send a search party.'

'You shouldn't joke, we nearly did that for Asha when we lost her during the summer gathering.' Aiden smirked. 'See you in a few.'

With a nod he slipped inside the study.

Lorna turned a full circle in the middle of the hallway before investigating the long corridor that ran through the heart of the ground floor. Finding the lounge, games room, cinema, swimming pool, two further offices and a den that doubled as a library, Lorna soon ended up falling back through the kitchen door to see if Sookie needed another pair of hands.

'I get this crew in every year for the Halloween meet, it's the only one almost everyone attends, they know what they're doing,' Sookie said with a smile as another steaming hot plate was carried past them out to the lengthy table. 'If you can carry anything out to the dining room, they'll soon throw it at you, don't worry.'

'I'm sorry if I monopolise Aiden's time,' Lorna said quickly, remembering Acheron's words.

'Nonsense, it's been interesting to observe the changes in him.' Sookie looked Lorna up and down. 'I should probably apologise for any bad habits he's got, he never really expected to live anywhere but here or college, there must be some wolfish habits you wouldn't have been used to.'

'Walking around half naked, even on the coldest days, for example?' Lorna smirked. 'He didn't do that in my house for very long.'

'Oh?'

'I happened to mention that the idea of walking around scantily clad on frosty spring mornings made me shiver. He hasn't done it since.'

'Huh,' Sookie mused as her eyes swept the room to make sure everyone was where they needed to be. 'It took me until he was in his teens to get him to make sure he always wore shorts or jeans around the house.'

'He'd wander around naked?' Lorna gave an exaggerated blink.

'Every once in a while. He'd be caught raiding the fridge at midnight starkers.' Sookie chuckled. 'He was a kid.'

'Sounds like family life could get interesting.'

'You'd better believe it, one son running around nude, while the other could fly.' Sookie's eyes widened playfully.

Lorna pressed her lips together picturing the mayhem the house had seen over the years.

'Here, take these salad bowls and grab yourself a seat, we're almost done in here.' Sookie took the bowls off a passing caterer and handed them to Lorna. 'I'll be out in a moment.'

Doing as she was told, Lorna returned to the seat Nick had pulled out for her.

Sookie's timing was impeccable, as soon as Lorna sat down, a warm hand landed gently on her shoulder.

'Meeting over?' she asked softly as Aiden sat beside her.

'It won't really be a meeting until tomorrow, we were just catching up.' He smiled.

Catching his eyes Lorna found herself staring. Aiden at home was a different Aiden, he was even more relaxed than normal, which she hadn't thought possible.

'About time you two,' Asha teased as she took the seat on Lorna's other side, also looking into Aiden's eyes as she did so.

'About time for what?' Lorna scowled. 'Did you tell—'

'I didn't have to,' Aiden growled, cutting Lorna off as he shot Asha a look.

Sticking her tongue between her teeth in a sheepish grin, Asha shrugged.

Lorna glanced back at Aiden, but he was focused on the table as the rest of the pack began to file in.

EIGHTEEN

'Bet you didn't find the basement.' Aiden grinned at Lorna as he leant back in his chair, the caterers packing up for the night around them.

Acheron had declared drinking could go on into the night, as was customary for the first night of the meet, but many had opted for an early night in preparation for the run in the morning.

'There's a basement?' Lorna waggled her eyebrows.

'Well, it's more of a dungeon, but we'll let Aiden give you the tour,' Nick said with a wink as he and Kia left the room.

Getting up, Aiden inclined his head for her to follow. Glancing around for Acheron or Sookie in order to excuse herself, Lorna found neither and so went after Aiden, who was in the entrance hall opening a door next to the living area.

Flicking a switch on the wall, the staircase beyond came to life.

'Given everything else I've seen, what could you possibly be hiding down here?' Lorna asked as he motioned for her to go first.

She shot him a distrusting look, but went anyway.

It wasn't your standard basement, there were no cobweb-infested beams or creaky boilers, though she could tell everything the house needed was all down there, just enclosed in their own room.

'Boiler room, panic room, laundry room and . . .' Aiden paused to turn her around. 'Dance studio and gym.'

'Panic room?!'

'That's what you took from that?'

'The fully loaded gym is impressive, but I've never seen an actual panic room before.' Lorna grinned.

'It's a fairly recent addition,' Aiden admitted.

'I see.' Lorna glanced back at it before wandering off towards the gym equipment. 'You've got everything down here.'

'Just about.' Aiden nodded. 'It's all here if you need to blow off any steam. You've been through a lot this week.'

'I suspect my limits might not be what they were . . . for better or for worse.'

'Care to test them?' Aiden asked, picking up some sparing pads.

'What if I'm stronger?' Lorna said pointedly. 'What if I'm not?'

'You can't hurt me,' Aiden chuckled. 'Come on, we've sparred plenty of times in the training arena. Aren't you curious?'

'Yeah, a bit . . .' Lorna smirked as she stared at the pads.

Dodging to the left, knowing he always expected her to go right, Lorna tested her speed, shocking them both when she managed to kick Aiden's feet from beneath him, sending him crashing to the floor.

'What was that for?!' He laughed from the flat of his back as he gazed at the ceiling.

'Just to see if I could.' Lorna chuckled in return, placing her hands on her hips. 'And whaddya know . . .?'

'That was sneaky.' Aiden got back to his feet. 'But impressive. Shall I just get rid of these if that's the kind of mood you're in?' He waved the pads at her and tossed them to one side anyway.

Sauntering towards her jovially, Aiden seized the moment to swing a hook of his own, the aim being to get her in a headlock.

When Lorna ducked his manoeuvre and socked him with a jab to the ribs, he wheezed and fell back.

'Oh shit.' Lorna quickly backed off. 'Did I crack something? I think we need these after all.' Biting her lip, she reached for the pads, but he tackled her from behind and they both crashed to the padded flooring.

Thankful the space had been designed with underhanded fighting techniques in mind, Lorna placed her hands flat on the padded floor tiles and shoved herself to her feet, despite Aiden's weight on her back.

'OK, maybe that's enough of that for tonight, before I hurt you.' Lorna extended a hand to help him up.

Aiden had moved into a sitting position and was looking up at her with a strange look in his eyes. She couldn't fathom what he was thinking, but she knew what the smirk on his lips meant.

'Don't even think it.' She warned him. 'Not here.'

'Bed, then?' He grinned, standing up.

'I think that's best, you have an early morning ahead of you.' Lorna turned as he approached her, reaching for her, and headed up the stairs, leaving his fingertips reaching for his own hair in frustration instead.

Waiting for Aiden to power down the basement, she then followed him up the main staircase and into the room next to Nick's. Lorna looked up and down the dark corridor where most of the pack were sleeping in their various rooms.

'Which room is mine?' Lorna asked quietly.

'This one,' Aiden answered casually.

'We're sharing a room?'

'It's just easier.'

'For who?! Won't the pack ask questions?' Lorna frowned.

'No.'

'What? They don't question you?' Lorna snipped, her voice lowered to a whisper.

'One day, hopefully, I'll be able to explain it to you, for now, let's just get some sleep.' Aiden's voice was a low rumble as he turned the light on.

Lorna should have been over the jaw-dropping sights the house was hiding, but the floor to high-ceiling bookshelves covering Aiden's bedroom walls still came as a surprise.

'And to think, I brought a book with me.'

'Fiction to your left, non-fiction, mostly world history, over by the terrace doors.' Aiden waved an arm towards the terrace as he made for one of two doors in the wall opposite his bed. 'Also, ensuite to the left, walk-in wardrobe to the right.'

'Can the pack adopt me?' Lorna quipped. Aiden threw her

a look over his shoulder. 'Or not,' she whispered as he shut himself in the bathroom.

Rounding the bed, Lorna walked to the terrace doors and peered out. Aiden's room was on the south side of the house and so his windows looked out over the extensive grounds, including a forest, beyond which was a lake.

When the bathroom door opened, Lorna turned, expecting it to be her turn to get ready for bed.

Aiden hadn't changed for bed.

He stood looking at her with his hands on his hips.

'What's the matter?' Lorna asked, the swirling in her stomach returning.

'They would.'

'What?'

'Make you a pack member,' Aiden said, unmoving. 'They might even table the motion tomorrow.'

'What? Why would they do that?'

'Because they all know.'

'That we . . .?' Lorna looked horrified.

'No. How I feel about you.'

'Is that really why you put us in the same room?'

'I didn't have to, it was assumed.' Aiden held her gaze. 'And it would have caused more questions if I hadn't.'

'How would they know?'

'It's a werewolf thing, there are certain things we do when we're . . . never mind.'

'Like Nick,' Lorna mumbled, remembering what he'd said, but even as the thought sank in, her body started to go cold.

'It's not something I control, Lorna.' Aiden's voice sounded strained.

'It happens when you fall in love with anyone?' Lorna asked, forcing the words out, needing to know the answer.

'Not just anyone.' His eyes narrowed. 'We shouldn't be talking about this. For my safety, remember.'

Sitting on the end of the bed, Lorna ran her fingers through her hair and took a moment to breathe before looking up at him.

'That's a lot to take in,' Lorna whispered to herself.

'I'm sorry.' Aiden's voice softened in realisation as he crossed the room to crouch in front of her. 'I know you've been through a lot, that's why I hid it, I didn't expect working with you to hit me this way. But when I thought I'd lost you . . .'

'Shit.'

'That's an understatement,' Aiden agreed with a smile. 'Seriously, we don't have to talk about it yet. Let's just go to bed.'

Lorna met his eyes. The anguish she'd seen there moments before had been tamed, she felt reassured despite the somersaults her insides were making. With a nod, she got up and headed for the bathroom, retrieving her overnight bag on the way.

Locking herself in the ensuite, Lorna met her haunted reflection head on, wondering what Fate was up to.

He'd been with her through the worst of times. In a way Daniel never could have been.

But the stakes were so much higher.

Slipping into shorts and a t-shirt, Lorna returned to the bedroom to find Aiden walking around in his boxers. Given Sookie's words, she was thankful he'd stopped there. Their relationship was getting muddied enough as it was. He'd closed the curtains and turned the bedside lamps on, a book open and face down already on the terrace side of the bed.

'If anything breaks in, it'll get me first,' he quipped when he found her looking at it. Lorna knew her faced visibly paled at his words when his face fell. 'Shit, sorry.'

'You don't get it,' Lorna muttered, still staring at the book.

'What don't I get?'

'You're so wrapped up in whatever it is your genetics are telling you to really consider how I'm feeling.'

'I know how my genetics work well enough to guess, thank you, you just need to admit it to yourself.' Aiden tipped his head, his eyes challenging.

'When have I ever given you the impression your feelings were reciprocated?' Lorna's eyes blazed as she stormed up to him.

'If you think back to what you just said, you know when,' Aiden said, his voice dangerously low. 'What are you going to do about it?'

'We can't be together,' Lorna breathed, her eyes falling to his lips.

'No one else needs to know, but it's not a secret in this house.'

Lorna remained frozen for a moment, her eyes locked on his lips as her brain fought with her heart.

'They already know,' she whispered to herself.

Reaching up to grab the wolf's tooth choker around his throat, Lorna pulled his head down and his lips to hers.

With a possessive growl Aiden picked her up and carried her to the bed where he sat her on his lap.

With a grin, Lorna peeled her t-shirt off, giving Aiden full access to her breasts. His hands on her backside pulled her hips closer before sliding up her back until they were chest to chest.

Pressing his lips to her neck softly and feeling her breath hitch, Aiden began trailing kisses down her torso, one hand at her back, the other sliding around to run a thumb over one of her nipples, causing her to squirm on his thighs, forcing a growl from Aiden's throat.

'I thought we weren't doing this?' Aiden muttered against the other nipple before he ran his tongue around it.

'I'm not doing anything,' Lorna breathed, unable to think clearly, her head tipped back as he continued to explore her skin with his mouth.

'You're everything,' Aiden whispered as he slid his palm over her shoulder and into her hair before he kissed her deeply.

'You've found one of my favourite positions,' Lorna panted as their lips parted. 'But there's a slight drawback.'

'What's that?' Aiden asked, nudging the underside of her chin with the tip of his nose.

'Too many clothes.' Lorna reached for his shorts and drew them down to his knees as she shifted back off his thighs.

As soon as she was on her feet he grabbed two fistfuls of her shorts and tugged them down. Giggling, Lorna kicked them off and, without giving him a chance to reach for her, she climbed back onto his lap, sinking him deep inside in one swift manoeuvre, causing breath to rush from his parted lips and his hands to grip her hips hard.

'Fuck,' he whispered before she silenced him with kisses

and proceeded to rock them to the stars.

Lorna lay awake long after Aiden had nodded off. He was flaked out on his front beside her, hugging his pillow. She smiled sadly and stretched her legs out, feeling the luxurious bedding against her skin.

Scrubbing her hands over her face for the thousandth time, she rode out another wave of the bone-deep ache that had set in.

How could she have been so stupid?

Glancing across the bed again, Lorna let herself watch him sleeping for a fraction of a second too long.

Covering her mouth with one hand as she tried to steady her breathing, she slipped out of the bed and grabbed the first item of discarded clothing she could find, which turned out to be one of Aiden's shirts. Rolling her eyes and not wanting to wake him, she threw it on and headed for the bathroom.

Leaning over the sink and splashing her face with water, Lorna found her hands shaking. Tears welled in her eyes and she choked back a sob as she dried her face.

Turning, considering sitting on the closed lid of the toilet until she'd calmed down, she gave a yelp of fright to find Aiden peering into the light with bleary eyes.

'Hey,' he soothed. 'I'm going to have to buy smaller shirts if you're planning on wearing them like that.' He raked a heated gaze across her body.

Lorna tried to smile, but it must have looked as unpleasant as it felt.

'What is it?' He stepped into the light and tugged her gently against his chest.

Nestling her head on his shoulder, Lorna tried to ignore the fact that he was naked and let him hold her.

'You're still worried for my safety.' He stroked her head. 'You don't have to be, especially not here.'

'They'll try to kill you, and I don't think I could handle that,' Lorna whimpered.

'I'm not going to let that happen.'

'I'm not willing to take that risk.' She buried her face in his collarbone. 'We need to go back to how it was.'

'I don't know if I can,' he said softly, running his hand up and down her back.

Lorna lifted her head. 'Aiden, I'm terrified, please be patient with me.'

'Patient with you? Lorna, I'd wait forever if I knew you were mine alone.' He kissed her on the nose. 'Can't say I'd enjoy it, though.'

'Right now, if a Baxter doesn't kill you, my brother will.'

'I'm not going anywhere. Now, will you please come back to bed and get some rest.' Aiden sighed into her hair.

Nodding, Lorna let him turn the bathroom light off and they headed back to the bed. Lorna left the shirt on as she climbed onto her side of the bed.

Tugging her closer, Aiden let her curl up against him.

'You're leaving the shirt on?'

'It smells of you.' Lorna shrugged.

'I smell of me,' he said, amused.

'Yeah, but . . . you know.' She pulled the sleeves down over her hands and brought them to her nose to sniff his cologne.

'Alright,' he whispered, and kissed her on the forehead as she began to drift off.

NINETEEN

Lorna stumbled out of Aiden's room much later than planned with a yawn. He'd slipped out ready for the pack run at daybreak, but had left the thick velvet curtains closed, fooling her into thinking it was still dark and three extra hours sleep she hadn't meant to take. After a luxuriously lengthy shower, she decided to wander downstairs to see who was about.

She found the ladies of the house lounging around the remnants of breakfast on the island in the kitchen.

'Morning, Lorna,' Sookie sang brightly as though she'd known her for years. 'Welcome to the wives and girlfriends club.'

'Not me.' Asha laughed.

'Well, except for Asha.'

Lorna grimaced, realising where that meant the women had placed her. Though she couldn't bring herself to deny it, knowing there was no point.

'Sleep alright?' Asha shot Lorna some side-eye, which Lorna pointedly avoided.

'Amazingly well, I don't think I moved from the moment I fell asleep.' Lorna looked around at the pile of dishes in the sink and discarded oven trays and skillets, the kitchen looked as though a stampede had passed through. Then she remembered, it had.

'Help yourself to breakfast.' Sookie handed Lorna a clean plate. 'There's pancakes, eggs, bacon, pastries . . . there might even be some waffle batter left.'

'There is,' Kia said around a mouthful of pancake. 'And one sorry looking lump of steak.'

'How the hell did they manage that?' Lorna lifted an eyebrow as she began nosing through the offerings. 'So, the men of the house all bugger off and leave you to the washing up?'

'They'll do the washing up when they get back,' Sookie replied. 'They run off some steam, get anything they need to off their chests, throw each other in the lake, then come back here and discuss the important points with us. We're not left out.'

'Where's Nick in all this?' Lorna asked, curious, as she piled her plate with the steak, eggs and a bread roll.

'He's usually here,' Kia explained. 'But this year, given the circumstances, he's gone with them.'

'Have you left Kieran hunting vamps?' Asha asked.

'I assume so.' Lorna sighed. 'He stormed off when I said I'd accompany Aiden this weekend.'

'It's not like you ever really get a holiday,' Asha said nonchalantly.

'No visions this week?' Kia asked quickly.

'Not since the second bite,' Lorna admitted, her voice low

as she returned to the island and settled herself on a stool to construct an egg and steak baguette.

Asha poured and slid her a hot chocolate.

'Thank you,' Lorna breathed into the steaming cup as she lifted it to her lips. 'I'm not going to worry about it until after this weekend. I'll see what my brother comes up with, if he's still talking to me, and we'll take it from there.'

Until Nick had asked her the night before, it hadn't really dawned on Lorna that she might not get her visions back. While she waited and observed the other side effects, she wouldn't allow herself to dwell on what that would mean for her, HQ, Kieran or Aiden.

'Will they think you're dead, if you're inactive for a few days?' Sookie asked, pouring herself a fresh cup of tea.

'They'll be looking for proof, for sure.' Lorna nodded. 'And if they see Kieran out in the field but not me, they could think that way. The question is where that leaves them.'

'They're drinking witch blood for a reason, it's the kind of thing we'd expect from Casey Baxter, but not so many others,' Kia stated.

'A group I tracked down the other night made it sound like they thought drinking our blood would prevent their misdemeanours from featuring in visions,' Lorna replied. 'Sounds like propaganda to me, but it's got enough of them trialling it.'

'Fuck,' Kia breathed, leaning back on her stool. 'So, we'll see an increase of this bullshit.'

'Most likely,' Lorna agreed. 'However, we have now killed several between us who tried it, so let's hope the rumour mill slams into reverse on that one.'

'Shouldn't we warn other guardians?' Kia met Lorna's eyes.

'I've got Mia on it.' Lorna nodded.

'I'll inform the college and my network.'

'You prefer to stay underground?'

'Given that Nick and I are also pack security, it's in my best interests to remain underground.' Kia offered Lorna a twisted smile. 'I'm the daughter of Evelyn Henderson, and as a hybrid I have other uses elsewhere.'

'Your mother is a shadowdancer, isn't she?' Lorna queried.

'Yes, but I can't teleport through the night or shadows, more transition through appearances.' Kia grinned. 'I'm also a morph.'

Lorna blinked stupidly, so that was the part of Kia she couldn't quite put her finger on. Morphs were almost as rare as angelings. Beings who could change into any living thing they had touched in the previous seventy-two hours.

'If you ever lose Kia, just look for a black cat or wolf.' Asha giggled.

'I've managed to retain the ability to shapeshift into those two animals specifically.' Kia wrinkled her nose. 'Comes in handy.'

'I'll bet,' Lorna agreed.

Sookie peered over her shoulder. 'I think I hear the thundering of paws.'

'Grab anything else you want for breakfast, they'll have these plates picked clean before they clean the kitchen,' Kia warned Lorna. 'Then they'll be after lunch.'

'I have several meat joints slow roasting in the ovens already,' Sookie reassured Lorna's wide eyes.

'I'd noticed Aiden can eat, but until last night I didn't appreciate it was a werewolf trait.'

'Especially after a run,' Sookie confirmed and jumped down from her stool.

A building wave of camaraderie could be heard drawing nearer as the pack ascended the terrace steps from the lawn below. Lorna held her breath and hoped she wouldn't act any differently around Aiden.

She wanted to trust him, wanted to embrace his words from the night before, but every fibre of her being locked up at the thought of letting herself get too involved.

The pack piled into the dining room through the bi-fold doors, some looking worse for wear and heading straight for their rooms to clean up.

'You weren't supposed to be beating each other up.' Kia gasped to cover her own laughter at the state of Nick when he approached the kitchen.

He, like so many of the werewolves, was covered in mud.

'We played an impromptu game of rugby.' Nick looked down at the state of his clothes.

'With what?' Kia arched an eyebrow.

'A rock.' Aiden chuckled as he slid around from behind his brother.

'That was no rock, it was a boulder.' Nick shot his brother a look, but Aiden, who seemed to have come out of the match mostly unscathed, was making his way towards Lorna.

'Hey,' he said softly, laying his hands on her shoulders to lean in and bury his face in her hair, placing a soft kiss to the back of her neck.

'Good run?' Lorna asked as brightly as she could manage, swallowing down the urge to kiss him back as her eyes darted about the kitchen.

Nick and Kia were already leaving, Sookie simply offered her a smile and Asha had disappeared.

'It was interesting. A lot of ground covered . . .' He seemed fresh and alert and smelled of the pine trees they'd run through. 'In more ways than one.'

'How come you aren't filthy?'

'I refereed.' Aiden grinned, his hands slipping to her waist as she hopped off her stool.

'Right, Sookie, put us to work!'

Lorna startled as two of the wolves appeared in the kitchen doorway. Though when Aiden didn't let her go she bristled inwardly, the panic she couldn't shake starting to return.

'Aiden, put her down for five minutes, we're starving!' the shorter of the two wolves teased.

Oakley and Ramsey, a trendy couple of Aiden's age who lived in the city and ran their own hairdressing salon, moved into the kitchen and began raiding the leftovers.

'You best be willing to share those scraps,' Dante rumbled as he followed the younger wolves into the kitchen, rubbing his hands. His brother Danyl was close behind. The brothers were nearer Acheron's age and, Lorna estimated, three hundred pounds of pure muscle a piece. Dante's son Seth was also a pack member.

Feeling her cheeks flame, Lorna looked up at the wolves advancing on the kitchen from the dining room, just in time to see Kia and Nick mobilise towards the bi-folds.

The look on Kia's face alone had her pushing herself out

of Aiden's grasp on autopilot and heading after them.

'Friend of yours?' Kia asked, staring out at the grounds when Lorna joined her.

'Li,' Lorna hissed, glaring at the dark, gangly figure lurking in trees to the side of the house. 'He's Jake's right-hand man and all-round thug. He'll be looking for me.'

'Demon,' Nick growled and grabbed for the door.

The demon in question was too busy looking at Lorna to notice he was about to have a problem as Nick crossed the terrace, spreading his black wings in threat.

Lorna huffed. 'Seems they sent a scout after all.'

'They wouldn't dare send vampires onto the grounds to find that out,' Aiden agreed, stepping up beside them.

The werewolves quickly went back to their business of hunting down lunch. Lorna leant against the terrace doors, staring out at the morning sunshine.

'They can't touch you here.' Acheron also appeared. 'And should vampires enter this property while you're here, you have my permission to do what you must.' With a pointed look he retreated to the kitchen.

'They know where I am now,' Lorna muttered, turning to Aiden who was stood behind her, his arms folded. 'And that I lived.'

When Nick reappeared, wings retracted, he met Lorna's look of concern with a smile.

'Li fled in the direction of the city, he didn't hang around.'

'He got what he wanted,' Aiden said.

'And so will Jake.' Lorna scowled. 'He's going to come after me.'

'Not here he won't.' Aiden rubbed her arms.

'That really would be an idiot move,' Kia said with a smirk.

'I should leave.' Lorna looked up into Aiden's eyes.

'Nonsense,' Kia said with a smile. 'If they send anyone else this way, they'll find out what we're really made of.'

'If he comes back with more fire power, someone could get hurt. I don't want to risk that.' Lorna shook her head.

'Hardly, we're forewarned, prepared, any casualties won't be on the furry side of the fight.' Ramsey grinned as he approached the group. 'While you lot were gossiping about the fang brigade, we got going in the kitchen, make yourselves useful.' He grinned from beneath a mop of curly hair and retreated to the kitchen, chased by Danyl.

'As you now carry vampire DNA, can they place you under military arrest?' Acheron asked thoughtfully as they began setting the table between them, Kia showing Lorna where everything was as they went.

'They probably can, but perhaps not here?' Lorna shrugged. 'Maybe protocol states that to use a military arrest here would void it? I wouldn't put it past them in the city.'

'If that becomes a real risk, you will be welcome to stay here as long as you need,' Acheron announced.

'Thank you, but I don't want to put the pack in danger. Plus, I can't lock myself down to one place, visions won't allow it.'

'If he sends anyone else,' Aiden muttered.

'We now consider you a member of this pack, it's not just vampire DNA you're now carrying.' Acheron shot her a look that made her stomach churn, it was one of pure acceptance, but that didn't stop the bile. 'Of course, given the events of March, I'll offer our pack members the opportunity to leave after the lunch meeting should anyone feel the need to do so.'

'We're not going anywhere,' Dante said for the pack members in earshot. 'It's obvious that Lorna isn't just part of this pack now, she's family. Whatever that brings, we're still a pack and that's what we do.'

'We'll do our best to keep the trouble away from the pack directly. You are all my responsibility too,' Aiden said, looking up at Dante, his hands on his hips.

'Then we should go back to the city and take this up with Mia and Ben.' Lorna shook her head, her face set in an attempt to pull rank she knew she didn't have. 'That's the best way to avoid the pack coming to harm.'

'You've got us, inside or outside of this house,' Kia said, tugging fondly on Nick's muddied jumper and realising her mistake with a grimace. 'Whether you like it or not.'

'I'm not sure what I'm signing myself up for here, but me too!' Oakley nudged Lorna with his shoulder as he passed by with a hot tray of lamb. Shaking his glossy shoulder length mane out of his eyes, he offered Nick and Kia a grin.

'Maybe pay more attention, Oak.' Kia rolled her eyes.

The smell of the food turned Lorna's stomach rather than settled her. She knew leaving was the safest thing to do, but that Acheron had basically placed her under pack hierarchy. She knew that if she left, Aiden would follow her, and the thought of that made her chest tight.

TWENTY

Sinking gratefully into one of the eight sumptuous sofas in the lounge, Lorna took in the large roaring fire and the even bigger cinema-sized television above it, and tried to relax.

The pack mood seemed buoyant, but Lorna's own sense of unease had only increased as the afternoon had worn into evening.

It had gotten dark earlier than usual as the weather had closed in and the pack had been for a second run in the rain, partly to ensure the grounds were clear of intruders. Nick and Kia had retired to their room and Nick had promised to make a sweep of the upper floors and terrace before going to sleep.

The wolves had returned empty-handed, most slumping down in front of the fire to dry off.

Sitting curled up on the sofa, Lorna watched the steam rising off Aiden's pelt and tried to enjoy the peace. He made eye contact with a huff, as if to tell her that if he could relax then so should she.

At the sound of low growling, everyone looked up as

Ramsey caught hold of Oakley's ear and nudged him for attention. With a snort, Oakley tried to sit on his husband, until Acheron cracked one eye open and batted the pair of them with his tail.

As the wolves began to return to their human forms and head for bed, Aiden and Acheron also shifted and moved to the sofas.

While Sookie began to nod off in her husband's arms, Lorna curled up in the opposite direction to Aiden when he sat down.

Pretending he hadn't noticed, he lay his head back and pretended to doze, closing his eyes in a manner that told Lorna he was listening to or for something.

Taking a deep breath, Lorna rested her head on her palm and considered resting her eyes ready for whatever the night might bring.

'Relax, you're surrounded by family,' Aiden muttered, eyes still closed. 'If there was anything looking to get into this house any one of the wolves, Nick or Kia would sense it. Hell, you'd sense it. We also have a pretty sophisticated alarm system we can set if you're that worried.'

'Aiden, this isn't my family. I can't place it at risk. I'll have to head back to the city tomorrow, for my own sanity if nothing else. It's best I inform Mia and Ben of what's happened too. I can't keep my side of the story from them forever.'

'While you're with Aiden, you're a member of this pack and, therefore, this family,' Acheron said, making Sookie startle awake.

'The implications that could have simply aren't worth it,

Acheron, I can't do that to this pack,' Lorna replied quietly. 'I'll try to keep the vampires as far away from your affairs as possible. I'm sorry there has already been disruption this weekend.'

'What are you saying?' Aiden growled, making Lorna look across to him.

'They overstepped the mark today, and we can't have that. Full pack membership . . .' swallowing hard, she glanced at Acheron, hoping he would listen to reason, 'at this time, would bring you both, and the whole family, more trouble than you need after the atrocities you have already dealt with this year.'

Tipping his head in acknowledgement, Acheron pondered her words and gave a slight nod. 'I accept your reasoning, but the whole pack stood by this decision earlier today, understand that it will stand firm. You have full pack protection at least until this weekend is over.'

'Sookie, is there another spare room?' Lorna asked, her voice quavering slightly, unable to look at Aiden and equally shocked at how much of his rising agitation she could feel.

'The rooms across the hall from Aiden's are free,' Sookie replied, groggy and concerned. 'Why?'

'Should anyone try to break in tonight, I don't want them to see me in Aiden's room.' Lorna felt her throat constrict under the weight of their stares, but forced herself to continue. 'It's safer that way.'

Aiden opened his mouth to speak, but before he could say whatever was on his mind, there was a small knock on the front door.

The tension only partially broken, they all jumped up, but

Acheron waved Sookie and Lorna back while he and Aiden went to answer the door.

'Was that too polite for a vampire knock?' Sookie asked with a slight smile.

'It could have been less so,' Lorna drawled, knowing exactly who was behind the door. 'What are you doing here?' she hissed at her brother when Aiden led him into the sitting room, Acheron bringing up the rear.

His features relaxing as he laid eyes on his sister, Kieran had the decency to look a little uncomfortable.

'I'm sorry to call so late into the evening, I needed to know my sister was alright. What happened this afternoon?' Kieran looked first to the alpha, then to Aiden and his sister, with a polite nod at Sookie.

'Jake's manservant paid us a visit, looking for Lorna, nothing we couldn't handle.' Aiden shrugged, though his voice was low.

'Yet you waited until now to decide you needed to come out here?' Lorna bit out. 'As you can see, I'm fine.'

'The threat level hasn't receded, you know that as well as I do,' Kieran muttered.

'You really need to keep the fuck out of my head,' Lorna hissed, folding her arms.

'I don't have to be in your head to know you're under attack,' Kieran admitted softly. 'You haven't slept a wink and you're not planning to. I think it's time we headed back to the city.'

Kieran locked eyes with his sister as though no one else was present. Lorna felt Aiden turn his attention on her.

Prickly heat seared up her back in agitation. Despite the

conversation she'd just had with the alpha, her brother telling her what to do was another ballgame.

'I'm not going anywhere. If the vampires return for me tonight, it will be to this house. I won't leave the pack to deal with that without me, that wouldn't be fair.' Lorna gripped her arms with her nails and stared her brother down. 'My duty is to all supernatural beings, and it would be my fault if anything were to happen after I left.'

'Kieran, you're welcome to stay.' Acheron stepped in. 'Should there be an attempted break-in in the next few hours, we'd be glad of the extra man on deck.'

'Thank you, I'll stakeout with Lorna, no need to make up an extra bed,' Kieran replied, far more gracious with the alpha than he was with Aiden.

Lorna glanced at Aiden as he flinched. Kieran caught the movement and turned on Aiden, his eyes wide. 'You have no claim over my sister.'

'I'll have no violence in my house,' Acheron said forcefully from across the room as Aiden, his fists balled and shaking, took a step towards Kieran.

Lorna tried not to smirk, Oakley and Nick had already informed her that the house had taken several batterings over the years, internally as well as externally. The pack could get heated within its own ranks.

Though Kieran didn't break eye contact with Aiden, he did relax his stance at Acheron's command.

Sighing angrily, Lorna returned to her seat on the sofa. She was more than accustomed to ignoring her brother when he was in protective mode.

'You're not staying in my room,' Lorna stated without

looking at Kieran, instead she was watching Kia – half asleep and in her pyjamas – entering the room.

'Because you two have been sharing a bed?!' Kieran began to shake with rage at the realisation. Aiden shifted his stance, putting himself between the twins.

'No, because . . .' Lorna paused as Kia walked towards Kieran, her eyes hardening as she woke up.

Kia's fist connected with Kieran's jaw a fraction of a second before she took out his ankles. Biting the inside of her cheek to stop herself laughing, Lorna arched one eyebrow and peered down at her felled sibling.

'. . . Because sharing a bed with your twin at our age is wrong,' Lorna finished, the amusement alight in her eyes while Kieran, dazed and confused, didn't move. 'Was that really necessary?' She looked up at Kia.

'The waves of threat woke me up. Why the hell didn't you stop him?' Kia's eyes blazed as she glared at Lorna.

'I had hoped Aiden would knock some sense into him before it came to that,' Lorna drawled sarcastically, but felt the mood in the room blacken.

'You should have been prepared to protect your alpha,' Kia snarled, seeming to forget who she was talking to as Lorna heard footsteps on the stairs.

'He's not *my* alpha.' Lorna got to her feet again, her voice rising as Nick walked in.

Kieran, who was in the process of getting to his feet and dusting himself off, had the decency to look confused.

'But you are officially under my watch,' Aiden said with sudden authority.

'Your six-monthly review is almost due,' Lorna pointed out

darkly, throwing her own authority behind her voice, but feeling her chest constrict.

'And until the review, the fact still stands, so don't even think about leaving this house with anything less than a full escort from Mia or Ben Sanderson.' Aiden crossed the room to stand in front of Lorna.

Keeping her arms folded, she stood her ground even as they glared at each other, Aiden bearing down on her.

'This pack doesn't need your protection, but it would have been home if you had wanted it.'

His words hit her square in the chest and Lorna forgot to breathe as Kia took a sharp intake of breath. It was enough for Lorna to glance at the younger guardian as Aiden turned away from her and left the room. Meeting her eyes only briefly, Nick followed his brother from the room.

The ache in her chest grew the larger the distance Aiden put between them, and Lorna found herself feeling cold, despite the raging fire in the room.

'Lorna . . . you know that when they find the right one, werewolves mate for life, right?' Kia whispered without moving.

Unable to meet Kia's eyes, Lorna sank back into her seat.

'I think it's time we all went to bed. This isn't over yet, let's get some sleep,' Acheron said calmly and ushered Sookie and Kia out of the room, leaving the twins alone.

Staring at the carpet, Lorna felt the itch to leave stronger than ever.

'I felt that,' Kieran said, breaking the uncomfortable silence.

Lorna shot her brother a black look. 'You'd better take the

room next to mine. If I catch you in my room, I'll break your neck.'

When he held his hand out to help her up, she slapped it away, getting up slowly before she led her brother upstairs. They found the door to the two rooms open and ready for them. Showing Kieran into the one furthest from Aiden's room, she waited until he'd crossed the threshold and closed the door for him.

Running her fingers through her hair, she turned back towards Aiden's room. His door was closed and her overnight bag was in the hall. Reaching down to pick it up, she realised there were voices coming from inside, Nick and Aiden were deep in debate over something.

Shutting herself in the opposite room, she tossed the bag on the bed and leant back against the door, feeling a crushing weight on her chest as she tried not to sob.

Swiping angrily at the tears welling in her eyes, she willed herself to feel relief that she had implemented at least part of her plan. He'd be safer across the hall.

'Lorna?' Kieran said quietly as he tapped on the door. 'Let me in for a moment, please?'

'I have nothing to say to you.' Lorna fixed a glare on her face and opened the door a crack.

Kieran took the opening and squeezed himself through the door regardless. Ignoring the black look she shot him, he helped himself to a seat on the bed.

'Lorna, I walked out the other day, I can't just go to bed on another argument.'

'Why the fuck not?' Lorna hissed as she shut the door. 'It's never stopped you before.'

'Because I've never felt *that* before. Barbed words from Daniel never took your breath away the way Aiden's did tonight.'

'Daniel never threw barbed words at me,' Lorna mumbled as she turned back to her brother. 'There were definitely times when he should have, though.' A sad smile tugged at her lips.

'Relationships with guardians are no picnic.' Kieran shrugged.

'You know that just as well as any of us,' Lorna agreed.

Kieran nodded and stared down at the carpet. Her brother hadn't been immune to heartbreak, he just hid it more fiercely than she did.

Sitting next to him on the bed, Lorna sighed. 'I'll leave in the morning, whether Aiden follows or not is his choice, but it's too late tonight. Whatever is coming for me will already be on its way. I'll just have to be ready for them.'

'We need to find a way to end this,' Kieran said.

'End what?' Lorna eyeballed him, remembering the words unsaid in her apartment.

'Whatever the vampires are up to, we need a strategy that will keep all guardians safe. The lid is unlikely to go back on the can of worms if the rumours start spreading like wildfire that you have survived a vampire bite.'

'I'm not sure issuing all guardians with an EpiPen laced with werewolf saliva is going to suffice here.' Lorna narrowed her eyes.

'Then we need to be able to take out the source.'

It was Kieran's turn to meet her eyes, the look in his was fierce and loaded.

'We'll never get the visions or the clearance for that.'

'So? What if we do it anyway?' Something flashed behind his eyes that Lorna had never seen before. 'What will they do to us if we remove a threat that could take hundreds of lives before it has the chance to become vision worthy.'

'We'd need proof.'

'You don't have enough already?'

Lorna thought back to the way Casey had been watching her. Her memory of his face wasn't enough on its own.

Then she realised Kieran was looking at the marks on her neck rather than waiting for an admission of facts.

'We can't use me as proof, that would send the wrong message.' Lorna shook her head.

'You lived. That's all they'll focus on,' Kieran stated.

'And the vampire who bit me didn't.'

'Damn. Good point.' Kieran got up, raking his fingers through his hair in agitation. Lorna noted that he'd clearly been doing that a lot, he rarely let his hair get too long, but whatever style he'd been opting for during his training had grown out and it was sticking up all over the place where he kept fluffing it up. Guardians had the ability to alter aspects of their appearance, so she wondered why he'd let it get so out of control.

'That mop of yours will be long enough to stick in a ponytail if you let it grow much more,' Lorna teased.

'It's already long enough to tie up.' Kieran's eyes drifted upwards to a section sticking out over his forehead. 'It was better for training.'

'You? A man-bun?!'

'Shut up.' His lip curled, affronted.

'Guess we'd better get some kind of rest before the party gets started.' Getting to her feet, Lorna followed him to the door.

'Though it all makes sense now, I can't say I'm happy with the turn of events. I had no idea . . .' Kieran said, tossing his hair in the direction of Aiden's room.

'That makes two of us,' Lorna admitted, her eyebrows heading for her hairline.

Shutting the door behind her brother, Lorna crossed the room to look out of the terrace doors. The room faced north, towards the city and onto the driveway. The mountains between were framed by light pollution from the city beyond.

Something was coming, there was a niggling at her temples, like a storm brewing. For the first time in months, she found herself hoping for a vision.

TWENTY-ONE

Though Lorna slept, it was fully clothed across the end of the bed.

Her senses on high alert, she got up and slipped her sneakers on before peering out of the door into the dark hallway.

Kia was stood outside Nick's bedroom, the door closed behind her, in her pyjama bottoms and a t-shirt. She'd also put shoes on.

'Woke you too, then?' Lorna whispered, noticing how awake and alert Kia was. 'Vision?'

'No, something else,' Kia whispered back. 'You?'

'Same,' Lorna admitted as she moved down the hall towards Kia.

'Someone's downstairs.' Kia peered towards the hall.

Lorna listened for a moment and noticed there was a crack of light in the hall below. The faint sound of whistling reached their ears.

'It's only Lazlo.' Kia relaxed a little.

The sound of breaking glass in the bedrooms up and down

the corridor behind them put the guardians back on high alert as they span around.

Quiet thumps followed, accompanied by footsteps running up and down the terrace.

Sinking to a crouch, they watched through the gallery as a large shadowy figure ran across the terrace above the front door.

Without thinking, Lorna stood as soon as they were out of view and reached for Aiden's door, but Kia caught her arm, shaking her head furiously as wisps of smoke began appearing from beneath the door.

'Some form of knock-out gas. They're not here for the wolves,' Kia whispered and began moving down the hall. 'We should get downstairs. That's where the party will be.'

Lorna followed Kia past the main stairwell, to the far end of the west wing where there was another staircase leading to the kitchen. Both guardians triggered their shields, Lorna marvelling at how Kia's shimmered like black glitter over her skin.

'How are you awake and Nick isn't? Is your radar stronger?' Lorna asked.

Kia glanced back. 'He was awake, I told him to go back to bed while I checked it out.' She rolled her eyes. 'Too late now.'

'Oh.' Lorna bit her lip.

'He'll be fine.' Kia shrugged.

Giving Kia a dubious look, Lorna then glanced back over her shoulder towards the brothers' rooms.

Spotting shadows moving down the east wing corridor, Lorna grabbed Kia and tugged her back against the wall.

They watched in silence as two large figures, shrouded in black, began peering inside each room.

Lorna held her breath as they inspected Kieran, Aiden and Nick's rooms in turn. She was grateful her room didn't look slept in. Her chest was burning by the time Kia nudged her. The rooms were left undisturbed.

Lorna looked down at Kia, who was peering around her at the figures for a better look.

'*They're big buggers, aren't they?*' Kia communicated clearly.

'*Could be more demons working for Jake, wouldn't surprise me if he has a brute squad,*' Lorna offered back with a smirk.

With the intruders approaching the west wing, the guardians continued their journey to the kitchen. Though Kia was smaller, Lorna realised that she couldn't hear their footsteps at all. And Lorna knew she had never been that soft-footed before.

'Hey girls,' Lazlo said brightly before taking another bite of the sandwich he was devouring whilst sitting at the kitchen island. As he chewed, he glanced at Kia's folded arms with amusement. 'Break-in? I'll be damned if I'm not going to finish my sandwich first. Who or what have we got?'

'We're not sure what they are,' Lorna replied with a backwards glance up the dark stairwell.

'With all that racket going on, the others will deal with them before they realise anyone's downstairs.' He shrugged.

'You have all the lights on in here and the dining room, they will be well aware someone is awake and down here. Probably why they started upstairs,' Kia informed him. 'Besides, that racket was the intruders gassing everyone else, they'll all be out cold for a few hours.'

Lazlo mulled the information over as he chewed the last mouthful of his snack. 'All of them?' he asked before swallowing.

'All of them.' Kia nodded as Lorna peered into the dining room.

'I can hear them talking,' Lorna whispered.

'What?' Kia looked at her with a frown of confusion. 'From where?'

'Upstairs.' Lorna walked over to a door leading to the downstairs hallway.

Everyone was silent for a moment as Kia listened in too. Lorna held up seven fingers, Kia inclined her head and nodded in agreement.

'Should we assume they're all as big as the two we already clocked?' Lorna raised her eyebrows.

'Probably.' Kia nodded, 'Lazlo . . .'

'I'm already on it . . .' He held his hands up and casually slid off the stool.

'Actually, I was going to suggest you make yourself scarce.' Kia turned to him, placing her hands on her hips. 'They're here for Lorna, they clearly don't intend on harming pack members.'

'Uh huh, and when was the last time anyone in this pack just sat back and watched a break-in take place? If I shift, I'll heal faster.' He shrugged. 'Sound fair?'

'Hmm.' She looked doubtful. 'Alright, but don't put yourself in any unnecessary danger, they're not here for you.'

'I won't, I won't.' He took up position behind the guardians, ready to switch into his wolf form.

'As we think the others are safe, we should technically find a place to hide,' Lorna offered. 'But I think I'd prefer to teach them a lesson.'

'I know which is more fun.' Kia grinned and joined Lorna at the door.

As they carefully peered around the door frame, there were sounds of footsteps on the stairs behind them.

Lazlo padded forward and nudged his head between them, looking up at Kia for permission to go further.

Kia nodded.

'You can investigate, but remember, don't do anything stupid.' She wagged a finger at him. 'I'm surprised your brother wasn't sitting guarding your door.' Kia glanced at Lorna as Lazlo backed up and set off in the direction of the entrance hall through the dining room.

'He might have taken a mild sedative to get a nap in, he usually gets visions if I'm in danger and they wake him up through almost anything.'

'Except an extra dose of night-night gas?' Kia smirked.

'It's going to be like double dosing, right?' Lorna rolled her eyes playfully. Kieran had already pissed Kia off, she didn't expect him to be her favourite person any time soon.

'*They don't look armed, but let's not assume . . . demons or vampires?*' Kia asked as they shifted into the dark hallway, the tentative steps on the stairs were getting nearer.

'*Go for the head for safety's sake,*' Lorna replied.

Making their way carefully down the hall, both guardians kept their ears on the rooms around them as well as the entrance hall and the kitchen behind.

Before Lorna could think to give them extra cover, the lights in the dining room and kitchen went out. Kia held up a hand to claim responsibility.

Keeping to the north wall gave them extra leeway on any intruders in the entrance hall.

By the time they could see the main doors to the dining room, Lazlo was stood guarding it, his hackles raised as he growled at something by the front door.

Kia signalled for him to back off or lay low, Lorna couldn't be sure.

Baring his teeth, he growled again, it was too late, whatever he was staring at had already seen him.

Crouching low, he prepared to pounce.

Kia threw her shield at the door, but it was too late. Lazlo charged into the hall.

With a thud the intruder hit the deck, gurgling in surprise as Lazlo tore his throat out.

Boots thundered through the kitchen and into the dining room, but no one came into view.

'What the hell?' They heard a male voice hush as the guardians tried to venture forward to see whether Lazlo had managed to hide.

'Seems we missed one,' came another voice.

Lazlo turned on hearing them and growled, his muzzle bloody, ears back, teeth bared as he readied himself to launch again, stood over the body of one of their colleagues.

Lorna willed him to get out of the way or for Kia to intervene.

When Kia shifted her position, Lazlo twitched and charged into the dining room. They both lurched forwards to assist him, but a round of automatic gunfire brought them up short when it was accompanied by a sickening thump.

The sound winded Lorna and she fell against the wall as Kia ventured forward more slowly.

Forcing herself to keep moving, Lorna used the wall to pull herself to where Kia was peering into the dining room, her breathing was hard, but she made little sound.

'You idiot,' one of the men said. 'You could have asked him where the fucking guardians have run off to first.'

'A building like this, there's probably a panic room somewhere . . . this dude was just in the wrong place at the wrong time,' the other said dismissively.

Hearing the guns fall apart, Lorna followed Kia as she broke cover.

'Hiding isn't our style, boys,' she sassed.

Reaching for the knife she'd hidden in her jeans, Lorna moved swiftly, the blade glowing hot as it sliced through the air.

Kia slid in next to Lazlo just as the two headless corpses bounced off the dining table.

Lorna froze in place, listening for the others, listening for a third person breathing in the room, waiting for Kia to confirm her worst fears.

A pack member had been killed. On her watch. Because of her.

'He's gone,' Kia said quietly.

Swaying slightly, Lorna reached out and gripped the table. 'Kia, I'm so sorry . . . I . . .'

'I told him to be careful.' Kia shook herself off and stood up before laying a hand on Lorna's shoulder. 'Three down, four to go.'

Kia's eyes were dark as she turned towards the main

staircase, just in time to see two cloaked figures land in the middle of the hall.

'Going somewhere?' The taller of the two grinned from beneath his cloak as they moved forward to block the doorway.

'No, you are though.' Kia's shield shimmered as she threw a punch that hit him in the solar plexus.

The added energy sent him and his partner crashing back out into the hall and sliding into the marble staircase in a heap.

Before anyone could gather their senses, Kia stormed after what Lorna could now tell quite clearly were demons. Holding her hand out, a sword Kia kept stashed in the umbrella stand obediently flew into her grasp.

The ruckus hadn't gone unnoticed and the last two mystery guests appeared in the kitchen, ready to charge after Lorna.

'Hang on a second.' Lorna glanced over at them as she threw a telekinetic bind on the kitchen door. 'I want to see this.'

Kia's blade had the glow of heated steel as she made two expert swings, decapitating the two in the hall before they could fully regain consciousness. Lorna smirked, playing with swords was always fun.

'Now then, want to make something of it?' She let the shield on the kitchen door down and joined Kia in the hall as they charged after her.

Waiting until the last two entered the hall, Lorna unleashed streams of fire from outstretched palms as Kia held them in a bind.

The demons roared only briefly before their core

temperatures soared to such an extreme that they crumbled to ash on the spot.

'Nice,' Kia chirped at the resulting piles of dust before returning her sword to its hiding place. 'You really do have a boiling point.'

Lorna nodded once. 'Think we got them all?'

'Yep,' Kia said simply. 'I'm not hearing any movement from anywhere else in the house.'

The silence reminded Lorna of Lazlo's body beyond the threshold of the dining room and her stomach rolled before hot angry tears found their way onto her cheeks.

'I need to get out of here.'

'Don't be ridiculous, we'll patch up whatever hole the cockroaches crawled in through and keep an eye out for the rest of the night.' Kia shrugged and returned to Lazlo's body, retrieving a tablecloth from a cupboard and laying it over him.

'How am I going to tell Aiden?' Lorna swiped at her tears.

Kia looked up, her face relaxing in realisation when she saw Lorna shaking.

'There was nothing we could do, you know that,' Kia reassured her. 'Fate had her way, sure Lazlo didn't help himself, but he wanted to help us. Acheron, Aiden and the pack will give him a proper burial in the morning. He was doing what he thought was right.'

'This wouldn't have happened if it wasn't for me.' Lorna backed up. 'I have to leave.'

'He took his orders from me. You don't need to go anywhere. I wouldn't have allowed him out of the kitchen if

I'd thought he would charge them.' Kia stood up with a shrug.

'I need to take my shit as far away from Aiden and the pack as possible . . . Next time it could be . . .'

'He told you, you can't leave,' Kia said darkly.

'He might outrank you, but he doesn't outrank me, not on this.' Lorna backed up, inching towards the stairs.

'You know he'll follow you.' Kia crossed the hall to stand at the bottom of the stairs as Lorna backed up the first two. 'This isn't your fault.'

'Maybe not directly.' Lorna moved to the banister. 'But I have the power to stop it hurting anyone else in this house. You need to tell him to stay away from me.'

'You think he'll listen to you? Or me, for that matter?' Kia bit back.

'Just remind him I can't go through that again.' Lorna stared through Kia, her eyes seeing an unwelcome memory. 'He'll know what I mean.'

'You do love him.' Kia scowled, but the realisation in her voice sounded more like surprise.

'I've been trying not to.' Lorna looked down at her hands fidgeting on the rail with a smirk.

'We thought he was nuts, running off the way he did in March, we thought he was barking up the wrong tree as a distraction. But as the months have gone on . . . well, I've never seen him so content,' Kia said gently.

'Then it's best I go now, while he's angry with me from earlier and now there's blood on my hands.' Lorna glanced up the staircase to the rooms above. 'I won't risk killing your alpha the way I killed Daniel.'

'You didn't kill Daniel.' Kia shook her head. 'Aiden knew he needed to go to you, that he'd been drawn to you since college. When news reached him of what had happened, he stormed out of this house and down to Sanderson Central. He only came back to pack a bag. It had been Acheron's idea to take the pack back, telling him to lay low for a year or so while we hunt down the assholes who attacked us. We were encouraged to let him go and get whatever he was feeling out of his system.' Kia rolled her eyes but there was fondness and amusement behind them.

'I wouldn't call working with the head guardian laying low,' Lorna muttered.

'In werewolf terms it is. The attack was orchestrated by someone from Acheron's past, someone with unfinished business, Acheron didn't want to pass his grudges on to the next generation.'

'Shit, and that's all still going on, isn't it? The rogues you've been tracking?'

'Yes, the mutt Acheron ousted before Aiden was born seems to have been building a pack of his own ready to challenge this one. Aiden came of age too soon for his liking, we think. The fucking coward didn't even come here in person in March,' Kia grouched.

'Great, so with a rogue pack out there somewhere you can't keep an eye on both Aiden and the pack . . .' Lorna chuckled with a crazed look.

'We're a pack, we work as one. If Aiden has chosen you, then that includes you too. It's clear you have his best interests at heart.'

'He really could have dealt with my brother earlier, you

know, if you'd let him. Kieran's not as scary as he thinks he is.'

'Instincts.' Kia shrugged with a grin.

'We need to clean up.' Lorna stepped back down the stairs.

'I've got this. Go back to bed,' Kia offered.

'But the break-in points . . .'

'All the upstairs windows are shattered, I'll secure the downstairs, by the time I've done that it should be getting light.'

'I won't sleep anyway,' Lorna suggested.

'How about you keep watch over upstairs and the terrace, then we're even. I'm only going to burn these bastards anyway.' Kia flicked a wrist at the bodies of the intruders, they all slid into a pile in the hall.

'OK, that sounds fair,' Lorna agreed, though she was reluctant to move.

'Goodnight,' Kia called after her.

'Night.' Lorna smiled back before ascending the stairs.

As she went a fiery glow appeared behind her, which was eerily comforting. The body of a pack member was one thing, but at least she didn't have to worry about the reanimation of the intruders.

Once at the top of the stairs, knowing he was going to be out cold, Lorna considered slipping into Aiden's room.

Unable to face him, even when unconscious, she retreated into her own room to throw on a sweatshirt before heading out onto the terrace to walk laps until the sun rose.

TWENTY-TWO

Lorna listened as she lapped the perimeter of the house for signs of Kia below her, for sounds of stirring from the inhabitants of the rooms she passed, for movement from Aiden's balcony door.

The smell of autumn was her only company until, just after the world around her had started to go blue with the early signs of dawn, she heard Nick and Kia speaking on the terrace below.

Uncertain whether they'd hear her or not, Lorna continued her round until she reached her room.

If Nick was awake the others soon would be. She slipped back indoors and across her room to step into the hall, but the hall was as deathly silent as outside had been.

Her pulse quickened at the thought that the wolves might have been more affected than Kia had given them credit for. Her only consolation being the fact Nick was awake.

Debating whether to go downstairs and face Nick first, or see if she could wake her brother, Lorna found herself staring at Aiden's door.

Sucking in a deep breath, knowing that the truth would be better coming from her own lips, Lorna grasped the door handle and went in.

The room was cold where the splintered door had been letting the night air in for hours while she'd walked.

But so was the bed.

Aiden wasn't in it.

Hurrying across the room to check the walk-in closet and ensuite, Lorna felt a cold dread start to spread across the back of her head and shoulders.

Her vision blurring in panic, she ran from the room and downstairs to where Nick and Kia were in the kitchen hunched over mugs of tea.

'Hey—' Nick said softly.

'Where's Aiden?' Lorna blurted, cutting him off, hoping that Nick's gentle smile would only increase as he told her his brother was out assessing the damage, or running off his anger.

When Nick's expression dropped, and Kia's followed it, Lorna's heart sank to her knees.

'What do you mean?' Nick stood from the stool he'd been sitting on.

'I've just been into his room to come clean before . . . He's not there . . .'

'I haven't seen him,' Kia confirmed, meeting Nick's eyes.

'I lapped the upstairs terrace all night, I didn't see anything either,' Lorna forced herself to say, though her tongue felt thick.

'He must be in the house somewhere,' Nick said softly. 'If you were both outside, maybe he's in the basement.'

'Lorna, was there any bl—'

'No,' Lorna snapped.

Nick took off for the basement, but was coming back up the stairs by the time Lorna and Kia joined him.

'No one down there.' He shook his head.

'Fuck.' Lorna ran one shaking hand through her hair and did a full rotation on the spot.

'Let's do a quick sweep of all rooms, he might yet turn up,' Kia said.

'OK, we need to make sure everyone's awake sooner or later anyway,' Nick agreed.

While Nick and Kia agreed between them who'd take the bedrooms, Lorna ran off down the east corridor, sticking her head in the pool room, the adjoining sauna, offices, dens, games room and lounge.

Kia took a more leisurely pace around the west wing, Lorna catching her up and completing the sweep with Acheron's office.

'Shit, shit, shit,' Lorna muttered, running up the marble staircase to the bedrooms.

Nick had opened almost every bedroom door by the time she got there except Kieran's or his parents.

'I'll wake him up,' Lorna offered, making a beeline for Kieran's room.

Nick nodded and crossed the hall, sounds of groggy, spluttering werewolves drifting up the corridor in his wake.

Knocking first, in case Kieran was aware of the situation and keeping out of it, Lorna let herself into her brother's room.

He was on the bed, fully clothed, snoring his head off.

'Dude, you need to sleep with your mouth closed,' Lorna said loudly, taking in the position of his body. The way he was sprawled suggested he'd been getting up to investigate too when the attack happened and hadn't made it across the room. 'Boy, are you going to have a headache.'

Nudging him on the shoulder, Lorna sat next to him on the bed.

When that didn't work, she rolled him over to stop the snoring.

Rolling him a second time when he remained unresponsive, Lorna watched him clatter to the floor.

'Owww!' he groused through a mouthful of carpet. 'What the fuck?'

'Morning!' Lorna leant over the end of the bed.

'Shit, did . . . did you just push me off the bed?'

'Oh, you were awake enough to feel that?' Lorna scowled. 'Get up.'

'Why? What's happened?'

'Aiden's gone missing.'

Having been in the process of heaving himself to his feet, Kieran gave up and sat back on his ass with a thump, looking up at his sister with wide eyes. 'What?'

'You heard me.' Lorna peered into her lap where she was picking at her fingernails. 'And a pack member was killed when a group of demons broke in here last night.'

'OK, OK.' Kieran got up onto the bed to sit with her. 'Go back to the beginning and fill me in.'

While explaining what had happened since bidding her brother goodnight, Lorna kept half an ear on the rest of the house. Knowing Nick was telling his father that not only was a pack member dead, but that his eldest son was also missing.

With Kieran processing the full story himself, Acheron timed his entrance perfectly, sweeping into the room with Nick and Kia.

'Acheron,' Lorna leapt to her feet, 'I'm so sorry, I never should have come here.'

'Aiden deemed it for the best and we agreed. These circumstances are unfortunate, but there is no use dwelling on that which we can't change. What I need now is for those of you in this room to find him.'

'What about Lazlo?' Kia asked quietly.

'We'll do as we always do when a brother is lost, we'll bury him in the pack cemetery shortly. The rest of us will get to work securing the house, Aiden is your priority right now.' He sighed. 'We'll have a proper grave-marking for Lazlo when we're next all together.'

Acheron met their eyes in turn, including Kieran.

'There's no sign of blood or a struggle in his bedroom,' Nick confirmed.

'That's not much to go on, but it's a start. If they took him alive, Lorna, I suspect you'll find out soon enough who is responsible.'

'I have my suspicions.'

'We all do.' Kia's eyes darkened as she folded her arms.

'Take breakfast to regroup, we may hear something before you're ready to head out,' Acheron said before leaving the room.

'I'll get changed and meet you all downstairs in ten.' Lorna nodded and headed for her own room.

'Don't even think about leaving this house without us!' Kia called after her.

Ignoring her, Lorna shut herself in her room and fell back against the door, the floor tilting beneath her feet as she finally dared reach for her phone from her pocket.

Nothing.

She'd barely had time to get changed when Kieran let himself into the room.

'You could have knocked!' Lorna barked.

'I didn't want to risk you bolting.'

Lorna didn't answer as she shot a glance at the terrace door.

'OK, I wanted to catch you before you did.'

'He could have been gone since the break-in, they could have taken him while we were downstairs . . .' Lorna rambled. 'How could they?!'

'It's probably just Jake trying to get his own way.' Kieran shrugged.

'Fucking stupid move,' Lorna hissed and stormed from the room.

'Lorna, he wants you.' Kieran grabbed for her arm as they reached the top of the stairs.

'Yeah, well, he got my attention.'

'Even Jake wouldn't be stupid enough to kidnap a pack alpha.' Kieran lowered his voice. 'He'd be mental to try and kill one.'

'I'm not so sure it is Jake.' Lorna glanced back at her brother and carried on down the stairs.

'What's that supposed to mean?' Kieran scrambled after her. 'Lorna! What do you mean by that? Who else is involved here?'

The twins found Kia and Nick in the kitchen. Sookie was bustling about with pre-arranged food trays left in the freezers by the caterers. The rest of the pack were drifting one by one into the dining room to see their fallen brother for the last time.

Lorna made eye contact with Oakley and Ramsey who, having grown up with the deceased, were pretty cut up and clinging to each other. They waved sadly in a manner she was certain was supposed to be reassuring, but it did nothing to ease the lead weight in her chest.

Nick had snuck up behind Kia to wrap his arms around her waist as she helped Sookie make a vat of tea. They'd been staring out of the window wordlessly when Lorna entered but Nick released Kia with a kiss to the top of her head when they saw her.

'Ready to go?' Kia asked as she reached for a bag of pastries.

'You kidding? She'd have already gone.' Kieran rolled his eyes as Acheron entered the kitchen. 'Where's Asha? We could do with her insight.'

'She had to go back to the city last night, something up with Joomba,' Nick informed them.

'I have a feeling we'll be seeing less and less of that tiny dragon.' Lorna smirked. 'Though maybe more of him.'

'Definitely more. You're not even going to try to tell us this isn't our business?' Kia asked brightly.

'Vampires just made it pack business,' Lorna shot back.

'Could it be to do with Nick stepping in the other night?' Kieran addressed the couple.

Kia gave an over-exaggerated shrug. Nick glanced at her with a look in his eyes that made Lorna's stomach turn.

If the angeling had reason to be worried . . .

Shaking herself off, she reached for one of the pastries Kia was holding, more to take her mind off that look than through hunger.

'Acheron.' Danyl appeared, resting a hand on his alpha's shoulder. 'What can we do?'

'We will lay Lazlo to rest and make the house secure.' Acheron glanced at him as Dante leant on the door frame.

'The vampires have killed one of our own and taken another, we can't sit back and wait to see what happens next,' Dante stated.

'Actually, demons, albeit sent most likely by vampires, killed Lazlo. We can't prove anything else yet,' Kia replied.

Acheron nodded his head slowly. 'Until Kia, Nick, Lorna and Kieran have ascertained further facts, we must wait.'

'It seems it was wiser than we gave you credit for to keep this meeting low-key,' Danyl mumbled reluctantly as he moved to lead his brother out of the kitchen.

'What does he mean by that?' Lorna asked Acheron directly.

'After the attack we sustained earlier in the year, I deigned it necessary to keep the numbers down. At Halloween meets pack partners and children are also welcome,' Acheron replied. 'However, that decision was taken months ago, it had nothing to do with Aiden bringing you here.'

'We should get going,' Nick said gently, saying goodbye to

his parents before ushering the group from the kitchen and into the hall.

'We'll take my car.' Kia reached into the pocket of her jeans for the keys.

'Good idea,' Lorna agreed when they reached the front porch, knowing Kieran's motorbike wouldn't carry them all and taking Aiden's car didn't seem right.

'Mine definitely isn't big enough.' Nick gestured to a sleek black two-seater next to Kia's SUV.

'Nor mine.' Kieran shook his head in the direction of the bike.

'Let's go find a needle in a haystack,' Kia said as they piled into her vehicle.

'Head for the apartment,' Nick stated. 'We'll use it as a base.'

TWENTY-THREE

Kia drove them to a high-rise apartment block in the centre of the city. As she pulled into her regular spot in the street-level parking garage, Lorna started to feel her head thicken; a storm or a vision was brewing.

'OK, so where do we start?' Lorna asked, jumping out of the car and trying her best to ignore the building pressure.

'I want to run up to the apartment first,' Kia said as she slid out of the driver's seat.

'Shall Lorna and I get a head start?' Kieran asked.

'This won't take a moment,' Kia answered, ignoring them and heading for the elevator.

Shooting Kieran a look and a shrug, Lorna fell in step with the couple.

'This place used to be my father's,' Nick explained as they entered a two-bedroom corner unit on the sixty-fourth floor with floor to ceiling glass walls. 'He thought he'd get away with a city base away from the pack house.'

'He doesn't get into the city much?' Lorna questioned, taking in more plush, warm surroundings and wondering whether Kia had had any say on the matter or if the pack in general loved their home comforts over style.

'He prefers the house.' Nick shrugged. 'He gave the flat over to me when I turned eighteen.'

'Aiden didn't want it?'

'Aiden was in line to be alpha.'

'Yeah, I didn't think that was how it worked with packs?' Kieran scowled.

'They're a human family before they're a canine one.' Nick smiled. 'He can be questioned or challenged for leadership at any time. It's been a few years since anyone has felt the need to give it a go, though.'

It was Kia's turn to shoot Nick a look as he shrugged.

'So, what are we up here for?'

'Ammo.' Kia grinned.

'We need weapons, with Nick around?' Kieran's eyebrows reached for his hairline.

'Technically, no, but I have a couple of little toys I like to keep on hand.' Kia headed for a partially concealed cabinet next to the wall-mounted television and opened it to reveal a selection of guns and knives.

'Now you're talking.' Lorna joined her to inspect the range.

'You're not the only one Aiden loaned his saliva to. These come in very handy.' Kia pocketed a handgun and some additional bullets. 'Do you have yours?'

'I have mine, but Kieran doesn't have one.'

Checking the safety was on the next one she grabbed, Kia tossed a second piece to Kieran.

With a nod of thanks, he tucked it in the back of his jeans.

After securing the cabinet, Kia reached out and grasped Lorna's wrist and they both zoned out as a vision took Kia under.

'That wasn't funny,' Lorna panted when the vision eased.

'That was gross,' Kia spat when she let go of Lorna's wrist.

'That's putting it mildly. Why rip out the heart?'

'It's a message. It's what he does. It's a trophy.'

'It's what who does?' Kieran's brow knitted in confusion.

'Casey Baxter. He's part of all this, he's been here in Pool Valley for some weeks.'

Kieran's eyes and voice darkened. 'How do you know that for sure?'

'He was there,' Kia looked from Kieran to Lorna, 'the night Lorna was bitten . . . she didn't tell you.'

'Fuck.' Kieran ran his hand through his hair and leant against the window to stare out across the city. 'How could you not tell me that rather significant detail?!' Kieran turned on his sister.

'What happened to "Mum dealt with him, don't worry about it, Lorna"?' Lorna bit back, though her eyes widened. 'You knew he wasn't dead,' she said slowly.

'Yeah,' Kieran admitted angrily. 'I knew.'

'You lied to me?'

'I thought when he left the city that he'd given up on his stupid venture.' Kieran scrubbed a hand over his face.

'What stupid venture?!'

'He'd been drinking from guardians for some time. Managing to keep it under the radar. When Skyler, our mother, was sent after him we thought he'd taken it as warning enough. Then when she . . . well, we thought that was it.'

'So, really he went away to regroup, practise elsewhere and wait for fresh meat to take the reins? Is that what you're saying?' Lorna advanced on her brother. 'And who's this WE?'

'Mia and Ben know.'

'For fuck's sake,' Lorna hissed. 'Well, now he has minions and they're closing in on us.'

Crossing the apartment, Lorna headed for the door.

'It wasn't your vision,' Kia said quietly. 'And getting one of his minions to carry out a copycat murder, triggering a vision . . .'

'It's a trap,' Nick stated. 'He's a monster, and when he slips up and we work out where he is, I'll deal with him.'

'It's not your fight either.'

'He wants Kia, that makes it my fight.'

'What?' Lorna's hand dropped from the door handle. 'How would he even know Kia would get that vision?'

'You didn't get it. Your incident the other night might have permanently altered your ability to receive them,' Nick said, a harsh reality but someone had to say it. 'Kia was always going to be his next target.'

'She's not next in line.' Kieran folded his arms, also looking confused.

Nick stared at Kia, his eyes holding a warning.

Kia looked to each twin in turn, then back at her angeling.

'No,' she said eventually, reaching for Nick's hand whilst holding his gaze. 'But I am Lucious trained.'

'Shit,' Lorna breathed slowly.

'Yeah, exactly.' Kia nodded.

'Kia can't come into contact with Casey,' Nick said bluntly, his eyes still locked on hers.

'He's taking that choice away from us.' Kia shook her head. 'His minion will keep killing until he gets an audience, and he'll be watching.'

'We can't even hand it over,' Lorna said, pacing near the front door. 'He kills anyone he can't find a use for.'

'It's what he does to the ones he keeps . . .' Nick looked from Lorna to Kia. 'He'll see a use in you very quickly.'

'Something we have always been aware of. This wasn't a secret I was likely to keep forever,' Kia soothed. 'Fate is just having her way a little sooner than we expected.'

'Kieran and I will take the vision,' Lorna ordered. 'You two look for Aiden while he's distracted.'

'Could work,' Kieran agreed. 'Though if Casey wants an audience with Kia, it's unlikely he's the one who pup-napped Aiden.'

'Let's not rule anything out.' Kia shot him a look. 'We don't know how far this goes or how many of his family are involved.'

'They all seem to be playing their own game so far,' Lorna huffed.

'Even more reason to be cautious,' Nick offered. 'We'll all go.'

'What?' Kia frowned at him. 'They'll be ready for that.'

'Then so will we.' Kieran shrugged, looking at his sister for confirmation.

Lorna answered by opening the door to the apartment and leading them all out.

'Considering the revelations back there, you're exceedingly

calm.' Lorna glanced back at Nick as they reached the elevator.

'Nick's impervious to adrenaline.' Kia grinned but not without a roll of her eyes.

'Is that an angeling thing?' Kieran asked Kia.

'It's a Nick thing.' She shrugged playfully.

'Training helped,' Nick said bluntly.

TWENTY-FOUR

Lorna's eyes slid towards Kia as they strode side by side through Pool Valley midtown, towards one of the less-frequented access tunnels to the Underground. Known as Monster Alley, the district was home to some of the lowest of the low who had clawed their way back out of the seedy underbelly of the Underground gambling district, which was where they were headed.

Those who made it back to the surface after a disastrous encounter with the Underground were often forever changed. Most were too broken by the experience to ever venture into the light again.

But it wasn't the lost the guardians needed to be wary of, it was those looking to exploit the weak or naïve. Those who controlled the lost.

She noted how Kia made eye contact fearlessly, something Lorna herself had taken some time to learn. Between Kia's training and Lorna's experience and upbringing, they had little reason to fear most of the nasties lurking in the shadows.

Ducking down an alleyway, they entered what looked like a derelict subway station and, kicking past the piles of rubbish on the ground, worked their way down a spiral staircase.

'That's handy,' Kia said quietly when they found a train waiting on the lower platform.

The station was at the end of the line and often train drivers turned back without waiting around for passengers.

Boarding the three-car service, they joined just four others, two of whom were barely conscious on God only knew what substance. Given the supernatural constitution in general, many of the popular drugs in the city were home-grown. Alchemy was alive and well as a career choice, both legally and illegally.

Mood enhancers were popular above ground, but below . . . potions existed for just about everything from ability enhancers to monstrous steroids.

'Do you ever wonder what your life would be like if you'd been born a spell-casting witch rather than an elemental one?' Kia suddenly queried.

'Some days I wonder if it would have been easier, but I doubt my parents would have been impressed, being who they were,' Lorna admitted, then smirked. 'Though it would have made life interesting if Kieran had been elemental and my powers had been potion based. Do you?'

'Not really.' Kia looked up and down the train as it began to move. 'Though I do wonder if it would be handy sometimes. Speaking of which, we'll go in the back way.'

When the train slammed on the brakes at the next station, Kia disembarked, catching Lorna unawares and leaving her to catch up.

'Do you know Mr Wu's Magick Emporium?' Kia asked.

'I don't,' Lorna said with a shake of her head.

'Then there's someone I'd like you to meet.' Kia grinned as they left the station and entered an underground row of shops.

Halfway down the street Kia swept into what looked like a nineteenth century sweet shop, but was in fact a store full of a vast array of curiosities.

Mr Wu himself was an elderly gentleman, a fox shifter. He ran his small shop almost rent free from the owner of the casino it backed onto. The owner, Reggie, was a hot-headed fire demon and didn't much care what the shop was used for so long as the odd punter accidentally stumbled through the curtain into his casino.

Wu sold random and often useless items associated with the practice of magic and the dark arts.

Some of it was genuine stock for the spell-casters, but the rest was for the often-deluded supernaturals wandering around the Underground. Occasionally the odd city-dwelling human would head into the store looking to prove they had power, the balls or both.

There was one such human peering into a book by the window. As they started muttering one of the spells to themselves, Kia nodded towards the book they were holding and it let out a poof of smoke. The book was hastily dropped.

'That was mean.' Lorna sniggered.

'But so much fun,' Kia muttered back, stifling a chuckle.

Wu took most of his takings from the drug-infested crazies who were locked into or living on their very own magical planet. The supernatural equivalent of a crack addict couldn't tell the difference between incense and tarot, and so whether an item worked or not was of little consequence.

The store wasn't just some giant joke on Wu's part, though he had a wicked sense of humour. Having studied alchemy, he knew how to get hold of rare herbal remedies and wondrous substances, which was how Kia had come to meet him. Wu was Nick's supplier of the wicked-strength painkillers and substance neutralisers he kept in his medi-kits.

'I like Mr Wu,' Kia told Lorna. 'I spent an afternoon in here waiting on Nick coming back from a rather bloody incident he didn't think I needed to see, and this woman came in dragging that book over there on a leash behind her.' Kia pointed to a book sat on the floor next to the cash register. The book was entitled "So You Think You're a Witch".

'It's not even about witchcraft,' Kia continued. 'Anyway, she insisted that the little devil had barked all night long and that she needed to return it to its rightful owner. Wu wasn't able to talk her into taking a refund, even though he remembered her buying it, but he now can't get rid of it either as the daft bat still visits it!'

'He should just tell her it died.' Lorna smirked.

'The man is sharp as a samurai sword, he may well do that one day, but for now it's entertainment.' Kia met Lorna's eyes, her own sparkling with the mischief of it all.

As they headed for the burnt-orange velvet curtain at the back of the store Kia spotted Mr Wu speaking with a spell-caster in the herbs corner. Catching his eye she offered him a wave, which he returned with a nod.

'Oh, wow.' Lorna grimaced as they entered Inferno. The volcano themed casino was heavily daubed with garish reds, yellows and oranges as though lava had been thrown on every wall and surface.

'Wonderful, isn't it?' Kia laughed.

'How does anyone ever stay in here long enough to lose their life savings?' Lorna pondered as they approached the bar.

'You get used to it.' Kia sniggered.

'You like it in here?'

'I've also been known to wait in here before meeting Nick at Wu's,' Kia replied. 'Thanks to the lighting it's easier to go undetected with a little shift of hair colour. Which is handy for keeping an ear out for any carelessly thrown around info.'

'Are they fully licensed?' Lorna nodded in the direction of a table where two scantily clad women sat.

'Mostly.' Kia glanced over Lorna's shoulder. 'I have had to liberate them of the occasional ill-acquired staff member.'

While Kia ordered them a couple of drinks that were mostly for show, Lorna claimed the table nearest to the two women.

'What are we waiting for?' The younger of the two fidgeted with a straw that had been abandoned on the table.

'All he said was that we were awaiting a very important client.'

As the exchange fell silent, Kia joined Lorna at the table, her eyes narrowing at the panicked tone of the older woman.

'There have been a lot of vampires around lately, I don't want vampires again tonight,' the first whined. 'I've barely recovered from last night.'

Lorna caught Kia's eye and nodded to the roulette table where there was a raucous group of vampires. One in particular, dressed to impress, kept glancing over at the two women. Both guardians were thankful that his attention was on what he was probably hoping his winnings would pay for and that he hadn't spotted them yet.

He was their mark.

'Did you find out what happened to Sonja?'

'No idea. No one can get hold of her.'

'She was sent out on special order last night.'

Lorna glanced at Kia as she sat up slightly. They both knew who made special orders when it came to sex workers. And they both knew why the poor girl was unlikely to return.

'Lil'

Their attention was dragged back to the room by the vampire in the sharp suit as he spread his arms wide and walked towards someone at the main entrance.

Kia's hand on the bottle of beer she had been slowly turning between her fingers stilled as Lorna looked back to the women at the table next to them.

Casually standing, as if she needed to borrow a menu, Kia put herself between the roulette table and the women as Lorna kept their target and his guest in view.

'Get out of here. Now.'

'What?' they squeaked in unison.

'Go out the back, take the door next to the men's room. Take this, head to that address if you need somewhere safe. They'll know what to do, tell them Kia sent you.' Reaching into her pocket, Kia handed them a business card with the address of the Barnes Shelters printed on the back.

Lorna held her breath as the pair hesitated. If Casey was about to follow Li through the front door the girls were already sold, bought for atrocities she daren't imagine.

Casey would eat just about anyone or anything, flesh as well as blood, and if the mood took him, he liked to have sex with his food, alive and dead.

As the older of the women finally reached out for the card, Lorna stole a glance at the table as the younger of the two reached up to rub one of her cat-like ears, sucking her bottom lip under her top teeth as she tried to compose herself.

'You need to move.' Kia lowered her tone to enunciate the urgency.

'Now,' Lorna added darkly, making them look over and spot the head guardian for the first time. 'Before you become Casey Baxter's new toys.'

Returning her gaze to the front of house, Lorna caught the girls scramble up backwards out of the corner of her eye.

Getting to her feet to aid their escape, Lorna watched as suited vamp was preparing to lead Li towards their table. He spread one arm wide, beckoning his contact to view the offering, but his smile dropped before his arm could.

'Hey, get back here! Where's security? Someone stop those two.'

The gang at the roulette table all turned at once, nearer to the guardians than their boss was.

Too focused on the runaways, they all ran head first into the wall of energy Lorna and Kia collectively threw at them.

'Why don't you pick on someone your own size?' Kia

cooed sweetly as they started to get back to their feet, shaking off the crackles of electricity Lorna had laced into the blast for fun.

Realising what she'd said, many of them started laughing when they saw how petite Kia was. Simply raising an eyebrow, and her right palm towards the ceiling, Kia drew her hand swiftly across her body.

The air between them glowed with heat and the laughing stopped abruptly as their heads left their bodies, hitting the carpet with heavy thuds, necks cauterized.

As the bodies teetered on dead legs before falling like dominoes, Lorna heard Kia's phone buzzing in her pocket and watched Casey walk in the door as Li ducked out of it.

She didn't need to ask her who was calling.

Nick knew. And he was on his way.

'Given you have just deprived me of two very important packages, I'll be needing you two to join us at our booth.' The suited vamp was suddenly stood in front of them with a self-assured grin on his face.

'You're not off the hook, Chuckles, we know what you did,' Lorna hissed.

'I brought you here.' His smile widened.

'You know that doesn't make you safe, right?' Kia rolled her eyes. 'We'll have to decline your request.'

'I'm afraid I'll have to insist. See, if you kill me, Li is under strict instructions to make sure your little rescue attempt was completely in vain.'

'In other words, they're already dead,' Lorna growled.

'Now, now, we can be men of our word, sometimes.' He pouted before turning to lead them to the table.

Lorna noticed that Casey's usual right-hand man, an inoffensive looking vampire called Marcus, had also appeared in the time it had taken their exchange to take place. He was short and slight, but highly trained and effective. She frowned to herself, wondering why Jake would want or need to loan Li to Casey.

They still hadn't heard from Aiden or anyone who might be holding him.

And now Casey had them right where he needed them.

A waitress was placing complimentary blood cocktails on the table with shaking hands as the guardians approached. She peered at them both through her hair and Kia held up a hand to decline refreshments, sending her scurrying back to the safety of the bar.

As Lorna slid into the booth, Kia grabbed a spare chair from a nearby table and parked herself at the end of the table.

Marcus prepared to protest but Casey, eyes locked on Kia, motioned for him to sit down before scooping up a cocktail to shove under his nose.

'What do you want, you murdering bastard?' Kia asked sweetly, offering him a wooden smile.

Casey glanced at Lorna. 'I just came here to pick up some takeout.'

'We know that's not all you're here for,' Lorna drawled.

'Ah, it seems dinner is not completely lost. Oh! Though it seems you'll have to excuse my associate, he seems to have taken it upon himself to discipline my first course.' Casey's gaze moved across the top of Kia's head to where Lorna watched a blood-soaked Li drag the younger prostitute to a whimpering stop.

Before Kia could react, the severed head of her companion hit the table to the tune of rattled glasses and a sickening thunk.

'Let her go,' Lorna bit out.

Kia inspected the head in front of her, careful not to react.

'Whyever would I do that? Although, stupid little girls are apparently very easy to come by in this city, I don't really want to have to wait for more to be delivered.' Casey's eyes flickered black as he let them see his annoyance.

'Let her go,' Kia repeated for Lorna, though they both knew there was little point in explaining how illegal his feeding choices were. In any city.

'Oh, I do love to find someone's weak spot,' Casey cooed as Li handed him one of Kia's business cards.

As Casey turned the card over in his fingertips, the card combusted in his grasp.

Casey let the ashes flutter to the table with an orgasmic shudder.

'The raw power, it's wonderful, do it again.'

Without flinching, every glass on the table rose into the air and doused Casey from head to toe.

Marcus shifted in his seat, expecting to be given an order, but Casey merely laughed joyously.

'That was me,' Lorna said darkly, wiping the grin off his face as Kia fought a smirk.

Wordlessly, Casey picked up a napkin and dabbed at his face.

Calmly placing the soaked item back on the table neatly, he paused before clicking his fingers.

In that instant the shifter in Li's grip started screaming.

Kia took a deep breath as Lorna twitched in her seat.

'Ah, ah, ah. Either of you move another muscle and I inform the whole of my network about your little safe haven full of sluts and runaways,' Casey warned.

Lorna felt herself pale and had to commend Kia for how impassive she managed to remain as the sound of material and flesh ripping continued behind her. The screaming intensified before becoming laboured with shock.

Li was watching his boss as Casey watched Kia with pure fascination. Though when he gave a single nod, the girl's screams were silenced with a nauseatingly wet splash, her intestines tumbling out of the gaping hole in her abdomen to the floor.

The metallic smell of blood washed over the occupants at the table as the body was dropped to the floor.

With a self-satisfied smirk, Casey inclined his head towards Li, who whistled, causing two additional vampires to appear from nowhere.

'Li, did you get the address on that card?'

Lorna caught the demon nod out of the corner of her eye and the tiniest flinch from Kia.

'Take a team down there and make a mess. It's time the werewolves were shown who's going to be in charge around here.'

Before anyone could move, the two new lackeys exploded, showering everyone with their remains.

Casey laughed again, running his fingers through his long blond hair and brushing the dust from his shoulders.

'Li, find a new team, but off you go.'

Neither guardian could ice a telekinetic demon that fast, and so he was gone before either of them could do anything about it.

'Now that I have your full attention.' Casey looked at Kia.

'Where's Aiden?' Lorna growled, feeling that Kia's core temperature was practically molten with rage.

'That mutt you hang around with? No idea,' Casey said dismissively, still staring at Kia. 'Thanks to my associate over there, I had hoped for an exclusive audience with Miss Henderson, but who knew it would draw our survivalist head guardian out of hiding too? Now I have both of you exactly where I need you.' Casey's eyes flashed as he side-glanced Lorna. 'How exciting!'

'That's what you think,' Kia hissed.

'Tell me, how long does it usually take the angeling to get to you?'

Given how close Nick and Kieran promised to stay, not this long, Lorna thought.

'Nick's not here.'

'Yet.' Casey pouted. 'Whatever happens, if this goes sideways and I have to kill either of you before I'm ready, at least I'll have repaid a debt to your mother.'

'Just how much is the price on my head these days?' Kia folded her arms in a bored manner.

Casey chuckled. 'It's negotiable.'

'Money's no longer enough to set the assassins on me now?'

'Not with so much more at stake.' Casey's toxic green eyes were alight.

'Dare I ask where Nick fits into all this?'

'Well, as Lucious' pet, I think he would make a very useful ally.' Casey lowered his tone as Kia frowned. 'I don't suppose Nick's ever told you what a vampire bite could do to him?'

'He's half demon and so, in a way, are vampires. Surely that's a no-brainer,' Lorna snarked.

'You don't think it would take the angel out of the angeling?' Casey pinned her with a look of delight. Kia remained composed.

'You have no proof that would work,' Lorna drawled and caught Kia's shield shimmer in warning, a fine black shimmer across her skin.

She threw her own shield up just in time as Kia stood, the wings she could borrow from Nick as a morph released. All glasses in the vicinity of the table exploded.

Their mark was dusted by a well-aimed shard in the fray but Casey and Marcus avoided death by beer bottle.

'Don't think for a second that you can get away from me. Once I get my fangs into either of you, you'll be under my control.' Casey stood and slid out of the booth to face Kia, plucking splinters of glass from his face.

Lorna's stomach turned when he slid one very long shard out from the corner of his eye.

'You deluded son of a bitch,' Kia said calmly as Marcus rose his hand and six more vampires, plants from the casino punters, joined the party.

'Deluded I could be, but you're here, aren't you? That's just step one.'

Stepping backwards carefully over the body of the shifter, Kia stole a glance at Lorna, who had her eyes on Marcus and the back of Casey. The head of the first girl was lying on the bar where it had been launched off the table in the fireworks. The bar staff were peering over the top of it, ready to evacuate.

With a demonic roar, Kia grabbed Casey telekinetically by the shirt before anyone could react and threw him towards the main entrance.

He took the double doors apart as he passed through them, landing out on the street just as Nick and Kieran arrived.

Lorna felt her brother's confusion as the six remaining lackeys homed in on her, and Marcus leapt over the debris in the direction of his boss. Kia stalked after them both, fire flowing from her outstretched palms as she attempted to set them alight.

As Lorna fought off the six determined to restrain her, Kieran appeared at her side and helped even out the numbers.

'About time,' she hissed as they danced through dust clouds.

'Sorry, didn't realise he brought backup,' Kieran bit back as he threw a vampire through the window out onto the street where Nick was throwing Casey from building to building and Kia was catching the stragglers.

As the twins stood in a settling cloud of dust some seconds later, Lorna caught a stray running towards the back door.

'Shit.' She sighed. 'You go help Kia, I'll get the defector.'

'You could just let him go.' Kieran chuckled.

'He was trying to kill or kidnap me not ten seconds ago. If I don't kill him, I might be able to beat Aiden's location out of him. Go help Kia.'

'As if she needs my help.'

'Good point.' Lorna smirked. 'I'll be back in a minute.'

Taking off at a run towards the back door, Lorna barely made it to the curtain when a vision struck hard.

When she regained consciousness, she was on the other side of Wu's shop, unsure how she'd got there or where the stray vampire might have gone.

Glancing back at the shop, and the casino beyond, Lorna took off in the opposite direction before anyone could stop her.

If Casey didn't have Aiden, she knew a vampire who would.

TWENTY-FIVE

Lorna made it to the nearest station without anyone trying to contact her. Though not without realising she had been followed.

The train lurched to a halt, causing Lorna to crack her eyes open and peer through her lashes at two commuters attempting to enter the carriage. They seemed intent on joining her for the last couple of stops she needed to make. However, when they spotted the two headless corpses on the floor, they swiftly moved to the next carriage.

'Wise decision,' Lorna muttered as the doors and her eyes closed again.

She'd been resting her eyes between stops, knowing it was going to be a long ass day. Stuffing her hands into her hooded sweater, she felt the hood tighten across her forehead.

Having chosen the rear-most carriage because it was empty, Lorna had dragged her two tails onto the carriage telekinetically from their hiding places behind the ticket machine, blade already in hand.

As the train trundled through the city's underground

network the bodies had oozed rivulets of blood into the grooved flooring, their severed heads rolling backwards and forwards with the movement of the train, occasionally bumping into handrails and disappearing beneath seats, only to reappear with a clang somewhere else.

Lorna smirked to herself when she considered one of them could easily roll out the door at the next stop, should it be in the right position.

As they approached Central, Lorna gave herself a little shake and sat up, blinking her eyes awake in time to see one of the heads spin into her foot, the lifeless eyes peering up at her.

'Sorry guys, no prisoners. Not today,' she rumbled. 'Just playing the same game you are.'

Fishing her phone out of her pocket she checked it again. She'd already called in with the clean-up team regarding her two companions.

Pleased to see there were no calls or messages, meaning Nick and Casey were still otherwise occupied, Lorna turned the phone off before returning it to her pocket.

She was confident she had a healthy head start and having called Chris, the clean-up supervisor, direct, she knew she could stay under the radar until he filed his paperwork. She knew he'd keep it off record for as long as necessary if she asked him to, even if it meant owing him a favour, but she decided not to ask him. That way, if anyone went looking for her, they'd know she was working.

When the train pulled up at Central, Chris and his crew were already waiting. He grinned at her as the doors slid open and she gracefully leapt over the pools of blood.

'Nice work Lorna, could you have left us a bigger mess for the end of our shift?' He peered around her pointedly.

'But there were only two.' Lorna smirked and began heading down the platform.

'Cause of death?' He yelled after her.

'Spite,' Lorna returned without turning back.

The standard answers were 'vision kill', 'self-defence' or 'victim'. Lorna didn't look back to see how he was processing her choice of words.

'I'll just put self-defence then, shall I?'

'I owe you one!' Lorna called back.

Winding her way through the network of stairs and tunnels within Central Station, Lorna was aware that she could be tracked in a multitude of ways, and that soon it would become clear where she was headed.

It had occurred to her to slip down through a series of access tunnels to get to the line she needed, but she wasn't in the mood for that either.

As it was, all council members, including herself – even though she wasn't privy to sitting in on the meetings themselves – had to have at least one registered address. Of course, they all had their safehouses too for when times became fractious.

Given his arrogance, Lorna didn't expect Jake to know she was coming and her vision had already suggested she would find him in his penthouse apartment in Crimson Towers. The purpose-built eighty storey beacon of deep red concrete and UV-blocking glass had some underground levels, but many floors stretched into the sky. It exclusively housed the elite, wealthy and celebrity of the vampire community.

Gaining access to the building wouldn't come easily. With thumb-print ID and retina scan technology as standard, Lorna had to rely on Jake's own arrogance granting her entry. She planned on ringing the doorbell.

It wasn't like he'd be in his crypt; the older they got, the less likely a vampire was to sleep at all.

As head guardian she was entitled to request a meeting with the head of defence, though with no love lost on either side, there had never been such a need. Certainly not at the last minute.

She was thankful that her "I'm working" strut kept most people out of her way. The deeper underground she went, working her way from station to station, connection to connection, the more they averted their eyes. Rolling hers to the ceiling, Lorna wondered when they'd realise that the head guardian was only going to go after them if they'd been really naughty. Those stupid enough to get caught up in the Pool Valley Underground, and still walk around in full view, were often too past-it to think straight, let alone plot a murder or city-wide domination.

Whatever drug run or shady business they were on would be dealt with by another guardian if it went too far. After all, Underground Main Street, near to where she found herself, was as bent in its offerings as its above-ground counterpart was affluent.

It was those who lurked in the shadows that made Lorna's flesh crawl.

Strolling down the street until she found the right avenue, Lorna wandered straight up to the gate and pressed the buzzer.

'Lorna Titan, how interesting to see you alive, what the fuck can I do for you?' Jake answered on the second press of the button.

'I'm requesting a meeting,' Lorna said casually as she peered around her for the camera clearly trained on the gate. When she found it, she offered him a wave.

Jake paused for a moment before tutting patronisingly. 'You can't just walk up to my front door and make demands. You'll have to make an appointment.'

'I'm afraid I'm in a bit of a hurry.' Lorna folded her arms and gazed up at the floor to ceiling blackened iron gates. The concrete above her had been tastefully painted to replicate a sky.

'What could you possibly need to talk to me about at this time of the morning?' He barely stalled, but she could tell she'd caught him off guard, after all, he'd probably been expecting her gift-wrapped from Casey or Li. 'Don't you know what nocturnal means?'

'I know it no longer applies in a creature as old as you are. I knew you'd be stewing the morning O-neg.' Lorna pressed the button again.

'Just why should I grant you an audience, witch?'

'Because you know that's not all I am anymore.' As much as it pained her to admit it, she knew her admission was the only way she was going to get anywhere near him.

A high-pitched bleep told her he'd disconnected the call.

Rolling her eyes again, she lifted her hand to repress the buzzer a second time, but the gate began to swing open with an ominous groan.

Slipping inside, Lorna found herself in a small courtyard

with two fountains running with red water.

Not water, blood.

Afraid to find out what her new senses might think of the tell-tale tang in the air, she held her breath as she walked.

Two black metal entrance doors opened before she could reach them to reveal two tall, muscular vampires wearing black head to toe, a small badge on the breast pocket of their shirts. The Baxter insignia. More of Jakes's personal bodyguards.

'You boys here to keep me company in the elevator? You shouldn't have!' Lorna cooed as she slipped between them and allowed herself to be escorted to the elevator.

As soon as she was inside, and leaning against the back wall, they moved in and blocked her exit.

'Are those restraints in your pocket? Or are you just pleased to see me?' she asked their backs, raising an eyebrow.

By the time the doors opened onto Jake's apartment, Lorna was stood over the bodies of two of his highest-ranking bodyguards, spinning a set of manacles on one finger.

Jake, who was balancing a glass of brandy in one hand, ready to receive a bound guardian, had the decency to look outraged.

Jacob Baxter was over seven hundred years old and, Lorna suspected, had spent most of his seven centuries wearing varying styles of leather. Long, dark, curly hair sat on his shoulders and around menacing eyes that had seen more death than Lorna could fathom. Besides the highly nutritious and fatalistic diet a large vampire of his stature needed to survive, he'd fought in every war he'd stumbled upon over the centuries.

'They started it.' Lorna dusted off her hands, splattering blood onto the carpet as she stepped over their corpses. 'Take it you'd been hoping for a guardian blood chaser with that night cap?'

Jake's eyes darted to the left. Lorna flicked her right hand with unnatural speed, stopping the advancing guard from her right dead in his tracks, her knife spinning through the air and into his throat, forcing his head off his neck backwards with the force.

'I would offer to pick up the tab for a carpet cleaner, but I believe you started that one,' Lorna said drily as the knife returned to her outstretched palm.

She stashed the blade as Jake took in the scene. Three of his strongest bodyguards dead inside his home, one of which was holding the elevator in place as the doors tried to close repeatedly on his feet.

Considering Jake's penchant for leather about his own person, his apartment dripped designer opulence. Lorna guessed being as old as he was meant he bored easily and therefore moved with the fashions.

'There was little need for that,' Jake mused. 'They meant you no harm.'

'Whips and chains are hardly my preferred welcome gift. A coffee would have sufficed.'

'To think, if Casey had bothered to bite you himself, you'd be practically family now.'

'And if that had been the case wouldn't adding a shot of my blood to your brandy have been almost cannibalism? Incest at best?'

'I should have you cut up and tests run on you for surviving as it is.'

'I'm not here to offer up a blood test.'

'Then what do you want? So far, you've barged into my private dwelling and killed three of my staff.'

'Oh, you know I've killed more than three of your staff this morning,' Lorna challenged.

'Have you had a vision for any single one of these? Think before you answer, you're under surveillance.'

Lorna laughed before she could help herself. 'I'm allowed a degree of self-defence.'

'And the others?'

'Well, I can't say whether there were cameras, but they were on pack land. And you as much as anyone should have known what that would mean.' Lorna cocked a hip as if bored. 'It's almost as if you wanted me to visit.'

'Well, I did, I just didn't expect it to be under your own initiative.' Jake grinned. 'Or against protocol.'

'I followed protocol. I asked you nicely.' Lorna returned the grin. 'However, since people started fiddling with my DNA, I've been less inclined to give a shit about following the rules.'

'So, revenge is what this little tryst is all about? Your brother came clean about how your mother didn't even get the chance to try and live through a vampire bite?'

'Changing the subject won't save you this time.' Lorna's eyes narrowed as he walked away from her, lifting his glass to take a sip of the reddish amber liquid.

'You intend on killing the Vampire Council Leader visionless too, I suppose?' Jake chuckled. 'Without a vision, it's murder, Lorna.'

'Ah, now who said I was here visionless?' Lorna asked with a smirk. 'The flunkies were simply collateral.'

On cue the elevator doors thunked against flesh again.

Jake glanced at his men and his cheek twitched as he ground his teeth. Lorna was glad he was easily riled. His gaze returned to her as the words sank in.

She had to admit that it was a rare and wondrous sight to see a vampire shocked, if she hadn't studied Jake's soulless face countless times before, she wasn't sure she'd have spotted the subtle shift of his brow.

'On what grounds?'

'Using guardian blood to keep a very long list of misdemeanours cloaked from us.' Lorna folded her arms, the veil on her anger finally dropping for the first time since the vision had kicked in. 'It seems that now I carry your DNA the loophole has been closed. Casey should have made sure I died.'

'A mistake I'm sure he won't make a second time.'

'He certainly won't. Not when Nick or I am through with him.' Lorna smirked.

'You're on the road to hell, Lorna, even if you best me, you won't beat him.'

Watching the colour in Jake's eyes start to turn darker, the green of his irises leaking and swirling into the whites of his eyes, Lorna knew she'd have to pick her moment carefully.

'I left Nick throwing him around the gambling district.' Lorna shrugged.

'You know,' Jake continued, barely an eye-twitch showing his annoyance, 'if this goes wrong for you, it would be fitting for me to kill you the way I killed your mother.'

'Even if that's true, you're only making my job easier,' Lorna bit back.

'Ironically, I think I'd prefer death by guardian than death by werewolf. That mutt you've undoubtedly been screwing would certainly want to boil my blood if I did to you what I did to Skyler.' He met her eyes with feigned guilt and a side-serving of glee when her breath caught. 'I guess I'll just have to kill him too.'

Lorna's stomach dropped at the mention of Aiden.

'Aiden is not my lover,' Lorna stated as evenly as possible, remembering the surveillance.

Jake laughed loud and hard.

'I'm not sure what an alpha werewolf would want with a witch, myself, but whatever he is to you, he became our problem and yours the day he enlisted in your silly little special force.' Jake took another mouthful of brandy and glanced out across the morning skyline. 'Alpha or not, we're not averse to removing people in our way, as you might have noticed.'

'You bastard,' Lorna forced through gritted teeth. 'Daniel didn't deserve the death you dealt him. It was unnecessarily cruel.'

'Neither did your father.' Jake shrugged, rolling the remnants of the brandy about in his glass. 'Skyler never saw me coming, couldn't stop me before I advanced on her. I'd been building up my tolerance to guardian blood long before I sank my teeth into her throat.'

Lorna's blood turned to ice at the very thought, her world tilting, though she tried to retain her grip.

'I wasn't greedy, I'd like you to know your mother's blood

was stored, savoured and has been used sparingly, it lasted almost two years. Head guardian blood, it's something else. Oh Lorna, I've had some great fun these last few years, you wouldn't believe the things I've done.' Jake laughed softly, reviewing his own memories as he leant against the window.

Digging her fingernails into her palms to prevent her anger rising enough to cause a telekinetic storm that would give her away, Lorna filed the new information about her parents away for processing later. She knew there was no point calling Jake a liar, sensationalism wasn't his style.

'Thank you for the history lesson, I think there was some useful stuff in there,' Lorna said, doing her best to sound bored.

'Casey has been drinking guardian blood far longer than I have, he's so much stronger than me.' Jake's eyes flashed in warning.

'Guess that's why we thought he was dead.' She shrugged.

'Dead to your world. He quite literally cut his fangs on guardian blood. Not through my choice, of course, his . . . tendency to attack and feed on just about anything taught us it could be done in the first place.'

Lorna fought the urge to scoff. Of course something as psychotic as Casey couldn't have been killed as easily as she'd been told he had. At less than a century old, his body count was higher than Jake's.

'Must have been missing his dose when my mother went after him,' Lorna said flippantly.

'If your mother hadn't had that vision, we wouldn't have realised the magnitude of the gift Casey had given himself. It was simply a case of working out what he'd been doing differently.'

'I wouldn't call it a gift exactly.' Lorna shrugged and stood straight. She had more information than she had hoped for and there was another on her list.

'You don't think gaining control over guardians who live is a gift?'

'Hardly anyone lives. And all guardians we've found lately were already dead.' Lorna's eyes narrowed to cover the sinking feeling in her stomach.

'Oh, but when they do, *if* they do, sometimes, just sometimes, it binds them in much the same way we bind to those we sire. Only in such a weak mind as a guardian's the level of manipulation is stronger. That's the real reason it's illegal.' His eyes flashed. 'Bet no one ever told you that. Though I suspect your council representatives know . . . would they have told your brother, do you think?'

'There's no need to goad me, Jake, you and your vampiric offspring are marked.'

'Bullshit. He's unstoppable.'

'Oh, really?' Lorna sauntered closer to Jake than was strictly sensible. 'But he's next on my list,' she said, lowering her voice and leaning forward with a grin.

Jake glared down at her, searching her eyes for the lie she wasn't telling.

Reality finally sinking in, Jake's body reacted defensively, his eyes flooded with green, his fangs extended and his nails grew to talons.

Just as he was about to lose control, Lorna smiled.

'That's it, come and get me.'

Time seemed to slow as Lorna watched Jake make his move. He flew at her, ready to barrel her to the ground, but with added speed of her own, Lorna took a casual step to the side and fired two handfuls of fire at his back.

Crashing to the floor, Jake rolled to put out the flames, charring what was clearly a very expensive rug, before springing back to his feet with a hiss.

Wasting precious little time, Lorna planted her foot against his rib cage and used a charge of electricity to send him crashing into his oak coffee table.

'You should calm down a bit, your aim is getting sloppy,' Lorna goaded.

Jake replied by throwing the coffee table at her.

Deflecting it telekinetically, but not quickly enough, she bit back a growl of pain when the table caught her right arm. Snatching the item up as it landed, she used her left arm to throw it back.

Jake's fist punched straight through the solid oak surface, splitting the table in two. As the splinters settled, he stalked towards her.

Throwing two more fireballs to slow him down, Lorna put everything she had into her shield, creating a telekinetic bomb, triggered when Jake reached for her throat.

At such short range the blast knocked Lorna off her feet and forced Jake backwards, straight through the reinforced window.

Closing her fist around a shard of oak from the table she found at her elbow, Lorna jumped up, ran to the window and fired the sharp end directly into his heart as he fell.

Jake Baxter was a dust shower by the time anyone on the

street below knew he was coming.

Rubbing her right arm and finding it sluggish to respond, Lorna peered down through the broken window and waited for the pain to break through her focus.

Before she could take stock of her injury, a gunshot rang out.

TWENTY-SIX

The ding of the elevator doors brought Lorna back to reality when the pain she had been waiting for materialised at her waist rather than her arm.

Turning from the window in confusion, she found Hillary stood at the emergency stairwell, gun still raised.

Using her rapidly diminishing energy to swat the gun out of Hillary's grip before she could make the kill shot. Though before the vampire could dive for the gun, she was hauled backwards and thrown to the floor when Li strolled through the same door with Casey in tow.

Swaying slightly, Lorna shuffled to the side, wondering what her best angle might be in the circumstances. Once she'd clocked Casey, she couldn't take her eyes off him, not even to look at the wound pumping hot streams of blood through her fingertips pressed to her waist.

Casey stalked through Jake's living space like a predator as he slowly applauded her.

She took in the torn and bloodied flesh of his shoulder, his head lopsided where Nick had attempted to tear it off. Lorna wondered whether the death of his sire had caused him to bolt or if he'd known he would lose if Nick got anywhere near his head a second time.

With a clearer daylight view of him, she also noticed how pale his skin was, he was almost translucent. His white hair cascaded down his back and was catching in the wind being sucked into the gaping hole in the side of the building.

'Lorna Titan, you're under arrest for crimes against the Baxter family, particularly the murder of council leader, Jacob Baxter.' Casey grinned

'You can't do that,' Lorna replied calmly.

'Do you or do you not have vampire blood in your veins?'

'Thanks for reminding me.' Lorna felt her temperature rise and knew it would sap her energy too fast to retaliate in that way.

'Then I can charge you for the death of my father.'

'Well, that's a complicated issue, you see.' Lorna sucked in a breath. 'Because he was marked.'

Casey's eyes narrowed slightly, but he chose to ignore her.

'I have to say, your kill was nicely done. You were quicker than I expected, I honestly thought you'd make your mother's murderer suffer. Someone messes with my family, I like to kill them slowly.' His fangs extended, no doubt at the thought of what he planned to do with her.

'Tell me something I didn't know about you,' Lorna drawled, monitoring how much pain was in her voice. 'You can skip the part about being a heartless, murdering, raping, enslaving, soulless bastard.'

Casey was well known for what he called *playing* with his food, or victims. The case studies Lorna had seen were horrific. Most of the bodies were left unrecognisable. Vampiric or demonic sex was notorious for getting violent and Casey was no exception, believing himself to be more of the demon than a vampire. But where two vampires or demons together would heal from the gauges, bruises and broken bones, the women Casey picked were often found ripped limb from limb.

Glancing at Li, wondering how he'd been dragged back from the shelter so fast, Lorna bit back a wave of pain and noticed he was stood over the pile of bodies he'd dragged out of the elevator whilst they'd been talking.

In her moment of distraction, Casey snuck closer, the tension caused her to grind her teeth in pain and wish that Nick might still be chasing him down.

'I'm sorry that my sister shot you.' Casey motioned to Hillary, unconscious next to the bodies where Li had broken her neck by throwing her against the wall.

Feeling her body temperature plummeting, Lorna knew she needed medical attention fast and that either killing or getting away from Casey would be incredibly difficult.

As he reached out to touch the wound, Lorna felt fire consume her entire body.

Casey arched an eyebrow as the flames swirled around them both, his gaze fixed on her features as he squeezed her waist harder, causing her to scream and the fire to stop.

'That's quite enough of that,' Casey said softly as he contemplated his bloodied fingers. 'I'm sure I don't need to tell you that you're not my first guardian, or even head guardian.'

'I'm not my mother.' Lorna beat down the inward shudder.

Creating a fireball with her free hand and adding an extra punch of energy to the mix, she let it explode between them, hitting him in the chest and forcing him backwards several paces.

Skidding to a stop he laughed to himself.

'Pity.' Casey shrugged.

'She came back alive, but I'm guessing that was only due to the personal interest your father showed in her?'

'He found the situation to his advantage, for sure, but I had better reasons to keep Skyler Titan alive.'

Reaching out for another sharp chunk of the coffee table, Lorna swallowed down the pain and hurled it at Casey's chest.

It shot off to the side, narrowly missing the unconscious Hillary, deflected by Li from where he stood, statuesque in front of the elevator, out of the way.

As Casey laughed again the elevator pinged, announcing the arrival of a new set of Li's demons, and Hillary began to regain consciousness.

Sitting herself up, her head lolling to one side, she groaned miserably as she took a fistful of her own hair and reset her neck with a yank and a sickening crunch.

With a wince, Lorna scowled down at her. Hillary was out of sync with the vision, she shouldn't have been in the building at all.

'That was uncalled for,' Hillary spat at her brother. 'It's not like I'm the one trying to kill you.'

Casey looked to Li, who made a gesture with one hand and

two of the new arrivals hauled her to her feet and held her fast.

'No,' Casey shot her a glare that could have melted steel as he cooed dangerously, 'but you know I want her alive. And this is the second time you've tried to waste her blood. I doubt you were thinking of protecting me from a guardian on a delusional mission?'

'What good is a council leader who destroys all his allies?' Hillary retorted, making Lorna frown in confusion.

'Seems one of you actually has some sense?' Lorna chimed in.

Casey's eyes turned on her, making her shiver for a very different reason.

'Li,' he said quietly. 'Get a tranq in her asap, she can't die here.'

'Who said anything about dying here?' Feeling that Kieran was on his way, Lorna turned and ran towards the broken window, taking a flying leap towards it with no other plan than to get them out of the apartment.

She had barely cleared the glass when she felt the unmistakeable pull of telekinetic energy around her throat as Li caught her and hauled her back inside.

Gasping for air, she landed on the carpet, wishing she could scream as pain throbbed through her torso.

'Not sure where you thought you were going, but that's quite enough of that.' Casey laughed as Li shot a tranquiliser dart into her arm.

TWENTY-SEVEN

'Well, that was a bust.' Kia sighed as she led Nick and Kieran out of the elevator.

'How could we be so far behind a vision?' Kieran's voice was hollow as he leant against the wall while Nick unlocked the apartment door.

'They were long gone before we made it to Jake's.' Kia folded her arms, the scowl on her face barely easing.

'What the fuck are you doing here?' Nick asked as he headed into the apartment first.

'Dad told me you were out looking for me, so I came looking for you . . .' Aiden was sat in the armchair with one of Nick's reference books on his lap. 'Where's Lorna?'

When no one answered, he stood up, dropping the book.

'What's happened?' he persisted.

'Where the fuck were you this morning?' Nick asked quietly, his tone gaining a glance from Kia and a dawning realisation across Aiden's face.

'I went for a walk after our talk last night. I was mooching about in one of Dad's workshops in the woods when I was hit with one of those gas cannisters.'

'We thought you'd been abducted.' Nick's tone grew deeper.

'You should have checked the grounds.' Aiden frowned. 'Is that really what you've been doing all day. Looking for me?'

'We were side-tracked with visions, but we'd hoped that if someone *had* pup-napped you it would have killed two birds with the same stone,' Kieran informed him.

'And Lorna . . .'

'Ran off on a vision while we were distracted,' Kieran said evenly. 'All we know is that she killed Jake, but is now in the hands of Casey Baxter.'

'Casey Baxter?' Aiden's face turned thunderous. 'What does that evil bastard have to do with any of this.'

'Just about everything, as it turns out,' Kia said gently. 'Kieran, tell him what you told us.'

'Can someone sedate him first?' Kieran looked nervously from Aiden to Nick.

'Might not be a bad idea.' Kia grinned at Nick beside her.

'I'll see to the drinks,' he said as he picked her up by the waist and sat her on the breakfast bar.

Smiling, Kia reached for his shoulders and pulled him close for a quick kiss.

'Don't mind us,' Kieran drawled.

'They won't,' Aiden replied bluntly, but met Kieran's eyes darkly. 'You were saying?'

'Casey Baxter has been feeding on guardian blood for years, so has Jake, it allows them to remain cloaked from Fate to some degree. It's a tolerance that must be built on, but the stronger the guardian, the more likely they get away with just about anything their black little hearts desire.'

'And now Casey has Lorna?!' Aiden took a step forward as if to run from the apartment, but Kieran dared to stop him, planting his palm to his chest.

'Calm down, we need to think our next steps through very carefully,' Kieran continued. 'We came back here to regroup. We thought he'd taken both of you. We also suspect he will have her locked down at the military prison. It's one of few vampire territories we need permission to enter.'

'Like fuck we do,' Aiden growled.

'I'm inclined to agree with that statement, but trust me when I say that Casey will be planning on keeping my sister alive for as long as possible.'

'I can't stand here and let him turn the woman I love into a living blood tap.'

'It's not that you have to worry about.' Kieran winced, making Nick look up from where he was reaching for mugs in the kitchen. 'Casey has discovered for himself that a guardian survivor of a vampire bite can, on rare occasions, be controlled mentally by the vampire who bit them. That's the real reason cross-species feeding is illegal.'

'How long have you known *that*?!' Aiden yelled.

'Since our parents died,' Kieran admitted, shame burning his cheeks.

Aiden's right fist connected with Kieran's jaw before Nick or Kia could think to stop him.

'Direct hit,' Kia said lightly, jumping off the bench ready to calm Aiden if necessary.

'It's OK.' Kieran touched the back of his hand to his split

lip as he retreated backwards to slump down onto the sofa. 'I should have told Lorna years ago, rather than thinking training would allow me to protect her from it.'

'Well, wasn't that stupid.' Aiden's voice dropped back to a growl.

When silence once again fell on the group, Nick flicked the kettle on.

'Are you alright?' Kia asked Aiden gently.

'No,' he admitted. 'What if we don't get there in time? What if she . . .' Aiden pulled himself up short but caught Kia's look. He knew she'd be able to tell what he was thinking, her look told him as much. She could tell when he was beating himself up, and why.

He was itching to get out and find Lorna, not just for fear of what Casey would do to her, he couldn't bear the thought that he had caused her more pain. He remembered the look in her eyes, known the last words he'd said to her had hurt her.

But he'd only expected her to sleep on it.

'She'll be fine,' Kieran said unconvincingly as he sat dazed on the sofa.

'What's the plan?' Nick asked from the kitchen.

'We need to get out of here and find her,' Aiden growled, staring at the floor, his face pale.

'I can't think straight,' Kieran said as he rubbed his eyes. 'Is anyone else feeling a bit wrecked?'

'That'll be the blow to the head,' Kia chuckled. 'And the aftereffects of the night-night gas. Nick's just fixing us something that'll help.'

With a glance over the mugs, Nick gave a slight nod and

slipped a small jar from the cupboard.

'Nick, I saw that.' Aiden put his hands on his hips. 'No funny shit in my tea.'

'It's just a pep-up.' Kia shrugged.

'I know your idea of a pep-up. We need to find Lorna.' Aiden let another growl slip as he spoke.

'I promise it's an energy boost, as much as we need rest, I'm not going to knock you out, we haven't the time,' Nick confirmed. 'I'll add a few neutralising elements though, that might help shift the fog.'

'How come you're not affected?' Kieran twisted his head to look over the back of the sofa at the angeling.

'Different DNA.' Nick shrugged.

'Ain't that the truth,' Kia said with a smirk as she sat down and curled up in the armchair Aiden had vacated.

'It feels so wrong to be drinking tea when Lorna could be . . .' Aiden's face was pinched, even as he took a seat.

Kieran looked inclined to agree.

'Are you going to be able to fight Casey feeling like that?' Kia asked. 'Honestly.'

When neither of them could bring themselves to answer her, Nick handed everyone their tea.

'Give your body a chance while we work out how to get into the prison,' Nick said persuasively as Aiden made no move to accept the mug.

'If anything happens to her . . .' Aiden took the drink with a resigned sigh.

'You can seriously maim me.' Nick smiled. 'I'll let you maul one of my legs or something.'

Kieran looked at Kia to see how that went down, she was

blowing calmly on her tea and ignoring the brothers.

When Nick turned back to the kitchen for his own cup, Aiden moved towards the coffee table to put the mug down.

'Don't even think it,' Kia said between sips. 'If this is going to affect Lucious, I have a feeling I'll get another vision if we take too long. As it is I think you're being very insulting to assume she can't handle this.'

With a smirk, Kieran watched Aiden consider Kia's words. With another growl, he took a large mouthful of tea.

Having already put his faith in Kia, and knowing Nick had to have some form of contact with Lucious when necessary, Kieran followed suit.

'That's not bad, considering it's drugged.' Kieran yawned.

The couple sipped their tea calmly, Nick stood against the counter, Kia curled in the armchair.

After several moments of reflection, Nick took his phone from his pocket and dialled Mia Sanderson.

TWENTY-EIGHT

When Lorna regained consciousness, which she hadn't expected to do, she found herself in a fully enclosed prison cell. She gave a groan and rubbed her eyes with the heels of her hands as it sank in that they'd incarcerated her on military property.

The prison was deep underground and almost impenetrable without authorisation.

There was no way of knowing how long she'd been out, but when she sat up without thinking, she was surprised to find bandages at her waist.

A tentative prod at the clean dressings didn't warrant anywhere near as much pain as she'd first expected and further prodding suggested she was well on the way to repair.

Testing herself again, Lorna stood up.

The room span, the floor tilted, and she had to sit back down.

As her butt hit the crude cell bunk, the lights went out and the door was thrown open.

Before she could process what was happening arms were pinning her down and a torch was in her face.

Heavy hands tugged the arm of her sweater up past a cannula she hadn't noticed and hooked her up to an empty blood bag.

'We thought it best to catch you unawares for this part,' Casey said bluntly, lit only by the emergency lighting in the corridor as he watched over proceedings from across the room. 'Take two.' He nodded to a second bag.

As the second bag filled, Lorna felt her strength wane and the dizziness increase.

Shooting Casey a filthy look as she was finally released and the light flipped back on, she noticed him siphon a shot of blood out of one of the bags and knock it back.

With a roar he convulsed and bent double.

Lorna raised an eyebrow.

When he looked up, the whites of his eyes had turned red and every vein on his face was risen. Black blood flecked the corners of his mouth.

'That's one hell of a side effect,' Lorna drawled as he wiped his lips.

Casey glared at her and muttered something to his advisor, Marcus, who promised to investigate.

'You don't need to look into it, you stupid bastard,' Hillary's voice squawked with laughter from the cell next door. 'Can't you work it out?'

'It's not the result of the vampire bite,' Marcus said quietly, pausing in the doorway, equally puzzled.

Casey motioned to one of the vampires charged with restraining Lorna. With a nod, they left the room, returning moments later with Hillary who, battered and bruised with broken limbs, needed to be dragged into the hall.

Even Lorna shuddered at the state of her.

'What do you know?' Casey's voice was so threateningly low, it was barely audible.

'It was werewolf DNA they used to save her life.' Hillary's laugh was deranged around a broken nose.

Lorna wondered why the vampire wasn't healing, then decided she didn't want to know the timetable of torture Casey had already put his sister on. A tiny part of her was scared for the woman's life.

'What. Was. That?' Casey's voice dropped even lower, his eyes turning black and thunderous.

'You honestly thought she'd randomly survived being bitten and taken on vampire characteristics? Just like that?!' Hillary laughed again as Marcus shoved her into the corner ready to take action if ordered. She wriggled her broken body into a sitting position against the wall as a couple of bones popped themselves back into place. 'It's the werewolf in the mix that's fucking with your digestive system.'

'You had no idea what that could have done to me!' Casey raged.

'It didn't really matter to *me* what the outcome was for *you*.' Hillary's sharpened but bruised eyes were locked on her brother.

Casey had murder in his.

'If Lorna lived,' Hillary continued, 'there was a chance it would poison you and Jake enough to make you see sense. And if she had died that night, my plan had been to slit her throat and wash all that precious blood down the drain before you could retrieve the body.'

Lorna blinked to herself at the revelation of Jake's first sire. Hillary was playing a very different game to the rest of her family. Though Lorna suspected it was one she was about to lose, permanently.

'Shame you didn't take a sample back at Jake's apartment. It would have been interesting to see that tear in your neck increase. I see it's healed already,' Lorna goaded. 'Pity.'

'Careful, Lorna, I aim to keep you alive a little longer. Best not piss me off,' Casey warned with a sick grin.

'Tell me, Casey, how did you let Nick get anywhere near your pretty little head in the first place?' Lorna's eyes lit with amusement.

Hillary joined in the merriment, laughing to herself in the corner. 'That's what happened?! You barely breathed on the hybrid and the angeling nearly took your head off?'

'I don't know what you're laughing at, you've done me a favour. With the use of Lorna's blood, I can get to Kia Henderson *and* begin building my tolerance to werewolf poisoning. I have to say, Lorna, your blood has a wonderful kick to it.'

'You stupid bastard,' Hillary ground out as she was hauled up onto her still-broken legs by two prison officers. 'You really think you'll be able to get chummy with Lucious through the angeling?'

'Chummy?' Casey roared with laughter. 'Hell no. I plan on using the angeling to bring Lucious to his knees. Then I'll kill him.'

'Wow,' Lorna deadpanned. 'You really are batshit.'

In two strides Casey was across the room, once there he

backhanded Lorna across the face hard enough that she wasn't sure her neck didn't snap.

Rage, all consuming, burned up her back and she lit up like a torch, engulfing the room in flames.

The guards and Marcus dove for cover in the corridor.

Casey remained where he was, only moving to lift his arms enough to shield his face.

'Regaining your strength already I see.' Casey grinned at the horror in her eyes as the flames died back, revealing his half charred but very much whole form. 'Good.'

Before Lorna could process what had, or more importantly, hadn't happened, the door was re-bolted, and she was alone again.

TWENTY-NINE

Listening to the silence that followed, and her own ragged breathing, Lorna found she was shaking. The urge to scream and rage out was strong, but she daren't give Casey the satisfaction if he was still in range.

It wasn't until she'd managed to calm her breathing that Lorna realised Casey hadn't mentioned Aiden, and neither had Jake.

Covering her mouth and nose with her hands as she tried to stave off a panic attack, her brain ran through the several reasons that might have been.

Perhaps he wasn't leverage.

Perhaps he didn't matter now they had her.

Perhaps they'd killed him back at the house and dumped him in the woodland.

Getting up off the bunk as her head and shoulders went cold, she instantly reached out for the nearest wall as her legs turned to jelly. Her head swam, taking her complete focus as she tried not to fall to the floor, and she wondered briefly if she might be able to add concussion to her problems.

Stumbling to the cell's sink, she ran the tap and, cupping her hands under the water, drank several large mouthfuls and splashed her face. The cool sting of the water against her cuts and bruises acting as just another shove to get moving.

'I need to kill that bastard and get out of here,' she hissed to herself as she crossed the cell and felt the door. 'Or get out of here and kill the bastard. Whichever works.'

Placing her ear against the door, despite knowing it was probably several inches of steel thick, Lorna chanced it that her new hearing might serve her well. At first she heard nothing, and wondered if there was even anyone out there.

Wondering what they would have done with Hillary after her revelations and how heavy the surveillance was, Lorna peered down at her fingertips. Rubbing her finger and thumb together, she gauged how much of a spark she could produce, despite knowing getting out of the cell would take more than she had left.

Placing her palms flat on the centre of the door, Lorna took a deep breath as she considered whether an energy blast or pure molten heat would work better.

Moments later, she was waking up on the floor of the cell, the sound of laughter ringing in her ears.

'Silly witch,' a disembodied voice said with a chuckle. 'You think these cells weren't invented to hold the very worst creatures of this city? Or did you think that just didn't include you?'

'Fuck you,' Lorna groused as she sat up.

Of course the guards were watching her.

Of course the cells were electrified.

Locating the camera in the corner above the bunk, Lorna

flipped her captors off before throwing a ball of energy at the lens.

No one was more surprised than she was when the ball of lightning hit the camera with enough explosive force to take out the power, plunging her into darkness.

'OK.' Lorna peered down at her hands in the dark, which were crackling with tiny blue sparks.

Not bothering to consider just how much energy she'd absorbed from the shock the guards had given her, Lorna jumped to her feet and blasted the door with another wave of energy.

The emergency lighting hadn't yet kicked in, so she lit a fire orb in the palm of her hand to get a better look.

The door to the cell wasn't just open, she'd fired it across the hall.

'O-fucking-K,' she whispered to herself.

Using the temporary darkness as cover, she made a bolt for the end of the corridor and the nearest stairwell. She knew the military prison was underground and, in its oldest parts, a rabbit warren of inhumane boxes where the lowest of the low were left to rot. But having never needed to go beyond the lobby, as her only business was usually dropping off, she knew nothing of the layout.

She also knew the lobby was nearer to the Aboveground and that meant the further down she went, the more secure the place was likely to be.

Pausing at the door to the stairs, she listened for activity above or below her. There came neither. Instead, a stairwell at the other end of the corridor was alive with the sound of running boots and harried voices.

'She won't have gone far,' Casey stated to whoever he was with. 'Not if she still thinks she can kill me. Find her before the inspectors find her.'

Scowling, Lorna tried to listen to the rest of the conversation, but the rush of blood in her ears blocked it out.

Who the hell were the inspectors?

She wondered briefly whether Kieran would send Mia and Ben in. Then, remembering how much her brother loved to handle a crisis by himself, scoffed at the very thought he'd even bother to tell them.

Backing carefully into the stairway, Lorna remembered Kieran telling her that the lower levels were rumoured to be full of laboratories and tried not to think about the potential purposes for which vampires would be conducting experiments in a prison, or worse, on prisoners.

With a shudder, she failed as her brain offered an array of unwelcome images.

Knowing she was likely to have been placed somewhere between the lowest of the low and the day-to-day criminals, somewhere out of the way, Lorna estimated she was somewhere in the middle of the twenty-five storey building.

Pushing the idea that Aiden might already be dead to the back of her mind, Lorna decided to head downwards. If they had him, chances were he'd be in a high-security cell.

If he was still alive.

Shaking her head violently to regain her focus, she stared at the inky black ahead of her.

Closing the door to the corridor as gently as possible, hoping that because she couldn't see them, they hadn't seen her either, Lorna took the stairs down, being as light on her feet as possible.

She expected the emergency lighting to kick in before she could get too far, but disconcertingly, it didn't.

She made it four floors before she heard the door above her open.

Stopping abruptly and holding her breath, she felt as gently as she could for the nearest door. Finding the handle and hearing the door above close, she let herself onto the level as carefully as possible and began making her way down another black cavern of a corridor.

Listening closely for the sound of any other prisoners pacing their cells and hearing nothing, she suspected she'd found the laboratories, though if they were active, she expected personnel to be hollering into phones and radios about the power being cut off.

Lorna wondered whether they were fucking with her by not turning the power back on. Even a vampire couldn't see where there wasn't even a shred of light, so unless they had a night-vision system, they were all feeling around in the black. Though she highly doubted she could have caused a surge large enough to knock out the mains and the backup.

Inching forwards she felt her way across a door and knew it wasn't a cell. She was able to locate a number and some lettering. Unwilling to know what went on in those rooms, she didn't linger to find out what the letters spelled.

Unwilling to light so much as a fingertip's worth of flame until she had to, Lorna kept moving, though she wasn't sure what she was looking for.

She was contemplating trying a handle to see if the doors

were locked, when the slightest noise from up ahead stopped her.

Footsteps, quiet, more of a shuffle, as someone or something moved down the corridor. That she could hear them at all suggested it wasn't a vampire.

Holding her breath again, Lorna froze as she realised that whoever or whatever it was, was moving in her direction and getting closer. Fairly certain she could take down a wayward guard or two, Lorna wasn't certain she was in any fit state to take on Casey if he was wandering about in the dark for kicks.

She knew it could have been Li, but although the footsteps were too heavy for a vampire, they were also too light for a demon of his size.

Fighting to see any kind of movement in the black, Lorna searched the space immediately in front of her when the shuffling drew level.

Hoping they would continue their journey, as she was struggling to hold her breath, Lorna wondered what would happen first. Would she pass out or would they bugger off?

Trying to be as light footed as possible, she turned towards the wall and took a shallow breath.

The shuffling stopped.

Cursing, she waited what felt like an eternity for something to happen. For the lights to come back on, for the creeper to move on, for Casey to reach out of the dark and sink his teeth into her throat.

Another slight rustle and the shuffler was at her back.

Daring to take another shallow breath, Lorna caught scent of the person behind her just as strong hands found her waist.

That smell was the only thing preventing her from screaming.

'It's only me.' Lorna heard the whispered words of reassurance riding on a sigh of relief as his forehead rested against the crown of her head.

'I know,' Lorna whispered back, choking down a sob as she leant back into her captor, his arms snaking around her waist. Finding her breath and sucking in a lungful of stale air and the smell of a hundred summer runs in pine forests, Lorna closed her eyes and ran her hands down his arms, her fingertips tracing their way to his wrists.

When she found his hands she squeezed them tight.

Another deep breath and she also smelled the dried blood on his clothes.

Aiden pressed a kiss to her neck even as she reached around to search for a wound.

'I'm OK. It's not mine.' He chuckled as he turned her around.

'You need to get out of here,' Lorna hissed, finding his eyes in the dark when sparks lit her skin. 'You shouldn't have come looking for me, you need to find a way out.'

'And let you run off into the hands of that psychopath again?' he challenged. 'You don't have to go through any of this alone, Lorna. I know I said—'

'I don't care what you said. I said some pretty dumb shit myself to try to protect you,' Lorna cut him off.

'Yeah, now look where we are.' He smirked.

'I'm sorry.'

'There's nothing to be sorry for.' Aiden frowned.

'There is. I'm sorry I hurt you, I'm sorry I didn't leave before they could take a member of the pack, and I'm sorry if I didn't make it clear enough that losing you would kill me.' Lorna watched him process her words, expecting him to want to know more about the pack member, and hoping he didn't assume she meant his kidnap.

'It's fate, Lorna. You just have to roll with it.' He grinned.

'Aiden, they killed Lazlo. How can you be so laid back about any of this?'

'Because I know you did everything possible to prevent his death. Fate had her way, sad as the outcome was. But right now, all that matters is the woman I've craved for years just admitted she loves me.' Aiden's grin only widened as she attempted to look outraged.

'I didn't say that.' Lorna scowled, remembering the surveillance and again wondering whether it was running despite the power cut. 'Wait, years?!'

'I'll explain later. Right now, we need to make sure you fulfil your vision or die together trying.' He ran his palms up her sides, scowling when he felt bandages.

Fire and electricity burned through Lorna's veins at his words and she dropped all defences and reached for him. As they gripped each other tight, Lorna felt her own blood run hotter and finally understood what he'd been trying to tell her.

Tears crept into her eyes as she realised that every time he'd appeared out of nowhere during the difficult months following Daniel's death, it had been because he'd known exactly when she'd needed him.

Looking up to nudge his jaw with her nose, Lorna found his lips waiting to kiss her with a hunger and passion she'd never before experienced, which left them both breathless.

'Let's wipe the earth of this scumbag, then we'll have the rest of our lives for kissing,' Aiden panted. 'However much longer that might be.'

'Oh great, work, work, work,' Lorna grumbled playfully as he picked her up. 'Maybe I should retire if we live through this.'

Laughing as he threw her over his shoulder, Aiden began moving back in the direction he'd come from.

'I've had a long day, so you're welcome to carry me, but it's not necessary.' Lorna wriggled out of his grip. 'Do you think Kieran, Nick and Kia are looking for us?'

'Mia escorted us through the gates personally,' Aiden answered. 'Not that Kia planned on playing nice once inside. I suspect that's why the power is out.'

'Oh, no, that was me, I think,' Lorna admitted sheepishly. 'Wait, you came with them?'

'Something else for me to explain later, I was never pup-napped as your brother keeps calling it.' Aiden rolled his eyes. 'But I did separate myself from them in the confusion, knowing Casey would move swiftly once he got word of our visit.'

'The inspection,' Lorna said slowly, 'yeah, he knows.'

'Let's just head up, I'm sure the party will find us one way or the other,' Aiden continued, 'Nick will tear this place apart to find us if he has to.'

As they made for the opposite end of the floor, the

emergency lights finally snapped on.

'Fuck.' Lorna blinked several times as her eyes adjusted. She made a quick 360 to check their surroundings.

The level they were on wasn't just a long straight corridor of cells. It was a corridor, but there were several junctions between them and the main stairwell.

For the first time, Lorna spotted an elevator in the middle of the floor. A floor that she could only compare to that of an abandoned hospital or science wing, if they were to be carved from solid rock. The doors all held windows and small plaques stating the room's purpose.

"DNA Testing Suite" made her blood run cold. Though she was relieved to see that all the rooms appeared to be empty.

'Do we think this area is abandoned? Or did they evac when the power went out?'

'I didn't see or hear any evac. Did you?' Lorna turned to Aiden.

His eyes were fixed on her face as he let out a low, incensed growl.

'What's the matter?'

Reaching up gently, his fingertips traced the welts across her face, specifically the shiner on her left cheekbone. Feeling the sting of each bruise beneath his touch, Lorna tried to smile in reassurance, though it looked more like a wince. She'd heal.

'I'm going to rip him to fucking shreds.' Aiden's growl grew deeper.

Lorna took his hand and kissed his knuckles. 'Not if I get there first.'

Raising his head to nod, Aiden instead reached out to pull her in tight and bundle her into the nearest lab as the thundering of boots on the stairwell alerted them company was coming.

As the door clicked closed, they heard the doors at both ends of the corridor being kicked in.

'Shit.' Lorna turned towards the room's interior.

'There's nowhere to hide,' Aiden said, his voice barely a whisper as he tugged her in tight.

With a sigh of resignation, Lorna closed her eyes and drank in his warmth for as long as she could while each room was raided and their inevitable discovery drew closer.

When the door flew open seconds later, kicked in hard enough to crack, it bounced off Aiden's shoulder back into the face of the guard who had booted it.

Grabbing a scalpel she'd spotted, Lorna staked the first two vampires to enter the room before Aiden pulled her back and Casey himself entered.

As Casey's eyes settled gleefully on the couple, a slow manic grin split his face.

'Someone separate them,' he ordered. 'And watch her, she's armed.'

'Bitch, I'm always armed.' Lorna wrenched one arm free of Aiden's grip and fired the scalpel at him encased in fire, though she wasn't surprised when he caught it and tossed it over his shoulder, amused.

Taking a gun off one of his entourage, Casey sobered suddenly and pointed it at Aiden's head.

'Lorna, I keep saying I want you alive, but this is not a game. I will cut my losses, farm what blood you have left and simply move on.'

'So do it already,' Lorna bit back, even though Aiden squeezed the arm he still had hold of hard.

'Li.' Casey glanced over his shoulder to where the demon was waiting silently, though he stepped forward when summoned.

'Take Mr Barnes here to the draining suite. With such an honoured guest, I'd like to run some tests on werewolf blood. Make it snappy, we have company.'

Lorna's mouth dropped open in horror, though her eyes continued to shoot daggers at their captor.

With a nudge of reassurance, Aiden let her go before Li could tear them apart.

'How much are we talking?' Marcus appeared behind Li, ready to escort them.

'All of it,' Casey replied, his eyes locked on Lorna's even as she stole a glance at Aiden, who remained impassive. 'Then throw him in the furnace or something . . . but, bring me the wolf's tooth around his neck.'

Blood was rushing in her ears as she tried to work out what to do. The gun was still trained at Aiden's head, she could dismantle it, but she didn't know how many more were in the hallway. That didn't stop her frowning in confusion at Casey's words.

'We need to follow *some* protocol and inform the pack that their alpha is lost.'

'Starting a war with the werewolves now, too?' Lorna bit out.

'When I have control of the guardian network, they'll have to obey me. No more of this pound of flesh bullshit. All will fall in line,' Casey informed her before grinning at Aiden, who growled in warning. 'Now are you going to come quietly or am I going to have to shoot him anyway?'

Wishing he'd just shoot her, Lorna took a resigned step forward and found her wrists immediately bound.

Casey took hold off the cuffs and began dragging her down the corridor behind Aiden until they reached a crossroads and went separate ways. The turning Casey took led them to an opening with a guardrail. They turned again to join a gantry framing an exercise pen below. At the corner, Casey made Lorna walk down the metal steps ahead of him.

As they descended there was another distant gunshot.

Winded, Lorna broke into a hideously familiar, feverish cold sweat.

Pretending he hadn't heard anything, Casey carried on walking, stopping only when he reached one of the cells on the perimeter of the pen.

Shoving Lorna inside the cell as the automatic lights flickered to life, he started talking to her even as she fell to her knees, all strength ebbing from her bones. Barely noticing the hands grabbing her hair and arms as she was dragged further into the cell, Lorna only looked up when Li appeared behind Casey.

Words were said but they sounded to Lorna as though they were through water.

When she continued to ignore the voice she didn't have the capacity to pay attention to, he strode over to where she'd crumpled to a puddle on the cold, hard floor.

Crouching next to her, Casey grabbed her hand and removed the cuffs, placing Aiden's white gold wolf's tooth into her palm.

Angry that she wasn't listening to him, Casey wrapped her fingers around the choker and squeezed until she felt the sharp point of the tooth pierce her skin.

Too numb to scream, it was only once he'd slammed the door behind him that she let her vision blur with tears.

As she tried not to hyperventilate, she felt consciousness start to slip, and as it did, she heard the unusually comforting sound of her brother's voice in her head.

'Hold on Lorna, we're coming.'

THIRTY

Tasting bile, Lorna found herself on her knees, gripping the edge of the bunk despite Casey having mashed the fingers of her left hand. The choker was still in her palm. With a sob and a sickening crunch, she peeled her fingers open just enough to look at it before using her other hand to shove it in the pocket of her jeans.

Her head still spinning, she knew she needed to find fluids before doing anything else.

Crawling to the cupboard-sized toilet in the corner, she managed to get her feet under her long enough to turn the tap on and drink a couple of glasses worth of water.

Her mouth still incredibly dry, she tried to remember how long it took the average guardian to replace each lost pint of blood. She knew they'd taken a couple of pints, and that her supernatural constitution could rapidly replenish, but had no idea how much she'd lost when shot.

With a sigh of resignation, she closed and locked the toilet cubicle before sitting with her back against the door.

Just when the room had stopped spinning long enough for

her to consider getting up for another drink, Lorna heard the cell door open. Rolling her eyes and pinching the bridge of her nose, she listened as footsteps drew nearer, then paused as whoever it was found the room empty.

'Lorna, get out here,' Casey demanded.

'Why should I?' Lorna asked childishly.

'Don't make me break down the door.'

'Now that could be very embarrassing for you and me both, don't you think?' Lorna teased from her ragdoll position on the floor.

'You have three seconds.'

'No good acting like my mother, she's long dead, as you may recall,' she shouted back, determined to buy herself as much time as possible.

His fuse running shorter than she'd expected, Lorna screamed in surprise when he began pounding his fists on the door, knocking it inwards on top of her.

Swivelling on the spot as he reached out and threw the door aside, Lorna waited for him to make a grab for her before throwing a snowball in his face.

She was still laughing when he walked into the wall of energy she'd created in the empty doorframe. When he stepped back, rage turning his face purple, she turned it into a wall of frozen water, just for fun.

With a roar, he smashed his way through the ice and grabbed her by the neck of her jumper.

Prepared to deadweight herself, Lorna realised her mistake when he threw her against the wall and pinned her by the throat.

Gripping him at the wrist she tried to freeze his hand and

only succeeded in lowering the temperature of the room to the point where his eyebrows froze.

'Chain her to the wall,' Casey instructed Marcus, who Lorna hadn't spotted in the doorway.

Offering him each of her hands in turn as he wrenched her grip off his arm, Casey ignored the scratch marks she left in her wake as Marcus cuffed her into manacles, her wrists bound at shoulder height, either side of her head.

Once each arm was secure, Marcus used a pulley system to retract the chains connected to existing iron fixings. He upped the tension until her arms were stretched to breaking point, restricting any range of movement.

'Aww shit, how am I supposed to kick your ass now?' Lorna whinged playfully, trying to ignore the way his thumb had started working circles over her jugular.

'I truly love it when someone's auto-response to fear is humour.' Casey leaned forward but glanced at Marcus. 'Leave us.'

'Sir?'

'I'll make sure there's enough left for you too.' Casey returned his gaze to Lorna's throat.

Her eyes tracked Marcus as he nodded without another word and left the room, closing the door behind him. Having realised what he was about to do, Lorna willed her mind to shut down. Despite her wisecracks, there had never been any stopping him.

'Now then, let's see if we can't make this whole nasty business a little more enjoyable.' Casey regained her attention by using his free hand to squeeze one of her breasts, hard.

He started to chuckle when she began to shake with rage,

her core temperature rising so swiftly that sparks flew from her pointless shield as he moved to the other breast.

'Thanks for taking the edge off,' he cooed gently as he brought his face close enough to hers that she could smell the blood of his last meal on his breath. 'It was getting a bit chilly in here. And I do prefer my food warm,' he continued softly before dipping his head to her throat and sinking his teeth into her flesh.

Willing the same shock from the first bite to kick in, Lorna bit back a scream as his teeth tore into her neck. His eyes glanced upwards with glee as she worked hard to fight through it. Casey never bothered to stun his victims.

Each slow, rhythmic pull he made on her jugular sent waves of excruciating heat through every vein in her body, as though his poison was pure lava. Feeling the muscles in her shoulder solidifying, Lorna vaguely noted her brain fogging as she began to lose control of her legs.

Unwilling to finish his meal before he was ready, Casey placed a hand firmly against her breastbone, his claws extending until they pierced her skin, pinning her in place one handed.

Wincing as his talons scraped past her ribs, Lorna took a breath to scream, but he increased the pressure on her diaphragm enough to wind her before she could even squeak.

'There now,' Casey hushed, retracting his fangs before swirling his tongue over the bite, catching a trickle of blood. 'That wasn't so bad, was it? I would have loved to fuck you at the same time, but given the mood I'm in, I probably would have killed you just a tad too early. I won't waste your blood on the walls.'

Watching him carefully, expecting him to change his mind and do it anyway, Lorna knew she was unlikely to survive a second bite anyway.

'Let's first see if we can't make you a little bit *more* vampire. *That* would be interesting,' Casey breathed in her ear before biting his thumb and smearing some of his blood into the fresh bite marks.

Leaning back to review his work, Casey offered a contented smile before releasing the hold he had on her ribcage.

Her legs instantly collapsing beneath her, Lorna screamed with everything she had left when the manacles at her wrists caught her, wrenching both shoulders to breaking point.

Wishing for oblivion to take her, Lorna barely registered the movement when the door was thrown open.

That was until Nick appeared and, reaching for Casey, grabbed the startled vampire by the throat and threw him out into the exercise pen.

As they disappeared from view, Kieran appeared in front of her, just as every muscle in her body went into spasm at once and she screamed again. Relief was quickly overthrown by the memory of Jake Baxter telling her exactly how her mother had died.

An inhuman anger began to spread beneath her skin as Lorna felt the demon in Casey already teasing at the back of her mind.

'Get the fuck away from me!' Lorna yelled at Kieran, making herself jump at the intensity of her own voice.

Kieran stopped just short of head-butting distance, what had burst from his sister's vocal chords had been gravelly, harsh and filled with pain.

He had expected her to be angry at him, for someone to have opened their mouth and for her to finally know. But nothing short of a vision could have prepared him for the state he found her in.

Beneath the bruises and the blood, he could just about make out the sister who had told him only hours before that she'd be right back, as she glowered menacingly at him.

'I bet you even knew exactly where to look for me,' Lorna bit out, her voice deeper as well as ragged.

'Kia brought us here, a vision,' he struggled to say, horror in his eyes as he surveyed the room and his twin.

'You knew! All the time, you knew.' Her voice softened suddenly, exhaustion taking over as she hung by her wrists from the wall.

Her eyes, when they met his, were deep crimson, making him afraid to get too close. Breaking into her mind easily, he saw exactly what Casey had done.

'Stop that! Get out of my head!' she snapped, before lunging forward with a roar.

The chains rattled as she fought against the minimal manoeuvrability they offered.

As Kieran took a step back, Lorna fell back against the wall, letting her body sink towards the floor, continuing to curse her brother.

Rooted to the spot, he wasn't listening, he was too busy mentally running through as many options as he could to try and save her, numb as he acknowledged there was nothing any of them could do.

Hanging limp, too exhausted for more accusations, Lorna

fell silent and raised her eyes to her brother, feeling sickened by the way he was looking at her.

'No wonder you had to leave,' she mumbled, 'you knew they had it in for me.'

Squeezing his eyes closed, Kieran took a steadying breath before he spoke. 'Are you going to let me get you down?'

It was Lorna's turn to freeze, her body stiffening as she realised how feral she looked hanging from manacles, snarling and growling.

'Sure,' she muttered apologetically.

With a gentle smile, Kieran closed the space between them and helped her to stand as her manacles opened.

'Pah, I could have done that,' Lorna scoffed.

Meeting her eyes, Kieran smirked and helped her to sit down on the cot.

'Eventually . . . maybe, I'd have gotten my strength back.'

'Maybe,' he agreed quietly and let her settle into the crook of his arm, exhaustion taking over as her eyes filled with tears.

'I don't think you understand how much I've missed you. Even when you were here, I missed you. Now I understand why you distanced yourself,' Lorna said between sobs. 'Why didn't you tell me what was going on? I could have been better prepared for . . . well, any of this shit.'

'It wasn't that I gave you up for dead, I could never do that,' Kieran said eventually. 'I never wanted you to know what they'd done. I hoped I could stop them before it got this far.'

'That's why you went away, isn't it?' Lorna said slowly. 'Why you wanted the training so badly? So you could deal with this behind my back? You fucking idiot.' Lorna shook her head with a sigh.

'Not that it did any good. The party started without me.' Kieran gave her a squeeze. 'I'm so sorry.'

'I'd have been the one to get the vision eventually, anyway.' Lorna found his hand and clutched it tightly. 'Speaking of which, I should probably give Nick a hand, it seems an army is needed to take that bastard down.' Lorna glanced up at the door as Nick flew into one of the other cells, having been thrown by Casey.

'You're in no fit state to go out there.'

'I'm dead anyway, well, hopefully, I certainly don't want to be that psycho's puppet. What does my neck look like? Will my head fall off any time soon?' Lorna asked. 'And keep out of my head when you look, I don't want to see it.'

Tilting his head to take a closer look, even though he'd been able to see the gaping wound from across the cell, his stomach turned when he saw that Casey had made more than just a couple of puncture marks, having wrapped his jaw around her throat.

Sitting back, he daren't admit that he wouldn't even know where to begin stitching it. Instead, he tore the pillowcase off the bed and, shredding it into strips, attempted to create temporary dressings.

'Your head won't fall off,' he muttered as he worked to secure the fabric.

'Well then,' Lorna said decisively as she tried to stand.

'Hey now, Nick isn't doing too badly out there, Kia is about somewhere too.'

'It's my vision, I need to kill the son of a bitch, for Aiden if nothing else.' Lorna forced herself to her feet and made for the door.

THIRTY-ONE

With Kieran's support, Lorna made it to the door of her cell. But that's as far as either twin got.

Across the pen things were taking a turn for the worse.

Or the better in Lorna's case.

As Li and Marcus appeared from the shadows, ready to outnumber Nick, Kia appeared on the upper gantry with Aiden.

The air knocked from her lungs to see him, Lorna fell against Kieran to watch Kia give Aiden instructions. He limped his way across the gantry and made his way to where the twins were standing, while Kia leapt the guardrail and landed in front of Marcus, who microseconds later, was a pile of dust at her feet.

Wasting no time at all Kia locked eyes on Li, stalking after him as he tried to retreat into the shadows.

Blissfully unaware of his audience, Nick was enjoying the fight. A couple of prison guards had tried to intervene, and a variety of body parts littered the blood splattered space around him.

He had allowed his demon to take full control and it had obligingly made a mess. Blood splattered the floor and walls, though not just that of Casey and his staff.

As Kieran kept his eyes on the fight, Aiden made his way around the edge of the pen, eventually reaching a tearful Lorna, who hadn't been able to tear her eyes away from him as he'd approached.

Ignoring the way she looked, though his gut churned, Aiden scooped her up as she looked set to lose all ability to stand.

'I'm OK, I'm OK,' Aiden hushed in her ear.

'I'm not,' Lorna sobbed.

'You'll be OK, we just need to get you out of here.' Aiden tried to sound reassuring even as his voice quavered. 'Kieran, how do we do that?'

'We hope Nick stops pissing about and kills Casey.'

'There must be another way out of here, how did you get in?'

'After Mia was only able to get you access, Kia and I blew up the reception desk.' Kieran grinned.

'And they just let you walk in after that?' Lorna looked up at her brother.

'They didn't get much choice, though Mia and Ben are up there, along with Declan, Jake's official deputy. We thought it best to call in backup on this one,' Kieran admitted.

'Of course, they knew too . . .' Lorna huffed.

'Yes, they do,' Kieran agreed. 'Aiden, if you can get Lorna to reception level, I'll help Nick and Kia end this.'

'No,' Lorna bit out. 'I'm as good as dead. Let me finish him off.'

'You could barely stand a moment ago.' Kieran shot her a look.

With an explosion of energy from across the pen, Kia and Li reappeared suddenly, Kia landing in a heap, unconscious, as the demon recovered himself from the blast.

'On second thoughts . . .' Kieran turned to Nick, just as Casey backhanded him hard.

'Walk away from me now, angeling, and I will make you watch me kill her,' Casey goaded Nick, also forgetting they weren't alone.

'Go help Kia!' Lorna instructed Aiden and Kieran, though Aiden was already moving. 'GO!'

Helplessly, Lorna sank to her butt on the floor as Aiden and Kieran took off in the direction of the telekinetic demon and Nick and Casey continued to tear lumps out of each other.

Putting her head in her hands and feeling a wave of pure rage engulf her core and form a ball of energy, Lorna forced herself to her feet and began to walk into the centre of the pen.

Li was too busy facing down Aiden and her brother as they tried to get Kia out of the way, he didn't notice Lorna running towards him.

As the demon prepared to strike her loved ones with another energy blast, Lorna took a running jump at his back and with an unholy roar, seated herself on his shoulders and wrenched his neck hard enough to snap it before he could counteract.

As the pair landed hard, Kia began to regain consciousness and it was Nick's turn to roar.

Jumping up, Kia ran to where her lover had fallen.

Casey was waiting for her, stood over Nick as he knelt in a puddle of blood on the floor. She noted quickly that Casey had broken one of Nick's wings and smashed his collarbone, leaving his left arm hanging useless against his hip.

There was too much blood on either of them to be sure where it was coming from.

While Kia pondered the reasons why Casey would incapacitate Nick without instantly killing him, Casey watched her fixatedly.

'Tell me, if I reached into his chest and took his heart in my hand, how much control would that give me over you?'

Kia flinched at the thought, but looked Casey up and down and saw where Nick had almost torn his head off for a second time. It was lopsided, with a fresh split in the flesh from chin to ear. There were several other chunks of flesh missing, all oozing numerous bodily fluids, but healing at the same time.

Meeting his eye, Kia glared at him. Nick wasn't coming to her rescue this time, but she had already shaken off all fear of the vampire stood looking at her like his new favourite chew toy.

'I think he might just have been the only living creature able to stop me, aside from Lucious himself—'

'Now *that* could be arranged,' Kia muttered darkly, cutting Casey short.

'A private audience with Lucious? Wouldn't that be perfect.' Casey tilted his head back as far as he dare, relishing the thought. But I don't even need to fight you to kill you, do I? As fun as it would be to strap that wild spirit of yours down and have my way with you, find out whether you taste as good as Lorna over there, if I were to kill him now, you'd go with him, else risk being parted for all eternity.'

Her breath catching in a way she knew he heard, Kia's heart skipped a beat. It was a little-known fact that angeling beloveds were so bound to their partner.

Balling both fists against the pain of Nick's injuries and sheer frustration, Kia kept her mouth shut. Black wisps of smoke began swirling around her hands. She stood a better chance of landing a blow or outsmarting him if he couldn't see her.

Advancing before she could think twice, Kia bounced off a wall of energy.

Lorna had crept up on them unnoticed.

'The *only* creature able to destroy you?' Lorna sidled up behind Casey tutting. 'Surely, I'm as much you as you think you are me now? Kia, see to Nick,' Lorna ordered.

Peering around Casey, Kia found Lorna glowing red ever so slightly, her eyes a swirl of red and black. There was something unnatural about the way she stood, her hands talons at her sides.

Kia swallowed hard but did has she was told.

With a look of disgust, Casey turned to face Lorna whilst Kia dropped to Nick's side. Casey opened his mouth to say something he probably would have considered clever, had Lorna not punched him so hard that the split beneath his chin grew another inch, and he lunged for her.

'It's OK, I'm not as bad as I look,' Nick said quickly as Kia contemplated whether it was best to help him to his feet or drag him out of the way. 'Breaking my collarbone was just a calculated way of getting your attention. Fuck, this hurts.'

Kia shot him a sarcastic look, smirking at his words. He rarely swore.

As she helped him to his feet, he accepted the shoulders of Kieran and Aiden when they moved in.

'It's not good that she can keep up with him so well, is it?' Kia turned to where Lorna, despite her injuries, was giving Casey the run around as though possessed.

'No,' Kieran agreed.

Feeling the extra strength from the blood Casey had infused into his bite, Lorna was focused on completing her job. She was also aware that the burst of energy was most likely the final flare of her own light and that the comedown would be her end.

With a boom that rattled the gantry and made the others cower, covering their heads, Nick using his good wing to cover Kia, Lorna punched Casey square in the chest with a flaming fist.

As Casey went up in flames, landed awkwardly and rolled to put himself out, Lorna was already going after him, gaining speed as he got to his feet so that she could leap over his shoulders, sinking her talons into his back as she flew overhead and used the momentum to throw him across the pen into a wall of concrete.

With a snarl, Aiden shifted into his wolf form and barked to get her attention.

When the call was ignored, Aiden looked at Kieran with a whine.

Persisting with a howl, he finally got her attention and, as Casey regrouped, Lorna glanced over her shoulder to where

Kieran was bent at the waist, his hand ruffling the fur at the back of Aiden's neck either in reassurance or attempting to hold him back, she couldn't be sure.

Expecting the lunge Casey made for her when he thought she was distracted, Lorna sank her claws into his arm and put him in as tight a bind as she could muster, lacing the talons of her other hand through the shredded flesh of his neck and shoulder.

Forced to kneel, Casey roared in pain and frustration.

'I think I'll let Aiden kill you,' Lorna's low rumble was amused.

'He can't kill me, werewolves don't get visions.' Casey's voice had turned guttural.

'Correction, asshole, the vision stands, and with the exception of Nick, who can kill you whenever the fuck he chooses, the rest all have my permission to assist. Including Aiden.'

With a nod from Lorna, Kieran let Aiden go.

Claws scraped concrete as Aiden charged over to Casey and sank his teeth deep into the attached side of his throat, shaking his head to loosen Casey's some more for good measure.

When Aiden let go, Lorna did too. Both jumping back as Casey roared again, rattling the cell doors around them.

At first, he tried to get up, to retreat, but he stumbled and fell to his knees after a couple of steps, the veins in his arms, neck and head black and risen, his flesh bruised and swelling.

Aiden sat down to watch, tongue lolling in a pant.

Wide-eyed, Lorna couldn't take her eyes off Casey, though she moved around the scene to join Aiden, absently rubbing the fur behind his ears, wishing she could feel it.

Whatever Casey was trying to say to her came out as a gurgle from the back of his throat, his body having swollen to twice its size, his features almost indistinguishable.

With a gargled scream of rage, Casey exploded with a loud wet splat.

'Gross.' Lorna stuck her tongue out in disgust as a flood of blood, body parts, bone and clothing spread across the floor in front of them.

Remaining on his backside, Aiden returned to his human form, looking unimpressed at the carnage in front of and all around him.

'Thank fuck for that.' Lorna fell to her knees next to Aiden as Kieran went back into her cell to get more fabric to strap Nick's shoulder.

'All that mess for one vampire,' Nick said, addressing the puddle of Casey. 'Anyone else left on your hit list?'

'No.' Lorna looked back at him, then to Kia who was easing his arm into Kieran's makeshift sling as gently as possible. 'Yours?'

'No, all good.' Kia smiled sadly, trying not to dwell on the state of Lorna.

'Everyone but me OK, generally?'

'Bones and bruises only,' Kia replied, before pursing her lips as she looked down at Aiden.

'Couple of bullet holes, but no silver used, I'll make it.' He turned to Lorna and got to his feet to help Lorna up.

Falling against him in relieved exhaustion, Lorna looked from Aiden to her brother.

'Don't you dare,' Kieran warned her.

'Let's just see how far I get,' Lorna offered, gripping Aiden's hand for all she was worth.

Her red eyes and general pallor looked worse with a curtain of exhaustion, Lorna couldn't keep Kieran out of her head any longer, she knew how awful she looked.

'I think everyone else got the hint, or Declan has control already,' Kieran said as they began heading for the exit. 'Do you know where Hillary went?'

'For all we know Casey dusted her,' Lorna said, her voice fading with exhaustion. 'She pissed him off pretty bad.'

'How so?' Kia asked as she and Nick brought up the rear.

'She tried to kill me, to stop him.'

'Oh.' Kieran's eyes widened, surprised.

'Yeah.'

Heading up the gantry to where the nearest elevator was, Lorna made it to the top of the stairs, but her legs gave out on the last step. Aiden only just caught her before she could tumble back down them.

Sitting her down wordlessly, Aiden could barely make eye contact with her. Falling back against the wall, he pulled her close. Kia watched helplessly, Nick and Kieran crouched beside the couple.

'I can't go any further,' Lorna breathed. 'And I don't think Aiden biting me is going to pack quite the same punch this time.' She tried to smirk, but the effect was lost under the pain on her pale features.

'You can't leave me,' Aiden said, paralysed by the denial building in his chest, tears clouding his vision.

'Aiden,' Lorna turned her head into his neck, her voice choked with tears, 'I'm sorry, I don't think I can crawl back from this, I'm too far gone. I love you, but I can't stay.'

Taking his hand, she squeezed it again, but lost grip, her hand slipping to her lap. Aiden scooped it up again.

Kia, looking from Aiden to Nick through her own tears, folded her arms tightly around her torso against the bitter ache in her chest, knowing she should suggest what no one else wanted to hear.

'Nick . . . maybe you should . . .'

Meeting Lorna's eyes, Nick lowered his head, he was crouched at her shoulder next to Kieran. Looking to Aiden, he held his hand out.

'Nick, don't you dare,' Aiden growled.

'She deserves a peaceful death, Aiden,' Nick said quietly. 'Lorna, I can help you slip away painlessly, but only if that's what you want.'

'Can we be certain another bite from Aiden wouldn't buy her time?' Kieran asked, stroking his fingertips down his sister's temple.

Tugging her arms out of her ridged stance, Kia reached around to the small of her back and produced the gun she had been carrying.

'I still have bullets with werewolf blood in them. These ones explode on impact.' Kia held the gun out to Kieran. 'It could be faster than a bite?'

Looking from Nick to Aiden and then to her brother, Lorna felt a pang of heartache. Her body was screaming for peace, her heart was screaming at her to live, and her head knew there was too much at stake to leave behind.

'Kieran, you'll have to do it,' Lorna said. 'You know where to hit me to give me the best chance of survival.'

'You can't,' Aiden whined. 'I'll let Nick help her slip away before I let you shoot her!' His eyes blazed as he looked to Kieran, who wasn't paying any attention to him.

With a nod and glistening eyes, Kieran leant forward and kissed his sister on the forehead. 'I'm sorry.'

'It's fine, I'll give you this one.' Lorna grinned through her tears.

'Aiden, you need to move away,' Nick said as he got to his feet and stepped back.

'I'm not letting go . . .' Aiden whispered to Lorna, who kissed him to silence him.

At the sound of Kieran taking the safety off the gun, he growled and pulled her in tighter, kissing her the way he had the first time, with a lingering desperation.

'You have to, we don't know what will happen,' Lorna reasoned when he pulled away, tears rolling down her cheeks. 'If I react, I don't want to hurt you.'

Stepping around Kieran, Nick helped Aiden to his feet, pulling him out of range.

As soon as Aiden was clear, Kieran fired.

THIRTY-TWO

Bracing himself as the car hit the ramp to the Aboveground at such speed he almost left his seat, Nick kept his eyes on the road. Lorna was drifting in and out of consciousness in the back of Mia's SUV, held firm by Kieran and Aiden. She had been feverish and murmuring incoherent nonsense since they'd left the prison.

'Bloody hell, Kia, we need to get there in one piece,' Aiden yelled.

Mia and Ben, strapped into the spare seats at the back looked to each other with fear as they held on for dear life.

Kia floored the accelerator again, they were approaching the early morning sunlight. Nick shot her a look, none of them were in a fit state to be thrown around. Kia ignored him and flicked her eyes to the rear-view as sunlight bathed the car.

With an ear-splitting scream, Lorna's eyes flew open, convulsing when the rays hit her skin.

Shucking his jacket off, Ben handed it to Aiden who threw it over Lorna's head and shoulders while Kieran prevented her from kicking Kia in the back of the head.

Stealing a glance over his shoulder, Nick surveyed the level of thrashing just as Kia hit a curve in the road and threw the car down a shaded street back towards the Underground road network that would get them back to guardian HQ.

'I expected that.' Kia checked the rear-view again as Lorna stopped screaming, but continued to hiss and growl intermittently.

'That's gonna piss her off,' Kieran stated, his voice strained as he tried to keep her feet and knees away from his own head.

Nick looked at Lorna again, then to Aiden as they entered the tunnel and she almost stilled.

'It might not be permanent,' Aiden bit back.

'How are her vitals?' Kia asked calmly as she joined the carway. When her phone began ringing in her coat pocket, Nick reached across and fished it out. 'That might be Oakley,' Kia said quickly as Nick sat back with a sharp intake of breath.

'Better than I'd expected,' Kieran confirmed.

Kia eased off the accelerator while Nick answered her phone.

'Did you have to shoot her in the shoulder?' Aiden asked, reapplying pressure to the wound.

'She'd already been shot in the side, where would you have shot her?' Kieran sniped, knowing Aiden was only pissed because the second bullet had missed her heart by mere inches.

'It was Oakley,' Nick confirmed after hanging up. 'He wanted to let you know that the shelter is locked down, only a few vampires showed up. They dealt with it.'

Kia sighed in relief as she steered the vehicle into the parking garage at HQ. 'Good.'

She'd barely put the brake on before jumping out to help Asha, who was waiting for them at the door with a gurney.

Nick worked his way out of the front passenger seat gently, while Aiden and Kieran saw to their injured cargo.

'Asha, keep the coast clear, Lorna doesn't need an audience,' Mia instructed as she and Ben slipped out of the back of the SUV.

Asha nodded, her dyed red curls bobbing, a Broomstyx apron still tied over her baggy jeans. When she disappeared back inside the loading bay a freckly redheaded teenager stepped out.

Confused, Kieran watched the kid, easily in his late teens, rush forward to help get Lorna inside.

'Joomba?' Kia asked curiously.

'Yeah,' he answered with an awkward grin, ruffling his hair self-consciously. 'It's Luca, actually. Hey, Aiden.' He raised a hand to the werewolf, who he knew had never been comfortable with him.

His eyebrows flying upwards, Aiden looked the dragon up and down in a curious canine manner, before holding out a free hand for Luca to shake. 'Welcome back.'

'Thanks.' The dragon flushed slightly, especially when he caught Kia grinning in his direction before she launched herself at him for a hug, making him laugh awkwardly.

As they entered the building, Asha reappeared and confirmed that it was clear to theatre.

By the time they had all crowded into the facility and locked the door behind them, Lorna was trying to climb off the gurney, struggling so much that they had to work as a team to move it and stop her falling off.

'When we get to the theatre, strap her down,' Mia instructed. 'I'll go get a surgeon from the medical department to attempt to fix that neck wound. I'll ask Thad, he's the best we have and won't breathe a word. Nick, come with me and I'll see to it that someone x-rays and straps your arm up properly.'

'What about Aiden?' Kia asked.

Mia took in the amount of blood, though mostly dried, on Aiden's clothing. 'We'll get to him.'

Pausing at the door, Mia ran her eyes over her granddaughter and chucked a bunch of keys at Kieran.

'Give her what you can to keep her comfortable.'

Nodding, Kieran moved to the locked cabinet in the far corner of the room knowing that there was only one thing Mia would give Lorna in such a state. He also knew it was probably the only thing they could do for her other than patching up her open wounds.

As Kieran sedated his sister as heavily as he dared, Asha, Kia and Luca helped to keep her still while Aiden paced, and Ben watched helplessly from a chair he'd fallen into.

When the screaming became a low purr-like grumble, they all fell away from the operating table, some taking a seat on the floor, others leaning against surfaces to wait for Mia to return.

'You got him, then?' Asha stated when simply listening to Lorna became too much.

'Lorna got him, but not before he got Lorna,' Kia said sadly.

THIRTY-THREE

Tossing the book she had been trying to read for over an hour onto the sofa beside her, Kia reached up to massage her temples. She had yet to make it past the first page.

'You should have gone back to college,' Acheron muttered over his own book on the adjacent sofa.

'Like I would concentrate any more there when I'm needed here.' Kia got up, placing the book on the arm of the sofa, and left the room.

The shrieking and yelling intensified in volume as she crossed the hallway, but Kia needed to get closer to the source by going into Nick's room to take some wicked-strength painkillers from the medi-kit.

Ascending the stairs, she looked to the closed door of Aiden's room and wondered how it was he could sit in there with her. The only way any of them were getting any sleep was by heavily drugging the fury out of her.

Whatever self-repairing coma Lorna had slipped into after being stitched up wasn't deep enough to stop her raging unconsciously. She hadn't opened her eyes since Kieran had knocked her out for surgery.

For fear of rumours spreading, Mia couldn't risk keeping Lorna at the complex for too long and Aiden had insisted the pack house was the safest place for her.

Both exhausted, Aiden and Kieran had been taking it in turns to sit with her through the night.

Kia poured herself a glass of water from the ensuite sink and perched on the edge of Nick's bed to gulp down the painkillers, noting that the blister pack she'd removed them from was almost empty.

As she finished the glass, the noise from the bedroom next door suddenly stopped. Sighing in relief, Kia considered taking a nap while the pills kicked in.

Looking up in time to see Nick appear in the doorway, she smiled. He, too, looked exhausted, his arm still in a sling, though she knew he was being overly cautious. It was almost fully healed.

'Headache?' Nick kissed her temple as he sat down next to her and held his hand out for the last two painkillers.

Kia punched them out into his palm and jumped up, slipping into the bathroom to refill her glass for him before returning to her perch beside him.

'Yeah. I've given up on my coursework for the week.'

'Early night for us, I think.' Nick knocked back the tablets and drained the glass. 'We have no idea how long she'll stay this way. You should go back to college next week. I might even sneak onto campus and stay with you.' Nick smiled, leaning over and nudging her playfully with his nose.

With the house unusually quiet, everyone took the chance to get a few hours' sleep, even Aiden, who was on night duty.

Awaking with a start, his heart rate already risen with adrenaline, Aiden sat bolt upright in the armchair in the corner of his room.

Unsure what had woken him so suddenly, he looked to the clock to see how long he'd been asleep.

It was past 3 a.m.

His eyes drifted to the bed, wondering why it was so quiet and what might have woken him.

Lorna wasn't there.

Hoping she'd finally come out of her coma and wandered to the bathroom, he turned his head, only to find two burning red eyes watching him, unblinking, from over the arm of the chair.

Her intense stare was partially hidden beneath her hair, a misshapen knotted mass surrounding her face, a result of thrashing about in bed for four days.

Her unnaturally pale face was less than half a foot from his.

Letting out a less than friendly shriek and exposing newly sprouted fangs, Lorna gripped the chair as if to launch herself at Aiden.

'Shit.' Leaping to his feet, Aiden jumped out of the way.

Awoken by the sound of furniture being thrown, Kia's head snapped up off Nick's chest fast enough to give her whiplash.

'What the fuck was that?' she asked him as their eyes met in the dark.

A second crash, followed by a loud bang, preceded what sounded like the rumbling of thunder.

Scrambling out of bed, they both ran to Aiden's room,

where they found Kieran and Acheron in the process of breaking down the door.

'Lorna's gone berserk and attacked Aiden,' Acheron said.

'Just as new werewolves can sometimes turn on their maker?' Kia asked.

'That's best-case scenario, yes.' Kieran slammed his shoulder into the door again. 'At least if that is what she's doing then we know that the werewolf in her is strong and healthy.'

'And the worst-case scenario?'

'She's gone vampiric,' Kieran said through gritted teeth as he concentrated on getting the door open. 'Either way, this is a telekinetic bind on the door, it's calculated, but at least part-guardian.'

Kia reached for the door, but Nick jumped in to add his strength.

'Nick, your shoulder isn't ready, I can help Kieran get it open telekinetically.'

'I'm fine, we need to get my brother out.' Nick leant back, lacing his fingers through her hair and pressing a kiss to her forehead.

Heaving the ceiling-high bookshelf off his shoulders, Aiden surveyed the mess as he looked for Lorna. A flying hardback book had split his lower lip. Ignoring the sting, he sucked it into his mouth in the hope Lorna wouldn't smell the blood.

Unable to instantly spot her as he stumbled over the mound of books strewn across the floor, he looked to the ceiling.

He found her sat cross-legged on the ceiling next to the

light fitting, looking down at him – or up, he thought, given the inverted position she was in. At first she didn't move, just watched him intently with her deep crimson eyes as he circled the room.

'Lorna?' he asked gently.

With a growl she launched herself off the ceiling, landing on all fours in front of him.

No longer in a recognisable form, Aiden found a wolf with fur the colour of chocolate facing him down.

Conflicting emotions ran through him as her hackles rose. She crouched slightly, ready to spring.

Finally recognising the challenge in play, Aiden readied for the attack. At least in wolf form, he knew how to stop her. Though he knew that if it came to a fight between wolves, in his home, his pack, he would have to hurt her.

He began to shift his own shape as Lorna launched herself at him.

The wolves collided, causing Lorna to lose control over the door and Kieran, Acheron and Nick to fall in. As they readied for a second charge, Kieran threw an energy wall between them, stopping Aiden in his tracks. Lorna crashed into it head first.

Dazed, and realising they were no longer alone, Lorna returned to her human form, with the addition of fangs, even as she landed on her backside on a pile of books.

Before Aiden had the chance to change back and stop her, she had turned on the three in the doorway.

Kieran threw another ball of energy at his sister to slow her down and all three tackled her, dragging her kicking and screaming back to the bed.

'Aiden, where did the sedatives go?' Acheron asked as his son returned to his human state and began trudging through the wreckage of his room.

'She's thrown just about everything. I didn't see where they went.' Aiden ran his fingers through his hair as he turned a full circle in the middle of the room.

'We've got her, for now, but don't take all day about it,' Kieran said, his voice raised.

Leaving Sookie in the hall, Kia rushed in and began shovelling books to one side, aiding the search.

Between them they lifted the bookshelf easily and pushed it back against the wall, pausing when it wobbled precariously before settling.

'That'll need fixing,' Acheron said calmly.

'It might need replacing.' Kia nudged a large crack in the bottom shelf with her toe.

'What's that over there?' Nick lifted his hand to point, easing the stress on his collarbone from where holding Lorna's shoulder and right arm down was beginning to ache.

'Nick, don't let go!' Acheron yelled as Lorna lurched forward and sank her fangs into Nick's forearm.

Everyone stopped what they were doing. Even Lorna stilled as part of her brain seemed to realise she'd done something wrong, causing her to let go.

'She didn't . . .?' Kia asked finally, her voice cracking.

'No. Just a warning nip.' Nick shook his hair out of his eyes, but wouldn't meet the worried glances of anyone in the room as blood began to trickle over his wrist and drip onto Lorna's clothes. 'I need to let her go, Kia, can you take over?'

Kia stepped over to him with a nod. 'Nick, what can a bite

do to you?'

'It shouldn't do anything,' Nick said bluntly, but wouldn't meet her eye as both Acheron and Aiden shot each other a look and watched him leave the room.

'What?' Kia felt her hold on Lorna wobble, the strength in her arms faltering as she remembered Casey's words.

'We'll just need to keep an eye on him,' Acheron said quietly.

Kia looked down at Lorna, who was beginning to get agitated by the close proximity of blood on her clothing, and felt a desperate need to follow Nick from the room.

'Aiden, hurry up with that fucking sedative.' Kia shot him a black look.

Snarling slightly at her attitude, Aiden caught the look of concern on his mother's face as she followed Nick to his room. Grabbing the kit Nick had spotted for him, he set about administering the sedative as quickly as possible.

'We can't continue to keep her sedated like this,' Kieran said sadly, sighing as he let Lorna go to sink back against the wall. Kia rushed past him. 'Are you OK?' He looked to Aiden, beating Acheron to the question.

'A few bruises, nothing serious.' He shrugged. 'She's hit me harder than that before.' Aiden smirked but hadn't failed to register the point Kieran was making. They needed to decide how much longer they could keep her in such a state.

Kia found Nick in his bathroom, holding his arm under the cold tap and squeezing the puncture marks to clear as much of the contamination as possible.

Having been watching him from the doorway, Sookie stepped to one side to let Kia in.

'Nicky?' Kia edged forward hesitantly.

'Hey.' He looked up with a weak smile as she reached him at the sink. Slipping his dry arm around her waist, he drew her close enough to kiss her softly. 'It should be OK.'

'And if it isn't?' Kia pulled a towel off the rail behind them and, taking hold of his arm, gently wrapped it around the wound and held it firm.

'It could aggravate my demon.'

Kia swallowed hard.

'Casey told me he wanted to see if he could bring out your dark side,' she whispered.

'Lorna isn't a full vampire, and it was just a bite, it doesn't even burn . . .' He raised both eyebrows playfully, but his expression dropped with a scowl and he let her go. 'Kia, step back.'

'What? Why?'

'Just step back.' He raised his voice slightly as his eyes flashed black and his wings appeared without warning, knocking a shelf and the curtain rail from their moorings, cracking several tiles as they were forced from the wall.

His scowl intensified as he dropped the towel from around his arm and turned to leave the bathroom so swiftly Kia and Sookie had to jump out of the way. Passing them both wordlessly, he left the room and headed down the stairs.

'Where are you going?' Kia asked, following him only as far as the hall, frightened to go after him when something deep within her shifted.

'I'm just going to get out for a while to see if the demon calms down. I'll be back in a bit,' he called back as he left through the front door, slamming it behind him.

'What was that?' Acheron appeared in Aiden's doorway.

'Nick's gone out to try and calm down,' Sookie answered.

'The demon?' Acheron asked, though it was more of a statement. Sookie nodded. 'He knows he needs to get a hold on it. We need to give him the space he asks for.' Acheron lay a hand on Kia's shoulder with a look that made her world crumble. 'If he doesn't get a grip in the first twelve hours, things could get rough. For now, I suggest we all go back to bed and hope he's back by morning.'

'And if it does get rough?' Kia asked.

'We know that he has kept some of what the demon is capable of from you, against our better judgement, but that's Nick. There will be parts of the demon you haven't met yet. It gets nasty when it gets too much control. However, we don't know how he will react to you, last time it happened he hadn't found you yet. Whatever happens, you are home, this is always going to be your home,' Acheron offered, making the pit in Kia's stomach only sink further.

'That doesn't sound ominous at all,' Kieran stated as Acheron and Sookie returned to their bed. He was stood leaning against Aiden's doorframe when Kia turned, his arms folded.

'Looks like Casey got more than one parting shot in after all.' Kia looked pointedly to where Aiden sat on the end of his bed looking shellshocked, before turning on her heel and disappearing back into Nick's bedroom.

Kieran headed back into Aiden's room and started telekinetically stacking books to make a path between the bed and the bathroom.

'I'll take over for the rest of the night,' he offered as he righted the armchair, which was on the opposite side of the room to where it had been. 'Did she throw this?'

'No,' Aiden mumbled, standing and scooping up an armful of books. 'I did.

THIRTY-FOUR

'Bugger off, Kieran!'

'All I asked was that you show me your teeth.' Kieran smirked as Lorna glared at him from the middle of the bed.

'Seriously? Back the fuck off. Any more prodding and I will bite you,' Lorna yelled, her voice rougher than it had been.

'Poor choice of words,' her brother chastised, glancing at the wall beyond Aiden's ensuite where Kia was sleeping in a spare room.

Nick hadn't returned for twenty-four hours, by which time Oakley and Ramsey had returned to see if they could help. He had been silent, ignoring everyone in the house. He'd managed to retract his wings, but his eyes remained black.

When he barricaded himself in his room, they all assumed he was dealing with it, or simply wanted a shower and some sleep. No one expected him to do everything in his power to prevent Kia from entering the room. He only let Acheron in for ten minutes to collect some of her things when it became apparent that she would need somewhere else to sleep.

Lorna hadn't woken again until the day after, though fully

aware and conversational the second time.

'Acheron said he's been stuck before,' Kieran explained. 'There's no knowing how long it will last. Lucious might have to step in.'

'Casey got what he wanted,' Lorna said quietly, peering down at the plate of food Sookie had sent up in case she was ravenous. She'd picked at the toast and a couple of rashers of bacon, but her stomach wasn't sure about any of it. 'Now what?'

'Kia's going to go back to college while Dad works with Nick, if he'll let him.' Aiden smiled softly. 'You need to focus on recovery, whatever that's going to continue to look like.'

Lorna looked up at him with a sad smile, her eyes bloodshot, their colour a muddle of red and blue flecks where her original eye colour was returning slowly.

'How long has the weather been shitty?'

'What?' Aiden looked to the balcony doors in confusion.

'All week,' Kieran said quietly.

'Fuck,' Lorna uttered.

'Yeah.' Her brother nodded. 'Your call.'

'Kia,' Lorna said simply and reached up to take her choker off.

'Why not Kieran?' Aiden asked quickly, realising they were talking succession.

'If it was temporary, I'd agree.' Lorna looked up at him. 'But I don't think this is temporary. I have a feeling that whatever Fate saved me for, it's to be at your side now, not at the head of guardian ranks.'

Sliding up the bed to be closer to her, Aiden kissed her temple before resting his forehead there.

'You sure about that?'

'As sure as I'll ever be.' Lorna met his eyes, then glanced at her brother.

'Don't look at me,' Kieran laughed. 'I'm not fighting this anymore, I'm just glad I still have a sister. I'll go and get Kia.'

Kieran found Kia packing her bag in the next room, aware Nick had raged out a second time when he'd caught her in his room looking for her earbuds.

'Are you OK?'

'I will be if he is,' Kia stated, laying another t-shirt in the bag. 'We're trained to fight each other if we have to, but not being allowed near him is a whole new experience.'

'Acheron's in there with him now.' Oakley appeared in the doorway alongside Kieran and headed over to pull her into his arms where he stroked her head affectionately. Thankful, Kia clung to him, she could always rely on an Oakley hug to cheer her up.

'Lorna would like a word, when you're ready,' Kieran said.

'Alright, I'll be in in a moment.' Kia nodded from within Oakley's arms.

When Kia finally steeled herself to enter Aiden's room, Lorna was sat looking at Aiden across the bed. They'd stripped the bed and thrown Lorna in the shower in the time it had taken Kia to finish packing. She was sitting in jeans and a jumper on the bare bed with wet hair, twisting the tiger's eye she wore on a leather cord between her fingertips in front of her, the gemstone spinning in the air.

When Aiden saw Kia, he turned sad eyes on Lorna.

'You're sure about this?'

'Yep,' she replied, her voice barely a whisper.

With a single nod, Aiden got up and moved to the armchair next to the repaired and re-stacked bookshelf.

'Kia, first of all I'm so sorry for what happened.' Lorna looked up, guilt blatant in her eyes.

'You weren't to know, and neither was I,' Kia said gently. 'You weren't in your right mind.'

'Doesn't make it OK.' Lorna shook her head. 'I'll help in any way I can. It seems I'm family now.'

'Hell yeah, you are.' Kia reached out with a smile and poked her on the knee.

'But as my DNA is bound by the blood of others, I need you to do something for me.'

'OK,' Kia forced from dry lips when she finally spotted the choker spinning between them.

'I need to pass this on. I can't wear it anymore.' Lorna's eyes met Kia's and Kia saw the anger etched below the sorrow.

'You're still a guardian at your core,' Kia pointed out gently. 'If you can't wear it, then I certainly can't, I'm a hybrid too. Your DNA has been added to, your natural state will settle, you just have to give it time,' she added flatly as she folded her arms.

'I don't think Fate sees it that way.' Lorna glanced out of the balcony doors where the storm continued to rage. 'And I don't think time can fix this.' Lorna settled the pendant on her palm for just a second, but Kia saw the instant burn it left on her skin. 'That thunderstorm last night wasn't just your conflict with Nick, the city will begin to believe another head guardian is dead if this weather continues.'

'How long for?' Kia asked, causing Lorna's shoulders to

sag in relief.

'Probably permanently.'

With a deep breath, Kia held out her hand and let Lorna drop the necklace into her palm. Almost immediately the weather eased and by the time Kia had tied the leather around her neck, the rain had stopped.

'We should talk to Mia about having a replica made,' Kia said quietly. 'Or ask Lucious to enchant another.'

'Let's not offer him the chance to keep tabs on any more of us.' Lorna pursed her lips. 'What if my visions don't return?'

'What if they do?' Kia smirked.

'I won't need to retake the reins to keep my hand in.' Lorna shrugged.

'We could pretend like you're still head guardian?'

'A head guardian with the ability to turn into a werewolf or vampire without warning and a killer temper bordering on the psychotic?' Lorna asked, heavy on the sarcasm, but she smirked.

'Being a little psychotic has its uses in our line of work, I find.' Kia shrugged with a grin.

'With your reputation as it is already, are you, and Nick, OK with this?' Lorna's bravado faltered as the magnitude of what she was asking of Kia sank in.

'I've always said I'll help in any way I can.' Kia shrugged. 'Nick knows that, and if you chose me over your hot-headed brother, then I should be honoured.' Kia shot Kieran a look as he joined them.

'Honoured my ass, I've seen what you're capable of.' Lorna rolled her eyes and got up off the bed with a whimsical glance at the terrace doors.

With a grin she wandered over to Aiden, who stood to meet her, and slid her arms around his neck to kiss him, making him smile against her lips.

Jumping back, Lorna turned and reached for the doors, throwing them open and disappearing out onto the terrace as the sun broke through the clouds.

In the silence that followed, Kia, Aiden and Kieran all looked at each other panic-stricken before rushing outside after her, practically yanking the curtains down in the process.

They found Lorna sat on the terrace wall, eyes closed, a single tear running down her cheek past the smile on her lips as the sun warmed her face.

ACKNOWLEDGEMENTS

Thank you to my long-suffering friends and family, you have had the patience of a saint with this one. This book was my very first, these characters have been with me over 25 years. I promise I will leave this book alone now. Though maybe not the characters. Thanks again must go to Jenny Lewis of writeintothewoods.com for proofreading, we still haven't managed to meet for cake, but there's time yet!

And if you were wondering, yes, this is where he came from.

FATE BOUND: A PREQUEL

Nick threw the dismembered head over his shoulder and reached for a nearby curtain, wiping the blood from his hands as he shook his shaggy blond hair out of his eyes. That was the welcome party dealt with. He'd already left one body, badly broken, stuffed in an air conditioning duct on the roof, the other three lay in pieces, scattered at his feet.

Checking his clothing for blood splatter, he realised there was a phone vibrating underneath one of the body parts. Plucking it from a puddle of blood, he peered at the caller ID and scowled.

Evelyn Henderson.

Having recently met the woman, though only very briefly when offering to rescue her daughter, he wasn't wholly surprised to discover her name on the ID. His offer of help had been refused. Not that he'd been totally shocked by her dismissal. The Henderson name was a tainted one.

Wiping the phone on the same curtain he'd used for his

hands, he accepted the call and lifted the device to his ear.

'Yes?' he asked, his voice clipped.

'Sam?' an irritated voice bit down the line. Nick raised an eyebrow and chose not to enlighten her. Instead, he replied simply with a bored grunt.

'You've got company coming. It's time to cut our losses, if you know what I mean.'

'What kind of company?' Nick bit out as though she was disturbing him.

'The angeling. He's looking for Kia. Get rid of her before he gets there or you're on your own.'

Nick didn't get the chance to answer back, the phone line went dead.

He lowered the phone with a sigh, what did he do with a girl he couldn't take home to her own parents? He was only there because he took classes with Jamie Henderson. He'd overheard him telling another classmate that his sister had gone missing.

It had been Jamie's reluctance to give Nick any information that had truly piqued his interest. He'd started looking for the girl himself, despite what he knew of the Hendersons.

When his own phone began vibrating in the pocket of his jeans, he already knew it was Aiden.

'Hey,' he hushed.

'Nick, where the hell are you?' Aiden yelled down the phone over the unmistakable din of the college bar.

'I'm in the city,' Nick replied bluntly.

'Trouble?' Aiden asked curiously, knowing his younger brother rarely left campus without a reason, and that Nick's instincts had been taking him wandering into the night more and more frequently.

'Not anymore,' Nick said as he surveyed the mess. 'Hey Aiden, where would you take a girl who couldn't go home?'

'My room,' Aiden laughed down the phone. 'Hang on . . . you're with a girl?'

'No, I'm in the process of looking for one I believe was kidnapped for trafficking. It looks like her parents arranged it.'

'That's a relief, I think I might have died of shock if you'd looked at a girl twice,' Aiden said as he calmed down a bit. 'I still think that's weird, you know.'

'Species trait,' Nick bit out, as he had countless times before. He'd learnt to ignore how much it amused his older brother when girls tried and failed to get his attention.

'Yeah, that,' Aiden responded. 'Bring her here for a beer and we'll take it from there.'

'You're no help.' Nick smirked.

'Well, if you're not planning to head back to campus tonight, I'll see you at home tomorrow.'

'Yeah, I doubt I'll be back tonight.' Nick began heading for the hallway, drawn to the room right at the back of the apartment as he signed off and slipped the phone back into his pocket.

Moving down the hall, he heard muffled voices from behind the door at the end. He paused as the voices began to shout and adrenaline spiked through him, hitting him like a truck. The sensation was so overwhelming he couldn't make out the words.

The sound of a shotgun loading brought him sharply back to reality.

Regaining his senses, he made for the back room again. The door was blown off its hinges as he approached, the body of an ex-werewolf landing at his feet, the gun still in his grip. Stopping short, Nick peered down at the body. There were no outward signs of trauma, except for the odd laceration caused by the door as he'd taken it apart with his corpse.

Nick stalled, a lack of puncture wounds often meant death by telekinesis. Jamie had told him his sister was a morph, but hadn't mentioned anything else. He knew that a morph could borrow telekinetic strengths briefly from a telekinetic demon or a guardian, but no one Nick had seen so far was either and Kia had been missing too long to come into contact with anyone else.

Nick stepped over the body and reached for what was left of the doorframe.

'Step one foot in here and I'll rip your throat out, I swear.'

Eyebrows flying upwards in surprise, he stopped again. She sounded exhausted but he admired her spirit.

'I know your brother, Jamie,' Nick stated as he glanced back at the body on the floor.

There was silence as she considered the information, so with a deep breath he stepped into the room, preparing for anything she might throw at him.

The room was barely furnished, with only a mattress on the floor and a single chair under the window, on which sat a radio. The curtains were drawn against a stark orange approach light on top of a nearby building.

'I don't know you. You're not one of his friends,' a delicate but calm voice came from across the room.

Turning around, it took him a moment to see her. She'd

tucked herself into the darkest corner. A ball of white light appeared in his hand as he inched forward. In warning, a wall of energy shimmered around her, the light bathing her skin. Nick stopped again, recognising the shimmer as that of a guardian's shield.

As the light touched her face, he found her peering up at him curiously, her long black hair a mass of curls which tumbled around her shoulders and down her back as tired violet eyes found his in the gloom.

'You must be Nick?' she frowned curiously. 'Jamie has mentioned you, but you're not friends,' she announced suspiciously.

He didn't realise he'd caught his breath until he needed to answer her. Shaking his head, as much to shake himself off than in response, he replied, 'I am and we're not.'

Taking his words in silently, her mind ran through a million questions.

'We should get you out of here, have they drugged you?' Nick continued, unsure whether anyone else would be coming back to the apartment. As if to make a point, he peered back down the hall.

'They tried to sedate me.' Kia nodded slowly, her head appearing heavy. 'Fat lot of good it did them, though, huh?' One limp arm tried to motion to the body in the hall. As she did so, the shimmer around her faded away.

Stepping forward, Nick reached down and took her hand, pulling her to her feet. She willingly let him stand her up, but when her legs refused to support her, she fell against him.

'Dratit, I'm not used to needing rescuing, sorry,' she apologised as she looked up at him, but he shrugged it off and lifted her into his arms.

'Can you do me a favour?' Nick asked as he moved towards the door.

'I'll try.' Kia tried to look mischievous but sobered quickly when she realised that she must have looked quite drunk.

'Keep your eyes on me,' he instructed. He didn't want her seeing the mess in the apartment.

'No problem,' Kia said quietly.

'OK then.' Nick smiled as he checked that she was doing as he asked before carrying her from the room.

Feeling her eyes on him as he manoeuvred through the discarded body parts, he found himself checking the walls and ceiling for blood splatter, finding that he didn't want her seeing that either.

Kicking the wedge he'd left to keep the roof door open to one side, he felt himself relax. He hadn't left a mess on the roof, the body in the vent only visible if you knew what you were looking for, or at.

He crossed the roof in a few strides and, stepping onto the ledge, Nick took a moment to check that Kia was still focused.

'How are you with heights?'

'I'm good.' Kia nodded as the night air whipped tendrils of her hair around her face.

'How about jumping from them?' Nick's eyes sparkled with mischief as her eyes remained locked on his features.

'Again, I'm good.' Kia grinned.

Nick spread his wings ready to leave the roof but paused, looking over his own shoulder in surprise. He'd expected his demon wings to appear given the night's events. His angel wings rarely made an appearance so soon after such a blood bath, but it was white feathers Kia was gazing at over his shoulder.

'Oh yeah, you're the—' Kia didn't get the chance to finish her sentence as Nick launched himself off the edge, her stomach flipping over the word "Angeling".

They landed a moment later next to his car, which he'd brazenly left at the front entrance. Reaching over the passenger door of the Boxster he put Kia down on the passenger seat before heading for the driver's side.

'I have some neutralisers back at my place. It's late and I have a spare room, you can stay there tonight if you like?' Nick looked over as he started the engine, hoping she wouldn't be able to tell he was lying. He had a pack in his pocket but needed to buy some time to think. 'Is that OK?'

Kia was looking around the car with interest as she sank into the soft leather gratefully.

'I bet you say that to all the girls,' she said with a smile as she visibly relaxed, curling up into the warmth of the vehicle as Nick put the roof back up. Catching something flash through his eyes she bit her tongue, wishing she'd engaged her brain before her mouth as she remembered what her brother had told her about Nick, and what she knew about the angeling species. 'Sorry. Yes, that's great. Thank you.'

Nick nodded and pulled away from the curb. Kia, focused on the world outside the window as he drove, slowly nodded off, waking only when the loud ping of elevator doors startled her. Realising they were at their destination, Kia allowed Nick to put her back on her feet. He made sure she could stand before letting her go so that he could open the door to his apartment.

'Aren't you in the same year as my brother?' she asked probingly as she stepped into the open plan kitchen-living area.

'I am. This was my father's city base before he became alpha of the Barnes pack. He gave it to me when I turned eighteen. My older brother has even less use for it than my father did.' Nick moved around the living area turning lights on and ensuring the room was warm enough before moving to the kitchen.

Kia nodded when he looked over. 'I know who you are. And what you are.'

It was Nick's turn to nod as he switched the kettle on and began spooning a range of tea leaves into a diffuser from four different jars on the counter.

'What's that?' Kia walked over to the breakfast bar and leant on it as she watched him.

'Tea. It's a mixture I keep handy, it's good for clearing unwanted drugs from the system.' Nick turned and looked her up and down, her blue jeans were torn and dirty, her black fitted t-shirt also covered in something that looked like mud. 'I can add something to help soothe away any shock . . .?' It was a loaded question, she didn't look at all phased by what had happened to her, just tired.

'Just another day in the office.' She shrugged and looked at him as brightly as she could muster, finding that, despite her better judgement, she wanted him to ask her about it.

'You've been kidnapped before?' Nick felt his gut tighten at the thought.

'No one's actually succeeded before but there have been

attempts, and bad guys are sort of my forte.' When the horror he was feeling met his eyes she looked down at the countertop thoughtfully. 'I'm guessing Jamie told you I'm a morph?'

'He did.' Nick moved forward to lean on the other side of the breakfast bar curiously as the kettle continued to boil.

She rolled her eyes and looked up into the pure aquamarine of his, knowing instinctually that she could trust him. 'I'm a guardian too.'

'Ah.' Nick nodded, knowing instantly why the Hendersons wouldn't have told him that.

The kettle clicked off and he turned to pour the boiling water even though he hardly wanted to take his eyes off her.

'It's not something the Henderson family like to admit and I don't think it's something they're aware I practise either, so please don't tell Jamie,' she pleaded calmly. 'I'm guessing that's why I was kidnapped. I've trained hard to get to the standard I am without my parents knowing, but someone must have noticed what I'm capable of.'

Nick turned back to her, sliding a mug across the counter in her direction, but kept quiet on the matter.

'Thanks.' Kia took a tentative sip. 'Not as bad as I expected.' She took a larger mouthful. 'I'm not your average Henderson and I'm very aware of the reputation my family has. I don't know the full extent to which Jamie gets involved and I'm not sure I want to.'

'Sit down and relax, it's all over for tonight,' Nick said as he headed around the bar to place his hands on her shoulders and, feeling heat spread up his arms as he did so, steered her towards the sofa. 'I'll find something for you to sleep in and you can have a bath or a shower while I get the bed in the spare room ready.'

'That would be wonderful, thank you.' Kia's shoulders relaxed beneath his touch.

He guessed that she was almost a foot shorter than his six foot two height and although she was of a petite build, he could feel strength far beyond her age beneath his fingertips.

'I'm five foot four,' Kia said suddenly.

'What?' Nick flinched, dropping his hands from her shoulders.

'You asked me how tall I was?' She turned and looked up at him as she took a seat at one end of the sofa.

Nick blinked. He was certain he hadn't said anything out loud and his DNA had him on telekinetic lockdown as a matter of personal security, another species trait and one he was thankful for.

'I'll run you that bath,' Nick said by way of excusing himself and disappeared into one of two doors at the far end of the living space.

Kia raised an eyebrow. She hadn't stated her preference, but had been swaying towards a bath. She watched him leave the room, marvelling at how the rumours of his strength and beauty were all completely true. Rubbing a shoulder absently with her free hand, she could still feel an electric heat dancing across her skin.

By the time he reappeared with some clothes for her to borrow she had finished the tea and got up to meet him at the doorway to the bathroom, which was next to his bedroom.

'You can wash your clothes overnight and use these to sleep in. I don't know how well my clothes will fit you so there are a few things here for you to try.' Nick held out a folded bundle of clothes.

Kia accepted the pile of clothing, spotting a shirt, a pair of shorts and some gym wear. 'Thanks. I won't be too long.'

'Take all the time you need.' Nick shrugged as he watched her step around him. 'Kia?'

'Yeah?' She looked back over her shoulder.

'Will you be starting at the college when summer ends?'

'Yes, why?' She frowned.

'Something Jamie said, that's all.' Nick shrugged and waved her off. 'Let me know if you need anything else.'

'I will,' Kia said softly with a smile and disappeared into the bathroom.

While she was in the bath he changed the bed in the spare room, his mind running through possible ways to keep her safe until she moved into college dorms in September. He had another week before college closed for the summer, but only one exam left to take. Then he was due to attend his regular two weeks training in the mountains with Lucious. To Nick, that was three weeks in which her mother could attempt something else.

He'd started to go around in circles, pacing the living area and running his fingers through his hair, when the door to the bathroom clicked open. Kia emerged, wearing a pair of his boxer shorts and a shirt, her hair already dried.

'Where's your washing machine?' She held up her dirty clothes.

'It's in the cupboard next to the kitchen. I'll switch it on before I go to bed.' He gestured across the room before putting his hands on his hips, trying to calm the thoughts in his head.

Kia slipped around the kitchen and threw the dirty bundle into the machine.

'Hope you've got something strong enough to get blood out. The vision I was out on was an execution. It got messy.'

'I'll throw my stuff in with them.' Nick pulled at the front of his shirt, also splattered with blood from his night's work.

'Nice.' She grinned darkly.

'Where do you intend to spend the summer?' he found himself asking as he unbuttoned the shirt, revealing a t-shirt that hadn't escaped the mess either.

'Where? I didn't really have any plans . . . why?' Kia looked a bit lost for a moment as she considered sitting back on the sofa.

'I've seen your trashed bedroom, I know they followed you home and took you from there. You don't have to worry about seeing anyone from that apartment again, but—'

'What did you do?' Kia stopped abruptly at the end of the sofa, her eyes meeting his again.

'You don't need to know what, just that they're gone. But if the trafficking ring is bigger, or there are more of them . . .' He took a step forward and stopped himself.

'I'm sure I'll work something out.' Kia shrugged. 'I'll know what to look out for next time.'

She walked over to where he seemed frozen to the spot next to his coffee table.

'Is something troubling you . . .?' she asked as she took hold of his arms, but let go quickly when heat sparked through her hands. 'Sorry, was that me?'

'I don't think so,' Nick replied, looking into her eyes briefly before looking away, focusing on the top of her head.

'OK . . . Look, you don't need to worry about me. I'll be fine. But thank you for your help tonight. I can admit when it's not looking good, though I promise you I wasn't out of ideas.'

With a smirk she tiptoed up and kissed him, catching the edge of his mouth, in the hope that it would shock him into moving from the spot.

Heat flared through the room as soon as their lips caught. Kia expected Nick to step back or push her away but when he reached for her, he pulled her in tight, moulding her body to his own. As the searing heat glued them together, she slid her arms around his neck to steady herself, but realised as he deepened the kiss and her fingers slid into his hair, that it was unnecessary, he held them both anchored to the spot effortlessly.

'Oh, shit,' Kia breathed as they paused for breath and found Nick's wings surrounding them both.

She didn't need to ask him what had happened. Looking up into his eyes she found all the answers in the heartbeat she could hear and feel as though it was her own.

'You don't ever need to go back to your parents,' Nick whispered as his hands held her safer than she'd ever felt before.

'I know.' Kia held his gaze with a smile and, as she reached up to kiss him again, whispered back, 'I am home.'

Fate Bound
Coming October 2023

www.ingramcontent.com/pod-product-compliance
Lightning Source LLC
Chambersburg PA
CBHW010550170726
48285CB00011B/2837